John Buchan was born in Perth. His father was a minister of the Free Church of Scotland; and in 1876 the family moved to Fife where in order to attend the local school the small boy had to walk six miles a day. Later they moved again to the Gorbals in Glasgow and John Buchan went to Hutchesons' Grammar School, Glasgow University (by which time he was already publishing articles in periodicals) and Brasenose College, Oxford. His years at Oxford – 'spent peacefully in an enclave like a monastery' – nevertheless opened up yet more horizons and he published five books and many articles, won several awards including the Newdigate Prize for poetry and gained a First. His career was equally diverse and successful after university and, despite ill-health and continual pain from a duodenal ulcer, he played a prominent part in public life as a barrister and Member of Parliament, in addition to being a writer, soldier and publisher. In 1907 he married Susan Grosvenor, and the marriage was supremely happy. They had one daughter and three sons. He was created Baron Tweedsmuir of Elsfield in 1935 and became the thirty-fifth Governor-General of Canada, a position he held until his death in 1940. 'I don't think I remember anyone,' wrote G. M. Trevelyan to his widow, 'whose death evoked a more enviable outburst of sorrow, love and admiration.'

His first success as an author came with *Prester John* in 1910, and he went on to write a series of adventure thrillers, or 'shockers' as he called them, all characterized by their authentically rendered backgrounds, romantic characters, their atmosphere of expectancy and world-wide conspiracies, and the author's own enthusiasm. There are three main heroes: Richard Hannay, whose adventures are told in *The Thirty-Nine Steps*, *Mr Standfast*, *Greenmantle*, *The Three Hostages* and *The Island of Sheep*; Dickson McCunn, the Glaswegian provision merchant with the soul of a romantic, who features in *Huntingtower*, *Castle Gay* and *The House of the Four Winds*; and Sir Edward Leithen, the lawyer who tells the story of *John Macnab* and *Sick Heart River*, John Buchan's final novel. In addition, John Buchan established a reputation as an historical biographer with such works as *Montrose*, *Oliver Cromwell* and *Augustus*.

# SICK HEART RIVER

John Buchan

**With an introduction by Trevor Royle**

PENGUIN BOOKS

Penguin Books Ltd, Harmondsworth, Middlesex, England
Viking Penguin Inc., 40 West 23rd Street, New York, New York 10010, USA
Penguin Books Australia Ltd, Ringwood, Victoria, Australia
Penguin Books Canada Ltd, 2801 John Street, Markham, Ontario, Canada L3R 1B4
Penguin Books (N.Z.) Ltd, 182–190 Wairau Road, Auckland 10, New Zealand

First published in this edition by
Macdonald Publishers 1981
Published in Penguin Books 1985

Acknowledgement is made to Chatto & Windus
for the use of certain material taken from
*The Golden Grindstone* by Angus Graham (1935)

Made and printed in Great Britain by
Cox & Wyman Ltd, Reading
Set in 9/11 Monophoto Photina

# INTRODUCTION

On 20 July 1937, John Buchan, in his sixty-second year and in the third year of his reign as Governor-General of Canada, set off on a tour of the North-West Territories. His trip – *Down North* as he called it – took him from Edmonton, down the Athabaska River, over the Great Bear Lake and the Great Slave Lake, down the Mackenzie River to the Arctic Ocean. He was not the first Governor-General to have ventured into the north lands – another Scottish Governor-General, Lord Minto, had visited the Yukon in 1900 – but he was the first to bring to the North a sense of personal purpose. There were two reasons for the trip. Firstly, he had long been fascinated by the North, a territory which satisfied his inner need for exploration and adventure. 'I can never find words to describe that curious quality of light that you get up in the North. Sometimes it is like looking at the world out of deep water' ('Skule Skerry', 1928). Secondly, he believed that the northern territories should be opened up, physically and imaginatively, to the rest of Canada which he believed had become introverted and suburban in its outlook. 'I look to the North as one of the great unifying factors in the future of the Dominion' (notes for a speech by the Canadian Prime Minister William Lyon Mackenzie King, summer, 1937).

The trip, covering some 7,000 miles by train, boat and plane, had a great effect on Buchan. Initially the lakes and the Mackenzie River offered nothing but pleasure. 'It is the essential romance of Nature with man left out' (this and subsequent quotations from his report *Down North*, September 1937). He was impressed by the sense of comradeship he found in the Hudson's Bay trading forts, of the overwhelming desire to be helpful, of the hard work and dedication of the Catholic missionaries, of the sturdiness and endurance of the half-breeds, many of whom had Scots parentage. The delta of the Mackenzie River where the great river pours itself out into the Arctic Ocean was a disappointment. In place of the hard crystal world which he had expected, he found the landscape of the midden beneath the midsummer sun. But the journey back to Edmonton by air restored to him the sense of 'the clean, antiseptic North'. There was time to fish, to trek and hunt, to ponder the awesome fact that 'the world was not created on your scale', to seek again a sense of adventure and to discover the existence of 'three geographical mysteries of Canada' – the Rivière de l'Enfer, the forests of the Thelon River, and the South Nahanni in the Great Divide.

The trip also gave Buchan the opportunity to see in the men of the North a stoicism and a feeling of duty and endurance that complemented his own philosophy. No privilege without responsibility – a recurring motif in his fiction – could have been the motto of the trappers, traders and miners he met along the route. There was, too, the presence, made manifest, of the division between comfortable civilization and nature, red in tooth and claw, another favourite Buchan theme.

Little wonder that the trip was so important for him as an administrator and as a writer. It did wonders for his health too. Since 1914 he had been a semi-invalid and contemporary photographs show him to be of a thin, spare build. He weighed little more than nine stones, yet on his return to Ottawa he felt reinvigorated and an aide was able to report that the Governor-General had put on weight for the first time in years. The trip had also been a mental tonic and memos to the Prime Minister and to the Hudson's Bay Company on the future of the North flowed from his active mind. There was a need for increased air transport, an extension of agriculture with the introduction of new breeds of cattle, ranching to renew the pioneer spirit and tourism for those in search of adventure. The Canadians began to look on the North as an integral part of their country and as an area that could yield much.

> Nothing could be better calculated to bring home to our people the fact that Canada's future destiny lies northward. Nothing is more calculated to give an impetus to the Northland's challenge to the inertia of centuries than Lord Tweedsmuir's visit to the northern empire over which he rules (*Winnipeg Tribune*, 20 August 1938).

*Down North* gave Buchan the theme for his last and, in my opinion, best novel, *Sick Heart River*. In 1938 and 1939 he was very ill and felt himself to be at an age when he was able at last to sit back and take stock – his autobiography *Memory Hold-the-Door* was completed during this period and *Sick Heart River*, 'a very odd book' as his secretary called it, was begun in the autumn of

1939. The novel draws heavily on his memories of the northern expedition and on some of the events and sights of the journey: the landscape is lovingly delineated, the trappers, priests, Hare Indians, Scots half-breeds and the mystery of the North all make their appearance. The central character, Sir Edward Leithen, one of the more shadowy figures in the Buchan group who, since he had made his first appearance in *The Power House* (1916), had acted as an interpreter of the action, seldom taking part in it, and when called on to do so as in *John Macnab* (1925), carrying out his allotted role with economy and little fuss: he was the ideal cipher. Other familiar Buchan touches are present in the novel: the shared ritual, the survival in the wastelands, the legal mind's ability to analyse and assess and a growing realization of the comforting strength of Christianity. The Buchan reader knew the signs of the territory from the very beginning of the novel.

To begin with, Leithen – who is under the death sentence of a terminal illness – plays the detached role that we have come to expect of him. (Tommy Deloraine had said to him in *The Power House*: 'Poor old beggar! To spend your days on such work when the world is full of amusing things. Life goes roaring by and you can only hear an echo in your stuffy rooms.') He seems to be so removed from the action that there is a blank instead of a character until he gets to Canada. Then the farther north he gets and the more involved he becomes in the redemption of Galliard and the Frizels, the hollow centre of his character becomes filled and he emerges as a true Christian stoic, a reflection of his creator's ideals. There are other similarities between Leithen and Buchan: the physical leanness, his involvement in the struggle between life and death, between good and evil and the need for hard work and stern application to duty.

Leithen goes north to find Galliard and to find his own death. On the way he becomes fixed to the idea of finding death only in the Sick Heart River, a place that Galliard thinks will hold the waters of atonement – divisions between good and evil are never simple in Buchan's novels. Leithen has to help Galliard and Lew Frizel to find true humility before they can return to the civilized world and he finds his own release by abandoning his new-found health in favour of the diseased and down-trodden Hare Indians. And in a novel that rings with the language of the psalms and the Old

Testament, a truly Christian novel, it is not to be wondered at that Leithen, whose 'castles had been tumbled down', should give up his life for the meek, the poor and the disinherited. Towards the end, for the first time in his life, Leithen is effective, directing the regeneration of the dying community, in all humility.

Most men had their lives taken from them. It was his privilege to *give* his, to offer it freely and joyfully in one last effort of manhood. The North had been his friend, for it had enabled him, like Jacob, to wrestle with the dark angel and extort a blessing.

John Buchan, Lord Tweedsmuir of Elsfield, Governor-General of Canada, and storyteller, died on 11 February 1940, still in the saddle, preparing for another day's duty. *Sick Heart River* was published after his death, in 1941, after being serialized in *Blackwood's Magazine*.

TREVOR ROYLE

*Edinburgh, December 1980*

# PART I

'Thus said Alfred:
If thou hast a woe, tell it not to the weakling,
Tell it to thy saddlebow, and ride singing forth.'
*Proverbs of Alfred*

# 1

Leithen had been too busy all day to concern himself with the thoughts which hung heavily at the back of his mind. In the morning he had visited his bankers to look into his money affairs. These were satisfactory enough: for years he had been earning a large income and spending little of it; his investments were mostly in trustee stocks; he found that he possessed, at a safe computation, a considerable fortune, while his Cotswold estate would find a ready sale. Next came his solicitors, for he was too wise a man to make the mistake of many barristers and tinker with his own will. He gave instructions for bringing the old one up to date. There were a few legacies by way of mementoes to old friends, a considerable gift to his college, donations to certain charities, and the residue to his nephew Charles, his only near relation.

He forced himself to lunch at one of his clubs, in a corner where no one came near him, though Archie Roylance waved a greeting across the dining-room. Then he spent a couple of hours with his clerk in his Temple chambers, looking through the last of his briefs. There were not a great many, since, for some months, he had been steadily refusing work. The batch of cases for opinion he could soon clear off, and one big case in the Lords he must argue next week, for it involved a point of law in which he had always taken a special interest. The briefs for the following term would be returned. The clerk, who had been with him for thirty years, was getting on in life and would be glad to retire on an ample pension. Still, it was a painful parting.

'It's a big loss to the Bar, Sir Edward, sir,' old Mellon said, 'and it's pretty well the end of things for me. You have been a kind master to me, sir, and I'm proud to have served you. I hope you are going to have many happy years yet.'

But there had been a look of pain in the old man's eyes which told Leithen that he had guessed what he dared not hint at.

He had tea at the House of Commons with the Chief Whip, a youngish man named Ritson, who in the War had been a subaltern in his own battalion. Ritson listened to him with a wrinkled brow and troubled eyes.

'Have you told your local people?' he asked.

'I'll write to them tomorrow. I thought I ought to tell you first.

There's no fear of losing the seat. My majority has never been less than six thousand, and there's an excellent candidate ready in young Walmer.'

'We shall miss you terribly, you know. There's no one to take your place.'

Leithen smiled. 'I haven't been pulling my weight lately.'

'Perhaps not. But I'm thinking of what's coming. If there's an election, we're going to win all right, and we'll want you badly in the new Government. It needn't be a law office. You can have your pick of half a dozen jobs. Only yesterday the Chief was speaking to me about you.' And he repeated a conversation he had had with the man who would be the next Prime Minister.

'You're all very kind. But I don't think I want anything. I've done enough, as Napoleon said, *"pour chauffer la gloire"*.'

'Is it your health?' Ritson asked.

'Well, I need a rest. I've been pretty busy all my days and I'm tired.'

The Chief Whip hesitated.

'Things are pretty insecure in the world just now. There may be a crisis any day. Don't you think you ought –'

Leithen smiled.

'I've thought of that. But if I stayed on I could do nothing to help. That isn't a pleasant conclusion to come to, but it's the truth.'

Ritson stood at the door of his room and watched his departing guest going down the corridor to the Central Lobby. He turned to a junior colleague who had joined him –

'I wonder what the devil's the matter! There's been a change in him in the last few months. But he doesn't look a sick man. He was always a bad colour, of course, but Lamancha says he is the hardest fellow he ever knew on the hill.'

The other shook a wise head. 'You never can tell. He had a rough-ish time in the War and the damage often takes years to come out. I think he's right to slack off, for he must have a gruelling life at the Bar. My father tried to get him the other day as leader in a big case, and he wasn't to be had for love or money. Simply snowed under with work!'

Leithen walked from the House towards his rooms in Down Street. He was still keeping his thoughts shut down, but in spite of himself the familiar streets awakened memories. How often he had tramped them in the far-off days when he was a pupil in chambers and the world was an oyster waiting to be opened. It was a different London then, quieter, cosier, dirtier perhaps, but sweeter smelling. On a summer evening such as this the scents would have been a compound of wood paving, horse-dung, flowers, and fresh paint, not the deadly monotony of petrol. The old landmarks, too, were disappearing. In St James's Street only Mr Lock's modest shop-window and the eighteenth-century façade of Boodle's recalled the London of his youth. He remembered posting up this street with a high heart after he had won his first important case in court ... and the Saturday afternoon's strolls in it when he had changed his black regimentals for tweeds or flannels ... and the snowy winter day when a tiny coffin on a gun carriage marked the end of Victoria's reign ... and the shiny August morning in 1914 when he had been on his way to enlist with a mind half-anxious and half-exulting. He had travelled a good deal in his time, but most of his life had been spent in this square mile of west London. He did not regret the changes; he only noted them. His inner world was crumbling so fast that he had lost any craving for permanence in the externals of life.

In Piccadilly he felt his knees trembling and called a taxi. In Down Street he took the lift to his rooms, though for thirty years he had made a ritual of climbing the stairs.

The flat was full of powdery sunlight. He sank into a chair at the window to get his breath, and regarded the comfortable, shabby sitting-room. Now that he seemed to be looking at it with new eyes he noted details which familiarity had long obscured. The pictures were school and college groups, one or two mountain photographs, and, over the mantelpiece, Raeburn's portrait of his grandfather. He was very little of a connoisseur, though at Borrowby he had three Vandykes which suited its Jacobean solemnity. There were books everywhere; they overflowed into the dining-room and his bedroom and the little hall. He reflected that what with these, and the law library in his chambers and his considerable collection at Borrowby, he must have at least twenty thousand volumes. He had been happy here, happy and busy, and for a moment – for a moment only – he felt a bitter pang of regret.

But he was still keeping his thoughts at a distance, for the time had not come to face them. Memories took the vacant place. He remembered how often he had left these rooms with a holiday zest, and how he had always returned to them with delight, for this, and not Borrowby, was his true home. How many snug winter nights had he known here, cheerful with books and firelight; and autumn twilights when he was beginning to get into the stride of his work after the long vacation; and spring mornings when the horns of elfland were blowing even in Down Street. He lay back in his chair, shut his eyes, and let his memory wander. There was no harm in that, for the grim self-communion he had still to face would have no room for memories. He almost dozed.

The entry of his man, Cruddock, aroused him.

'Lord Clanroyden called you up, sir. He is in town for the night and suggests that you might dine with him. He said the Turf Club at eight. I was to let him know, sir.'

'Tell him to come here instead. You can produce some kind of a dinner?' Leithen rather welcomed the prospect. Sandy Clanroyden would absorb his attention for an hour or two and postpone for a little the settlement with himself which his soul dreaded.

He had a bath and changed. He had been feeling listless and depressed, but not ill, and the cold shower gave him a momentary sense of vigour and almost an appetite for food. He caught a glimpse of himself naked in the long mirror, and was shocked anew by his leanness. He had given up weighing himself, but it looked as if he had lost pounds in the past month.

Sandy arrived on the stroke of eight. Leithen, as he greeted him, reflected that he was the only one of his closer friends whom he could have borne to meet. Archie Roylance's high spirits would have been intolerable, and Lamancha's air of mastery over life, and Dick Hannay's serene contentment.

He did not miss the sharp glance of his guest when he entered the room. Could some rumours have got abroad? It was clear that Sandy was setting himself to play a part, for his manner had not its usual ease. He was not talking at random, but picking his topics.

A proof was that he did not ask Leithen about his holiday plans, which, near the close of the law term, would have been a natural subject. He seemed to feel that his host's affairs might be delicate ground, and that it was his business to distract his mind from some unhappy preoccupation. So he talked about himself and his recent doings. He had just been to Cambridge to talk to the Explorers'

Club, and had come back with strong views about modern youth.

'I'm not happy about the young entry. Oh! I don't mean all of it. There's plenty of lads that remind me of my own old lot. But some of the best seem to have become a bit too much introverted – isn't that the filthy word? What's to be done about the Owlish Young, Ned?'

'I don't see much of youth nowadays,' said Leithen. 'I seem to live among fogies. I'm one myself.'

'Rot! You are far and away the youngest of us.'

Again Leithen caught a swift glance at his face, as if Sandy would have liked to ask him something, but forbore.

'Those boys make me anxious. It's right that they should be serious with the world slipping into chaos, but they need not be owlish. They are so darned solemn about their new little creeds in religion and politics, forgetting that they are as old as the hills. There isn't a ha'porth of humour in the bunch, which means, of course, that there isn't any perspective. If it comes to a show-down I'm afraid they will be pretty feeble folk. People with half their brains and a little sense of humour will make rings round them.'

Leithen must have shown his unconcern about the future of the world by his expression, for Sandy searched for other topics. Spring at Laverlaw had been diviner than ever. Had Leithen heard the curlews this year? No? Didn't he usually make a pilgrimage somewhere to hear them? For northerners they, and not the cuckoo, were the heralds of spring ... His wife was at Laverlaw, but was coming to London next day. Yes, she was well, but –

Again Leithen saw in the other's face a look of interrogation. He wanted to ask him something, tell him something, but did not feel the moment propitious.

'Her uncle has just turned up here. Apparently there's a bit of family trouble to be settled. You know him, don't you? Blenkiron – John Scantlebury Blenkiron?'

Leithen nodded. 'A little. I was his counsel in the Continental Nickel case some years ago. He's an old friend of yours and Hannay's, isn't he?'

'About the best Dick and I have in the world. Would you like to see him again? I rather think he would like to see you.'

Leithen yawned and said his plans for the immediate future were uncertain.

Just before ten Sandy took his leave, warned by his host's obvious fatigue. He left the impression that he had come to dinner to say something which he had thought had better be left unsaid, and Leithen, when he looked at his face in his dressing-table mirror, knew the reason. It was the face of a very sick man.

That night he had meant, before going to sleep, to have it out with himself. But he found that a weary body had made his brain incapable of coherent thought, so he tumbled into bed.

# 2

The reckoning came six hours later, when his bedroom was brightening with the fore-glow of a June dawn. He awoke, as he usually did nowadays, sweating and short of breath. He got up and laved his face with cold water. When he lay down again he knew that the moment had arrived.

Recent events had been confused in a cloud of misery, and he had to disengage the details . . . There was no one moment to which he could point when his health had begun to fail. Two years before he had had a very hard summer at the Bar, complicated by the chairmanship of a Royal Commission, and a trip to Norway for the August sea trout had been disastrous. He had returned still a little fatigued. He no longer got up in the morning with a certain uplift of spirit, work seemed duller and more laborious, food less appetizing, sleep more imperative but less refreshing.

During that winter he had had a bout of influenza for the first time in his life. After it he had dragged his wing for a month or two, but had seemed to pick up in the spring when he had had a trip to Provence with the Clanroydens. But the hot summer had given him a set-back, and when he went shooting with Lamancha in the autumn he found to his dismay that he had become short of breath and that the hills were too steep for him. Also he was clearly losing weight. So on his return to London he sought out Acton Croke and had himself examined. The great doctor had been ominously grave. Our fathers, he said, had talked unscientifically about the 'grand climacteric', which came in the early sixties, but there was such a thing as a climacteric which might come any time in middle life, when the physical powers adjusted themselves to the approach of age. That crisis Leithen was now enduring, and he must go very carefully and remember that the dose of gas he got in the War had probably not exhausted its effect. Croke put him on a diet, prescribed a certain routine of rest and exercise, and made him drastically cut down his engagements. He insisted also on seeing him once a fortnight.

A winter followed for Leithen of steadily declining health. His breath troubled him and a painful sinking in the chest. He rose languidly, struggled through the day, and went to bed exhausted. Every moment he was conscious of his body and its increasing frailty. Croke sent him to a nursing home during the Christmas vacation, and for a few weeks he seemed to be better. But the coming of spring, instead of giving him new vigour, drained his strength. He began to suffer from night sweats which left him very feeble in the morning. His meals became a farce. He drove himself to take exercise, but now a walk round the Park exhausted one who only a few years back could walk down any Highland gillie. Croke's face looked graver with each visit.

Then the day before yesterday had come the crisis. He went by appointment to Croke – and demanded a final verdict. The great doctor gave it: gravely, anxiously, tenderly, as to an old friend, but without equivocation. He was dying, slowly dying.

Leithen's mind refused to bite on the details of his own case with its usual professional precision. He was not interested in these details. He simply accepted the judgement of the expert. He was suffering from advanced tuberculosis, a retarded consequence of his gas-poisoning. Croke, knowing his patient's habit of mind, had given him a full diagnosis, but Leithen had scarcely listened to his exposition of the chronic fibrous affection and broncho-pulmonary lesions. The fact was enough for him.

'How long have I to live?' he asked, and was told a year, perhaps a little longer.

'Shall I go off suddenly, or what?' The answer was that there would be a progressive loss of strength until the heart failed.

'You can give me no hope?'

Croke shook his head.

'I dare not. The lesions *might* heal, the fibrous patch *might* disappear, but it would be a miracle according to present knowledge. I must add, of course, that our present knowledge may not be final truth.'

'But I must take it as such, I agree. Miracles don't happen.'

Leithen left Harley Street almost cheerfully. There was a grim satisfaction in knowing the worst. He was so utterly weary that after coffee and a sandwich in his rooms he went straight to bed.

Soon he must think things out, but not at once. He must first make some necessary arrangements about his affairs which would keep him from brooding. That should be the task of the morrow. It all reminded him of his habit as a company commander in the trenches when an attack was imminent: he had busied himself with getting every detail exact, so that his mind had no time for foreboding ...

As he lay watching his window brighten with the morning he wondered why he was taking things so calmly. It was not courage – he did not consider himself a brave man, though he had never greatly feared death. At the best he had achieved in life a thin stoicism, a shallow fortitude. Insensibility, perhaps, was the best word. He remembered Dr Johnson's reply to Boswell's 'That, sir, was great fortitude of mind.' – 'No, sir, stark insensibility.'

At any rate he would not sink to self-pity. He had been brought up in a Calvinistic household and the atmosphere still clung to him, though in the ordinary way he was not a religious man. For example, he had always had an acute sense of sin, which had made him something of a Puritan in his way of life. He had believed firmly in God, a Being of ineffable purity and power, and consequently had had no undue reverence for man. He had always felt his own insignificance and imperfections and was not inclined to cavil at fate. On the contrary, he considered that fortune had been ludicrously kind to him. He had had fifty-eight years of health and wealth. He had survived the War, when the best of his contemporaries had fallen in swathes. He had been amazingly successful in his profession and had enjoyed every moment of his work. Honours had fallen to him out of all proportion to his merits. He had had a thousand pleasures – books, travel, the best of sport, the best of friends.

His friends – that had been his chief blessing. As he thought of their warm companionship he could not check a sudden wave

18

of regret. *That* would be hard to leave. He had sworn Acton Croke to secrecy, and he meant to keep his condition hidden even from his closest intimates – from Hannay and Clanroyden and Lamancha and Palliser-Yeates and Archie Roylance. He could not endure to think of their anxious eyes. He would see less of them than before, of course, but he would continue to meet them on the old terms. Yes – but how? He was giving up Parliament and the Bar – London, too. What story was he to tell? A craving for rest and leisure? Well, he must indulge that craving at a distance, or otherwise his friends would discover the reason.

But where? ... Borrowby? Impossible, for it was associated too closely with his years of vigour. He had rejoiced in reshaping that ancient shell into a house for a green old age; he remembered with what care he had planned his library and his garden; Borrowby would be intolerable as a brief refuge for a dying man ... Scotland? – somewhere in the Lowland hills or on the sounding beaches of the west coast? But he had been too happy there. All the romance of childhood and forward-looking youth was bound up with those places and it would be agony to revisit them.

His memory sprawled over places he had seen in his much-travelled life. There was a certain Greek island where he had once lived dangerously; there were valleys on the Italian side of the Alps, and a *saeter* in the Jotunheim to which his fancy had often returned. But in his survey he found that the charm had gone from them; they were for the living, not the dying. Only one spot had still some appeal. In his early youth, when money had not been plentiful, he had had an autumn shooting trip in northern Quebec because it was cheap. He had come down on foot over the height of land, with a single Montagnais guide back-packing their kit, and one golden October afternoon he had stumbled on a place which he had never forgotten. It was a green saddle of land, a meadow of wild hay among the pines. South from it a stream ran to the St Lawrence; from an adjacent well another trickle flowed north on the Arctic watershed. It had seemed a haven of pastoral peace in a shaggy land, and he recalled how loth he had been to leave it. He had often thought about it, often determined to go back and look for it. Now, as he pictured it in its green security, it seemed the kind of sanctuary in which to die. He remembered its name. The spring was called Clairefontaine, and it gave its name both to the south-flowing stream and to a little farm below in the valley.

Supposing he found the proper shelter, how was he to spend his closing months? As an invalid, slowly growing feebler, always expectant of death? That was starkly impossible. He wanted peace to make his soul, but not lethargy either of mind or body. The body! – that was the rub. It was failing him, that body which had once been a mettled horse quickly responding to bridle or spur. Now he must be aware every hour of its ignoble frailty ... He stretched out his arms, flexing the muscles as he used to do when he was well, and was conscious that there was no pith in them.

His thoughts clung to this physical shell of his. He had been proud of it, not like an athlete who guards a treasure, but like a master proud of an adequate servant. It had added much to the pleasures of life ... But he realized that in his career it had mattered very little to him, for his work had been done with his mind. Labouring men had their physical strength as their only asset, and when the body failed them their work was done. They knew from harsh experience the limits of their strength, what exhaustion meant, and strife against pain and disablement. They had to endure all their days what he had endured to a small degree in the trenches ... Had he not missed something, and, missing it, had failed somehow in one of the duties of man?

This queer thought kept returning to him with the force of a revelation. His mood was the opposite of self-pity, a feeling that his life had been too cosseted and fur-lined. Only now that his body was failing did he realize how little he had used it ... Among the oddly assorted beliefs which made up his religious equipment, one was conditional immortality. The soul was only immortal if there was such a thing as a soul, and a further existence had to be earned in this one. He had used most of the talents God had given him, but not all. He had never, except in the War, staked his body in the struggle, and yet that was the stake of most of humanity. Was it still possible to meet that test of manhood with a failing body? ... If only the War were still going on!

His mind, which had been dragging apathetically along, suddenly awoke into vigour. By God! there was one thing that would not happen. He would not sit down and twiddle his thumbs and await death. His ship, since it was doomed, should go down in action with every flag flying. Lately he had been re-reading *Vanity Fair* and he remembered the famous passage where Thackeray moralizes on the trappings of the conventional death-bed, the soft-footed nurses, the hushed voices of the household, the alcove on the staircase in which to rest the coffin. The picture affected him with a physical nausea. That, by God! should never be his fate. He would die standing, as Vespasian said an emperor should ...

The day had broadened into full sunlight. The white paint and the flowered wallpaper of his bedroom glowed with the morning freshness, and from the street outside came pleasant morning sounds like the jingle of milk-cans and the whistling of errand boys. His mind seemed to have been stabbed awake out of a flat stoicism into a dim but masterful purpose.

He got up and dressed, and his cold bath gave him a ghost of an appetite for breakfast.

# 3

His intention was to go down to his chambers later in the morning and get to work on the batch of cases for opinion. As always after a meal, he felt languid and weak, but his mind was no longer comatose. Already it was beginning to move steadily, though hopelessly, towards some kind of plan. As he sat huddled in a chair at the open window Cruddock announced that a Mr Blenkiron was on the telephone and would like an appointment.

This was the American that Sandy Clanroyden had spoken of. Leithen remembered him clearly as his client in a big case. He remembered, too, much that he had heard about him from Sandy and Dick Hannay. One special thing, too – Blenkiron had been a sick man in the War and yet had put up a remarkable show. He had liked him, and, though he felt himself now cut off from human companionship, he could hardly refuse an interview, for Sandy's sake. The man had probably some lawsuit in hand, and if so it would not take long to refuse.

'If convenient, sir, the gentleman could come along now,' said Cruddock.

Leithen nodded and took up the newspaper.

Blenkiron had aged. Eight years ago Leithen recalled him as a big man with a heavy shaven face, a clear skin, and calm ruminant grey eyes. A healthy creature in hard condition, he could have given a good account of himself with his hands as well as his head. Now he was leaner and more grizzled, and there were pouches under his eyes. Leithen remembered Sandy's doings in South America; Blenkiron had been in that show, and he had heard about his being a sort of industrial dictator in Olifa, or whatever the place was called.

The grey eyes were regarding him contemplatively but keenly. He wondered what they made of his shrunken body.

'It's mighty fine to see you again, Sir Edward. And all the boys, too. I've been stuck so tight in my job down south that I've gotten out of touch with my friends. I'm giving myself a holiday to look them up and to see my little niece. I think you know Babs.'

'I know her well. A very great woman. I had forgotten she was your niece. How does the old gang strike you?'

'Lasting well, sir. A bit older and maybe a bit wiser and settling down into good citizens. They tell me that Sir Archibald Roylance is making quite a name for himself in your Parliament, and that Lord Clanroyden cuts a deal of ice with your Government. Dick Hannay, I judge, is getting hayseed into his hair. How about yourself?'

'Fair,' Leithen said. 'I'm going out of business now. I've worked hard enough to be entitled to climb out of the rut.'

'That's fine!' Blenkiron's face showed a quickened interest. 'I haven't forgotten what you did for me when I was up against the Delacroix bunch. There's no man on the globe I'd sooner have with me in a nasty place than you. You've a mighty quick brain and a mighty sound judgement and you're not afraid to take a chance.'

'You're very kind,' said Leithen a little wearily. 'Well, that's all done with now. I am going out of harness.'

'A man like you can't ever get out of harness. If you lay down one job you take up another.'

Blenkiron's eyes, appraising now rather than meditative, scanned the other's face. He leaned forward in his chair and sank his voice.

'I came round this morning to say something to you, Sir Edward – something very special. Babs has a sister, Felicity – I guess you don't know her, but she's something of a person on our side of

22

the water. Two years younger than Babs, and married to a man you've maybe heard of, Francis Galliard, one of old Simon Ravelston's partners. Young Galliard's gotten a great name in the city of New York, and Felicity and he looked like being a happy pair. But just lately things haven't been going too well with Felicity.'

In common politeness Leithen forced a show of attention, but Blenkiron had noted his dull eyes.

'I won't trouble you with the story now,' he went on, 'for it's long and a bit ravelled, but the gist of it is that Francis Galliard has disappeared over the horizon. Just leaked out of the landscape without a word to Felicity or anybody else. No! There is no suggestion of kidnapping or any dirty work – the trouble is in Francis's own mind. He is a Canuck – a Frenchman from Quebec – and I expect his mind works different from yours and mine. Now, he has got to be found and brought back – first of all to Felicity, and second, to his business, and third, to the United States. He's too valuable a man to lose, and in our present state of precarious balance we just can't afford it.'

Blenkiron stopped as if he expected some kind of reply. Leithen said nothing, but his thoughts had jumped suddenly to the upland meadow of Clairefontaine of which he had been thinking that morning. Odd that that remote memory should have been suddenly dug out of the lumber-room of the past!

'We want help in the job,' Blenkiron continued, 'and it's not going to be easy to find it. We want a man who can piece together the bits that make up the jigsaw puzzle, though we haven't got much in the way of evidence. We want a man who can read himself into Francis's mind and understand the thoughts he might have been thinking, and, most of all, we want a man who can put his conclusions into action. Finding Francis may mean a good deal of bodily wear and tear and taking some risks.'

'I see,' Leithen spoke at last. 'You want a combination of detective, psychologist and sportsman.'

'Yep.' Blenkiron beamed. 'You've hit it. And there's just the one man I know that fills the bill. I've had a talk with Lord Clanroyden and he agrees. If you had been going on at the Bar we would have offered you the biggest fee that any brief ever carried, for there's money to burn in this business – though I don't reckon the fee would have weighed much with you. But you tell me you are

23

shaking loose. Well, here's a job for your leisure and, if I judge you right, it's the sort of job you won't turn down without a thought or two.'

Leithen raised his sick eyes to the eager face before him, a face whose abounding vitality sharpened the sense of his own weakness.

'You've come a little late,' he said slowly. 'I'm going to tell you something which Lord Clanroyden and the others don't know, and will never know – which nobody knows except myself and my doctor – and I want you to promise to keep it secret . . . I'm a dying man. I've only about a year to live.'

He was not certain what he expected, but he was certain it would be something which would wind up this business for good. He had longed to have one confidant, only one, and Blenkiron was safe enough. The sound of his voice speaking these grim words somehow chilled him, and he awaited dismally the conventional sympathy. After that Blenkiron would depart and he would see him no more.

But Blenkiron did not behave conventionally. He flushed deeply and sprang to his feet, upsetting his chair.

'My God!' he cried. 'If I ain't the blightedest, God-darned blundering fool! I might have guessed by your looks you were a sick man, and now I've hurt you in the raw with my cursed egotistical worries . . . I'm off, Sir Edward. Forget you ever saw me. God forgive me, for I won't soon forgive myself.'

'Don't go,' said Leithen. 'Sit down and talk to me. You may be the very man I want.'

# 4

His hostess noticed his slow appraising look round the table, which took each of the guests in turn.

'You were here last in '29,' she said. 'Do you think we have changed?'

Leithen turned his eyes to the tall woman at his left hand. Mrs Simon Ravelston had a beautiful figure, ill-chosen clothes, and the weather-beaten face of an English master of foxhounds. She was magnificently in place on horseback, or sailing a boat, or running with her beagles, but no indoor setting could fit her. Sprung from ancient New England stock, she showed her breeding in a wonderful detachment from the hubbub of life. At her own table she would drift into moods of reverie and stare into vacancy, oblivious of the conversation, and then when she woke up would turn such kind eyes upon her puzzled interlocutor that all offences were forgiven. When her husband had been Ambassador at the Court of St James's she had been widely popular, a magnet for the most sophisticated young men; but of this she had been wholly unconscious. She was deeply interested in life and very little interested in herself.

Leithen answered, 'Yes, I think you all look a little more fine-drawn and harder trained. The men, that is. The women could never change.'

Mrs Ravelston laughed. 'I hope that you're right. Before the depression we were getting rather gross. The old Uncle Sam that we took as our national figure was lean like a Red Indian, but in late years our ordinary type had become round-faced, and puffy, and pallid, like a Latin John Bull. Now we are recovering Uncle Sam, though we have shaved him and polished him up.' Her eyes ran round the table and stopped at a youngish man with strong rugged features and shaggy eyebrows who was listening with a smile to the talk of a very pretty girl.

'George Lethaby, for example. Thank goodness he is a career diplomat and can show himself about the world. I should like people to take him as a typical American.' She lowered her voice, for she was speaking now of her left-hand neighbour, 'Or Bronson, here. You know him, don't you? Bronson Jane.'

Leithen glanced beyond his hostess to where a man just passing into middle life was peering at an illegible menu card. This was the bright particular star of the younger America, and he regarded him with more than curiosity, for he counted upon him for help. On paper Bronson Jane was almost too good to be true. He had been a noted sportsman and was still a fine polo player; his name was a household word in Europe for his work in international finance; he was the Admirable Crichton of his day and it was rumoured that in the same week he had been offered the Secretary-ship of State, the Presidency of an ancient University, and the control of a great industrial corporation. He had chosen the third, but seemed to have a foot also in every other world. He had a plain sagacious face, a friendly mouth, and deep-set eyes, luminous and masterful.

Leithen glanced round the table again. The dining-room of the Ravelston house was a homely place; it had no tapestries or panelling, and its pictures were family portraits of small artistic merit. In each corner there were marble busts of departed Ravelstons. It was like the rest of the house, and, like their country homes in the Catskills and on the Blue Ridge, a dwelling which bore the mark of successive generations who had all been acutely conscious of the past. Leithen felt that he might have been in a poor man's dwelling, but for the magnificence of the table flowers and silver and the gold soup plates which had once belonged to a King of France. He let his gaze rest on each of the men.

'Yes,' he told his hostess, 'you are getting the kind of face I like.'

'But not the right colour perhaps,' she laughed. 'Is that worry or too much iced water, I wonder?' She broke off suddenly, remembering her neighbour's grey visage.

'Tell me who the people are,' he said to cover her embarrassment. 'I have met Mr Jane and Mr Lethaby and Mr Ravelston.'

'I want you to know my Simon better,' she said. 'I know why you have come here – Mr Blenkiron told me. Nobody knows about it except in the family. The story is that Mr Galliard has gone to Peru to look into some pitchblende propositions. Simon is terribly distressed and he feels so helpless. You see, we only came back to America from England four months ago, and we have kind of lost touch.'

Simon Ravelston was a big man with a head like Jove, and a noble silvered beard. He was president of one of the chief private banking houses in the world, which under his great-grandfather had financed the first railways beyond the Appalachians, under his grandfather had salved the wreckage of the Civil War, and under his father had steadied America's wild gallop to wealth. He had a dozen partners, most of whom understood the technique of finance far better than himself, but on all major questions he spoke the last word, for he had the great general's gift of reducing complexities to a simple syllogism. In an over-worked world he seemed always to have ample leisure, for he insisted on making time to think. When others of his calling were spending twelve hectic hours daily

26

in their offices, Simon would calmly go fishing. No man ever saw him rattled or hustled, and this Olympian detachment gave him a prestige in two continents against which he himself used to protest vigorously.

'They think I'm wise only because I don't talk when I've nothing to say,' he used to tell his friends. 'Any fool these days can get a reputation if he keeps his mouth shut.'

He was happy because his mind was filled with happy interests; he had no itching ambitions, he did his jobs as they came along with a sincere delight in doing them well, and a no less sincere delight in seeing the end of them. He was the extreme opposite of the man whose nerves demand a constant busyness because, like a bicyclist, he will fall down if he stays still.

Leithen's gaze passed to a young man who had Simon's shape of head but was built on a smaller and more elegant scale. His hostess followed his eyes.

'That's our boy, Eric, and that's his wife Delia, across the table. Pretty, isn't she? She has the southern complexion, the real thing, which isn't indigestion from too much hot bread at breakfast. What's he doing? He's on the Johns Hopkins staff and is making a big name for himself in lung surgery. Ever since a little boy he's been set on doctoring and nothing would change him. He had a pretty good training – Harvard – two years at Oxford – a year in Paris – a long spell in a Montreal hospital. That's a new thing about our boys, Sir Edward. They're not so set nowadays on big business. They want to do things and make things, and they consider that there are better tools than dollars. George Lethaby is an example. He's a poor man and always will be, for a diplomat can't be a money-maker. But he's a happier man than Harold Downes, though he doesn't look it.'

Mr Lethaby's rugged face happened at the moment to be twisted into an expression of pain out of sympathy with some tale of the woman to whom he was talking, while his *vis-à-vis*, Mr Downes, was laughing merrily at a remark of his neighbour.

'Harold has a hard life,' said Mrs Ravelston. 'He's head of the Fremont Banking Corporation and a St Sebastian for everyone to shoot arrows at. Any more to be catalogued? Why, yes, there are the two biggest exhibits of all.'

She directed Leithen's eyes to two men separated by a handsome old woman whose hair was dressed in the fashion of forty years ago.

'You see the man on the far side of Ella Purchass, the plump little man with the eagle beak who looks like he's enjoying his food. What would you set him down as?'

'Banker? Newspaper proprietor?'

'Wrong. That's Walter Derwent. You've heard of him? His father left him all kinds of wealth, but Walter wasted no time in getting out of oil into icebergs. He has flown and mushed and tramped over most of the Arctic, and there are heaps of mountains and wild beasts named after him. And you'd never think he'd moved further than Long Island. Now place the man on this side of Ella.'

Leithen saw a typical English hunting man – lean brown face with the skin stretched tight over the cheek bones, pale, deep-set eyes, a small clipped moustache, shoulders a little stooped from being much on horseback.

'Virginian squire,' he hazarded. 'Warrenton at a guess.'

'Wrong,' she laughed. 'He wouldn't be happy at Warrenton, and I'm certain he wouldn't be happy on a horse. His line is deep learning. He's about our foremost pundit – professor at Yale – dug up cities in Asia Minor – edited Greek books. Writes very nice little stories, too. That's Clifford Savory.'

Leithen looked with interest at the pleasant vital face. He knew all about Clifford Savory. There were few men alive who were his equals in classical scholarship, and he had published one or two novels, delicate historical reconstructions, which were masterpieces in their way.

His gaze circled round the table again, noting the friendliness of the men's eyes, the atmosphere of breeding and simplicity and stability. He turned to his hostess –

'You've got together a wonderful party for me,' he said. 'I feel what I always feel when I come here – that you are the friendliest people on earth. But I believe, too, that you are harder to get to know than our awkward, difficult, tongue-tied folk at home. To get to know really well, I mean – inside your plate-armour of general benevolence.'

Mrs Ravelston laughed. 'There may be something in that. It's a new idea to me.'

'I think you are sure of yourselves, too. There is no one at this table who hasn't steady nerves and a vast deal of common sense. You call it poise, don't you?'

'Maybe, but this is a picked party, remember.'

'Because of its poise?'

'No. Because every man here is a friend of Francis Galliard.'

'Friend? Do you mean acquaintance or intimate?'

The lady pursed her lips.

'I'm not sure. I think you are right and that we are not an easy people to be intimate with unless we have been brought up with the same background. Francis, too, is scarcely cut out for intimacy. Did you ever meet him?'

'No. I heard his name for the first time a few weeks ago. Which of you knows him best? Mr Ravelston?'

'Certainly not Simon, though he's his business partner. Francis has a good many sides, and most people know only one of them. Bronson could tell you most about his work. He likes my Eric, but hasn't seen much of him in recent years. I know he used to go duck-shooting in Minnesota with George Lethaby, and he's a trustee of Walter Derwent's Polar Institute. I fancy Clifford Savory is nearer to him than most people. And yet ... I don't know. Maybe nobody has got to know the real Francis. He has that frank, forthcoming manner which conceals a man, and he's mighty busy too, too busy for intimacies. I used to see him once or twice a week, but I couldn't tell you anything about him that everybody doesn't know. It won't be easy, Sir Edward, to get a proper notion of him from second-hand evidence. Felicity's your best chance. You haven't met Felicity yet?'

'I'm leaving her to the last. What's she like? I know her sister well.'

'She's a whole lot different from Babs. I can tell you she's quite a person.'

Leithen felt that if his hostess had belonged to a different social grade she would have called her a 'lovely woman'. Her meaning was clear. Mrs Galliard was someone who mattered.

He was beginning to feel very weary, and, knowing that he must ration his strength, he made his excuses and did not join the women after dinner. But he spent a few minutes in the library, to which the men retired for coffee and cigars. He had one word with Clifford Savory.

'I heard you five years ago at the Bar Association,' Savory said. 'You spoke on John Marshall. I hope you're going to give me an evening on this visit.'

Bronson Jane accompanied him to the door.

'You're taking it easy, I understand, Sir Edward, and going slow with dinners. What about the Florian tomorrow at half past five? In these hot days that's a good time for a talk.'

# 5

The library of the Florian Club looked out on the East River, where the bustle of traffic was now dying down and the turbid waters catching the mellow light of the summer evening. It might have been a room in an old English country house with its Chippendale chairs and bookcases, and the eighteenth-century mezzo-tints on the walls. The two men sat by the open window, and the wafts of cool evening air gave Leithen for the first time that day a little physical comfort.

'You want me to tell you about Francis Galliard?'

Bronson Jane's wholesome face showed no signs of fatigue, though he had been having a gruelling day.

'I'll tell you all I can, but I warn you that it's not much. I suppose I'm as close to him as most people, but I can't say I knew him well. No one does – except perhaps his wife. But I can give you the general lay-out. First of all, he is a French-Canadian. Do you know anything about French Canada?'

'I once knew a little – a long time ago.'

'Well, they are a remarkable race there. They ought to have made a rather bigger show in the world than they have. Here's a fine European stock planted out in a new country and toughened by two centuries of hardship and war. They keep their close family life and their religion intact and don't give a cent for what we call progress. Yet all the time they have a pretty serious fight with nature, so there is nothing soft in them. You would say that boys would come out of those farms of theirs with a real kick in them, for they have always been a race of pioneers. But so far Laurier

30

is their only great man. You'd have thought that now and then they would have produced somebody big in the business line, like the Scots. You have young Highlanders, haven't you, coming out of the same primitive world, who become business magnates? We have had some of them in this country.'

'Yes. That is not uncommon in Scotland.'

'Well, Francis is the only specimen I've struck from French Canada. He came out of a farm in the Laurentians, somewhere back of the Glaubsteins' new pulp town at Château-Gaillard. I believe the Gaillards go right back to the Crusades. They came to Canada with Champlain, and were the seigneurs of Château-Gaillard, a tract of country as big as Rhode Island. By and by they came down in the world until now they only possess a little bit of a farm at the end of nowhere.'

'What took him out of the farm? The French don't part easily from the land.'

'God knows. Ambition? Poverty? He never told me. I don't just know how he was raised, for he never speaks of his early days. The village school, I suppose, and then some kind of college, for his first notion was to be a priest. He had a pretty good education of an old-fashioned kind. Then something stirred in him and he set off south like the fairy-tale Younger Son, with his pack on his back and his lunch in his pocket. He must have been about nineteen then.'

Leithen's interest quickened. 'Go on,' he said, as Bronson paused. 'How did he make good?'

'I'm darned if I know. There's a fine story there, but I can't get it out of him. He joined a French paper in Boston, and went on to another in Louisiana, and finished up in Chicago on a financial journal. I fancy that several times he must have pretty nearly starved. Then somehow he got into the bond business and discovered that he had a genius for one kind of finance. He was with Connolly in Detroit for a time, and after that with the Pontiac Trust here, and then Ravelstons started out to discover new blood and got hold of him. At thirty-five he was a junior partner, and since then he has never looked back. Today he's forty-three, and there aren't five men in the United States whose repute stands higher. Not bad for a farm boy, I'll say.'

'Does he keep in touch with his people?'

31

'Not he. That door is closed and bolted. He has never been back to Canada. He's a naturalized American citizen. He won't speak French unless he's forced to, and then it's nothing to boast of. He writes his name "Galliard", not Gaillard. He has let himself become absorbed in our atmosphere.'

'Really absorbed?'

'Well – that's just the point. He has adopted the externals of our life, but I don't know how much he's changed inside. When he married Felicity Dasent five years ago I thought we had got him for keeps. You don't know Mrs Galliard?'

Leithen shook his head. He had been asked this question now a dozen times since he landed.

'No? Well, I won't waste time trying to describe her, for you'll soon be able to judge for yourself; but I should call her a possessive personality, and she certainly annexed Francis. Oh yes, he was desperately in love and only too willing to do what she told him. He's a good-looking fellow, but he hadn't bothered much about his appearance, so she groomed him up and made him the best-dressed man in New York. They've got a fine apartment in Park Avenue and her dinners have become social events. The Dasents are a horsey family and I doubt if Francis had ever mounted a horse until his marriage, but presently she had him out regularly with the Westbrook. He bought a country place in New Jersey and is going to start in to breed 'chasers. Altogether she gives him a pretty full life.'

'Children?'

'No, not yet. A pity, for a child would have anchored Francis. I expect he has family in his blood like all his race.'

'He never appeared to be restless, did he?' Leithen asked.

'Not that I noticed. He seemed perfectly content. He used to work too hard and wear himself out, and every now and then have to go off for a rest. That's the tom-fool habit we all have here. You see, he hadn't any special tastes outside his business to make him keen about leisure. Felicity changed all that. She isn't anything of the social climber, or ambitious for herself, but she's mighty ambitious for her man. She brought him into all kinds of new circles, and he shines in them, too, for he has excellent brains – every kind of brains. All the gifts which made him a power in business she developed for other purposes. He was always a marvel in a business deal, for he could read other men's minds, and he would have made a swell diplomatist. Well, she turned that gift to social uses, with the result that every type mixes well at their parties. You'll hear as good talk at their table as you'll get anywhere on the civilized globe. He can do everything that a Frenchman can do, or an Englishman or an American. She has made him ten times more useful to Ravelstons than before, for she has made him a kind of national figure. The Administration has taken to consulting him, and he's one of the people that foreigners coming over here have got to see. I fancy she has politics at the back of her mind – last winter, I know, they were a good deal in Washington.'

Bronson lit a fresh cigar.

'All set fair, you'd say, for the big success of our day. And then suddenly one fine morning he slips out of the world like the man in Browning's poem, and God knows what's become of him.'

'You know him reasonably well? Is he happy?'

Bronson laughed. 'That's a question I couldn't answer about my own brother. I doubt if I could answer it about myself. He is gay – that is the French blood, maybe. I doubt if he has ever had time to consider whether he is happy or not, he lives such a bustling life. There can't be much of the introvert in Francis.'

A man had entered the room and was engaged in turning over the magazines on one of the tables.

'Here's Savory,' Bronson whispered. 'Let's have him join us. He's a rather particular friend of Francis.' He raised his voice, 'Hullo, Clifford! Come and have a drink. Sir Edward wants to see you.'

Clifford Savory, looking more like a country squire than ever in his well-cut grey flannels, deposited his long figure in an armchair and sipped the whisky-and-soda which the club servant brought him.

'We were talking about Galliard,' Bronson said. 'Sir Edward has heard a lot about him and is keen to meet him. It's just too bad that he should be out of town at present. It seems that Francis has got a reputation across the water. What was it you wanted to ask, Sir Edward? How much of his quality comes from his French blood?'

Savory joined his finger-tips and regarded them meditatively.

'That's hard to say. I don't know enough of the French in Canada, for they're different from the French in Europe. But I grant

33

you that Galliard's power is exotic – not the ordinary gifts that God has given us Americans. He can argue a case brilliantly with the most close-textured reasoning; but there are others who can do that. His real strength lies in his *flair*, which can't be put down in black and white. He has an extra sense which makes him conscious of things which are still in the atmosphere – a sort of instinct of what people are going to think quite a bit ahead, not only in America, but in England and Europe. His mind is equipped with no end of sensitive antennae. When he trusts that instinct he is never wrong, but now and then, of course, he is over-ridden by prosaic folk. If people had listened to him in '29 we should be better off now.'

'That's probably due to his race,' said Leithen. 'Whenever you get a borderland where Latin and Northman meet, you get this uncanny sensitiveness.'

'Yes,' said Savory, 'and yet in other things his race doesn't show up at all. Attachment to family and birthplace, for instance. Francis has forgotten all about his antecedents. He cares as little about his origin as Melchizedek. He is as rootless as the last-arrived Polish immigrant. He has pulled up his roots in Canada, and I do not think he is getting them down here – too restless for that.'

'Restless?' Leithen queried.

'Well, I mean mobile – always on the move. He is restless in another way, too. I doubt if he is satisfied by what he does, or particularly happy. A man can scarcely be if he lives in a perpetual flux.'

6

A figure was taking shape at the back of Leithen's mind, a figure without material mould, but an outline of character. He was beginning to realize something of the man he had come to seek. The following afternoon, when he stood in the hall of the Galliards' apartment in Park Avenue, he had the chance of filling in the physical details, for he was looking at a portrait of the man.

It was one of the young Van Rouyn's most celebrated achievements, painted two years earlier. It showed a man in riding breeches and a buff leather coat sitting on a low wall above a flower garden. His hair was a little ruffled by the wind, and one hand was repelling the advances of a terrier. Altogether an attractive detail of what should have been a 'conversation piece'. Leithen looked at the picture with the liveliest interest. Galliard was very different from the conception he had formed of him. He had thought of him as a Latin type, slim and very dark, and it appeared that he was more of a Norman, with well-developed shoulders like a football player. It was a pleasant face, the brown eyes were alight with life, and the mouth was both sensitive and firm. Perhaps the jaw was a little too fine-drawn, and the air of bonhomie too elaborate to be quite natural. Still, it was a face a man would instinctively trust, the face of a good comrade, and there could be no question about its supreme competence. In every line there was energy and quick decision.

Leithen gazed at it for some time, trying to find what he had expected.

'Do you think it a good likeness?' he asked the woman at his side.

'It's Francis at his best and happiest,' she answered.

Felicity Galliard was a fair edition of her sister Barbara. She was not quite so tall or quite so slim, and with all her grace she conveyed an impression, not only of physical health, but of physical power. There was a charming athleticism about her; she had none of Barbara's airy fragility. Her eyes were like her sister's, a cool grey with sudden lights in them which changed their colour. She was like a bird, always poised to fly, no easy swoop or flutter, but, if need be, a long stern flight against weather and wind.

She led Leithen into the drawing-room. Her house was very different from the Ravelstons', where a variety of oddments represented the tastes of many generations. It was a 'period' piece, the walls panelled in a light, almost colourless wood, the scanty furniture carefully chosen, an Aubusson carpet, and hangings and chintzes of grey and old rose and silver. A Nattier over the fireplace made a centre for the exquisite harmony. It was a room without tradition or even individuality, as if its possessors had deliberately sought out something which should be non-committal, an environment which should neither reflect nor influence them.

'You never met Francis?' she asked as she made tea. 'We have been twice to Europe since we married, but only once in England, and then only for a few days. They were business trips, and he didn't have a moment to himself.'

Her manner was beautifully composed, with no hint of tragedy, but in her eyes Leithen read an anxiety so profound that it was beyond outward manifestation. This woman was living day and night with fear. The sight of her, and of the picture in the hall, moved him strangely. He felt that between the Galliards and the friendly eupeptic people he had been meeting there was a difference, not of degree, but of kind. There was a quality here, undependable, uncertain, dangerous perhaps, but rare and unmistakable. There had been no domestic jar – of that he was convinced. But something had happened to one of them to shatter a happy partnership. If he could discover that something he would have a clue for his quest.

'I have never met your husband,' he said, 'but I've heard a great deal about him, and I think I'm beginning to understand him. That picture in the hall helps, and you help. I know your sister and your uncle, and now that I'm an idle man I've promised to do what I can. If I'm to be of any use, Mrs Galliard, I'm afraid I must ask you some questions. I know you'll answer them frankly. Tell me first what happened when he went away.'

'It was the fourth day of May, a perfect spring day. I went down to Westchester to see an old friend. I said good-bye to Francis after breakfast, and he went to the office. I came back about five o'clock and found a note from him on my writing-table. Here it is.'

She produced from an escritoire a half-sheet of paper. Leithen read –

*'Dearest, I am sick – very sick in mind. I am going away. When I am cured I will come back to you. All my love.'*

'He packed a bag himself – the butler knew nothing about it. He took money with him – at least there was a large sum drawn from his account. No, he didn't wind up things at the office. He left some big questions undecided, and his partners have had no end of trouble. He didn't say a word to any of them, or to anybody else that I know of. He left no clue as to where he was going. Oh, of course, we could have put on detectives and found out something, but we dared not do that. Every newspaper in the land would have started a hue and cry, and there would have been a storm of gossip. As it is, nobody knows about him except his partners, and one or two friends, and Uncle Blenkiron, and Babs and you. You see he may come back any day quite well again, and I would never forgive myself if I had been neurotic and let him down.'

Leithen thought that neurotic was the last word he would have chosen to describe this wise and resolute woman.

'What was he like just before he left? Was there any change in his manner? Had he anything to worry him?'

'Nothing to worry him in business. Things were going rather specially well. And, anyhow, Francis never let himself be worried by affairs. He prided himself on taking things lightly – he was always what the old folk used to call debonair. But – yes, there were little changes in him, I think. All winter he had been almost too good and gentle and yielding. He did everything I asked him without questioning, and that was not always his way ... Oh! and he did one funny thing. We used to go down to Florida for a fortnight after Christmas – we had a regular foursome for golf, and he liked to bask in the sun. This year he didn't seem to care about it, and I didn't press him, for I'm rather bored with golf, so we stayed at home. There was a good deal of snow at Combermere – that's our New Jersey home – and Francis got himself somewhere a pair of snow-shoes and used to go for long walks alone. When he came back he would sit by the hour in the library, not dozing, but thinking. I thought it was a good way of resting and never disturbed him.'

'You never asked what he was thinking about?'

'No. He thought a good deal, you see. He always made leisure to think. My only worry was about his absurd modesty. He was sure of himself, but not nearly so sure as I was, and recently when people praised him and I repeated the praise he used to be almost cross. He wrote a memorandum for the Treasury about some tax scheme, and Mr Beverley said that it was a work of genius. When I told him that, I remember he lay back in his chair and said quite bitterly, *"Quel chien de génie!"* He never used a French phrase except when he was tired or upset. I remember the look on his face – it was as if I had really pained him. But I could find nothing to be seriously anxious about. He was perfectly fit and well.'

'Did he see much of anybody in particular in the last weeks?'

'I don't think so. We always went about together, you know. He liked to talk to Mr Jane and Mr Savory, and they often dined with us. I think young Eric Ravelston came once or twice to the house – Walter Derwent, too, I think. But he saw far more of me than of anybody else.'

Her face suddenly stiffened with pain.

'Oh, Sir Edward, you don't think that he's dead – that he went away to die?'

'I don't. I haven't any fear of that. Any conclusion of mine would be worthless at the present stage, but my impression is that Mr Galliard's trouble has nothing to do with his health. You and he have made a wonderful life together. Are you certain that he quite fitted into it?'

She opened her eyes.

'He was a huge success in it.'

'I know. But did the success give him pleasure?'

'I'm sure it did. At least for most of the time.'

'Yes, but remember that it was a strange world to him. He hadn't been brought up in it. He may have been homesick for something different.'

'But he loved me!' she cried.

'He loved you. And therefore he will come back to you. But it may be to a different world.'

7

New scenes, new faces, the interests of a new problem had given Leithen a few days of deceptive vitality. Then the reaction came, and for a long summer's day he sat on the veranda of his hotel bedroom in body a limp wreck, but with a very active mind. He tried to piece together what he had heard of Galliard, but could reach no conclusion. A highly strung, sensitive being, with Heaven knew what strains in his ancestry, had been absorbed into a new world in which he had been brilliantly successful. And then something had snapped, or some atavistic impulse had emerged from the deeps, something strong enough to break the tie of a happy marriage. The thing was sheer mystery. He had abandoned his old world and had never shown the slightest hankering after it. What had caused this sudden satiety with success?

Bronson Jane and Savory thought that the trouble was physical, a delicate machine over-wrought and over-loaded. The difficulty was that his health had always been perfect, and there was no medical adviser who could report on the condition of his nerves. His friends thought that he was probably lying hidden in some quiet sunny place, nursing himself back to vigour, with the secretiveness of a man to whom a physical breakdown was so unfamiliar that it seemed a portent, almost a crime.

But Savory had been enlightening. Scholarly, critical, fastidious, he had spoken of Galliard, the ordinary successful financier with no special cultural background, with an accent almost of worship.

'This country of ours,' he told Leithen, 'is up against the biggest problem in her history. It is not a single question like slavery or state rights, or the control of monopolies, or any of the straightforward things that have made a crisis before. It is a conglomeration of problems, most of which we cannot define. We have no geographical frontier left, but we've an eternal frontier in our minds. Our old American society is really in dissolution. All of us have got to find a new way of life. You're lucky in England, for you've been at the job for a long time and you make your revolutions so slowly and so quietly that you don't notice them – or anybody else. Here we have to make ours against time, while we keep shouting about them at the top of our voices. Everybody and everything here has to have a new deal, and the different deals have to be fitted together like a jigsaw puzzle, or there will be an infernal confusion. We're a great people, but we're only by fits and starts a nation. You're fortunate in your British Empire. You may have too few folk, and these few scattered over big spaces, but they're all organically connected, like the separate apples on a tree. Our huge population is more like a collection of pebbles in a box. It's only the containing walls of the box that keep them together.'

So much for Savory's diagnosis.

'Francis is just the kind of fellow we need,' he went on. 'He sees what's coming. He's the most intellectually honest creature God ever made. He has a mind which not only cuts like a scalpel, but is rich and resourceful – both critical and creative. He hasn't any prejudices to speak of. He's a fascinating human being and rouses no antagonisms. It looks like he has dragged his anchor at present. But if we could get him properly moored again he's going to be a power for good in this country. We've got to get him back, Sir Edward – the old Francis.'

The old Francis? Leithen had queried.

'Well, with the old genius. But with an extra anchor down. I've never been quite happy about the strength of his moorings.'

# 8

Walter Derwent at first had nothing to tell him. Francis Galliard had not been interested in travel in far places. He was treasurer of his Polar Institute, but that was out of personal friendship. Francis had not much keenness in field sports either, though his wife had made him take up fox-hunting. He never went fishing, and in recent years he had not shot much, though he sometimes went after duck to Minnesota and the Virginia shore. He was not much of a bird-shot, but he was deadly with the rifle on the one occasion when Derwent had been with him after deer . . .

Derwent screwed up his pleasant rosy face till, with his eagle beak, he looked like a benevolent vulture. And then suddenly he let drop a piece of information which made Leithen sit up.

'But he did ask me – I remember – if I could recommend him a really first-class guide, a fellow that understood woodcraft and knew the northern woods. Maybe he was asking on behalf of someone else, for he couldn't have much use himself for a guide.'

'When was that?' Leithen asked sharply.

'Some time after Christmas. Early February, I reckon. Yes, it was just after our Adventurers' Club dinner.'

'Did you recommend one?'

'Yes. A fellow called Lew Frizel, a 'breed, but of a very special kind. His mother was a Cree Indian and his father one of the old-time Hudson's Bay factors. I've had Lew with me on half a dozen trips. I discovered him on a trap-line in northern Manitoba.'

'Where is he now?'

'That's what I can't tell you. He seems to have gone over the horizon. I wanted him for a trip up the Liard this fall, but I can get no answer from any of his addresses. He has a brother Johnny who is about as good, but he's not available, for he has a job with the Canadian Government in one of its parks – Waskesieu, up Prince Albert way.'

Leithen paid a visit to the Canadian Consulate, and after a talk with the Consul, who was an old friend, the telegraph was set in motion. Johnny Frizel, sure enough, had a job as a game warden at Waskesieu.

Another inquiry produced a slender clue. Leithen spent a morning at the Ravelston office and had a long talk with Galliard's private secretary, an intelligent young Yale man. From the office diary he investigated the subjects which had engaged Galliard's attention during his last weeks in New York. They were mostly the routine things on which the firm was then engaged, varied by a few special matters on which he was doing Government work. But one point caught Leithen's eye. Galliard had called for the papers about the Glaubstein pulp mill at Château-Gaillard and had even taken them home with him.

'Was there anything urgent about them?' he asked.

The secretary said no. The matter was dead as far as Ravelstons were concerned. They had had a lot to do with financing the original proposition, but long ago they had had their profit and were quit of it.

# 9

Leithen's last talk was with young Eric Ravelston. During the days in New York he had felt at times his weakness acutely, but he had not been conscious of any actual loss of strength. He wanted to be assured that he had still a modest reservoir to draw upon. The specialist examined him carefully and then looked at him with the same solemn eyes as Acton Croke.

'You know your condition, of course?' he asked.

'I do. A few weeks ago I was told that I had about a year to live. Do you agree?'

'It's not possible to fix a time schedule. You may have a year – or a little less – or a little more. If you went to a sanatorium and lived very carefully you might have longer.'

'I don't propose to lead a careful life. I've only a certain time and a certain amount of dwindling strength. I'm going to use them up on a hard job.'

'Well, in that case you may fluff out very soon, or you may go on for a year or more, for the mind has something to say in these questions.'

'There's no hope of recovery?'

'I'm afraid there's none – that is to say, in the light of our present knowledge. But, of course, we're not infallible.'

'Not even if I turn myself into a complete invalid?'

'Not even then.'

'Good. That's all I wanted to know. Now I've one other question. I'm going to look for Francis Galliard. You know him, but you never treated him, did you?'

Eric Ravelston shook his head.

'He didn't want any treatment. He was as healthy as a hound.'

Something in the young man's tone struck Leithen.

'You mean in body. Had you any doubt about other things – his mind, for instance?'

The other did not at first reply.

'I have no right to say this,' he spoke at last. 'And, anyhow, it isn't my proper subject. But for some time I have been anxious about Francis. Little things, you know. Only a doctor would notice them. I thought that there was something pathological about his marvellous vitality. Once I had Garford, the neurologist, staying with me and the Galliards came to dinner. Garford could not keep his eyes off Francis. After they had gone he told me that he would bet a thousand dollars that he crumpled up within a year ... So if there's a time limit for you, Sir Edward, there's maybe a time limit also for Francis.'

Leithen disembarked on a hot morning from the Quebec steamer which served the north shore of the St Lawrence. Chateau-Gaillard was like any other pulp town – a new pier with mighty derricks, the tall white cylinders of the pulp mill, a big brick office, and a cluster of clapboard shacks which badly needed painting. The place at the moment had a stagnant air, for the old cutting limits had been exhausted and the supply of pulp-wood from the new area was still being organized. A stream came in beyond the pier, and the background was steep scrub-clad hills cleft by a wedge-like valley beyond which there rose distant blue lines of mountain.

For the first mile or two the road up the valley was a hard, metalled highway. Leithen had not often felt feebler in body or more active in mind. Thoreau had been a favourite author of his youth, and he had picked up a copy in New York and had read it on the boat. Two passages stuck in his memory. One was from *Walden* –

'If you stand right fronting and face to face to a fact, you will see the sun glimmer on both its surfaces, as if it were a scimitar, and feel its sweet edge dividing you through the heart and marrow, and so you will happily conclude your mortal career. Be it life or death we crave only reality. If we are really dying, let us hear the rattle in our throat and feel the cold in the extremities; if we are alive, let us go about our business.'

The other was only a sentence –

'The cost of a thing is the amount of what I will call life which is required to be exchanged for it.'

How valuable was that thing for which he was bartering all that remained to him of life? At first Blenkiron's story had been no more than a peg on which to hang a private determination, an excuse, partly to himself and partly to the world, for a defiant finish to his career. The task fulfilled the conditions he wanted – activity for the mind and a final activity for the body. Francis Galliard was a disembodied ghost, a mere premise in an argument.

But now – Felicity had taken shape as a human being. There was an extraordinary appeal in her mute gallantry, her silent, self-contained fortitude. Barbara Clanroyden could not under any circumstances be pathetic; her airy grace was immune from the attacks of fate; she might bend, but she would never break. But her sister offered an exposed front to fortune. She was too hungry for life, too avid of experience, too venturesome, and more, she had set herself the task of moulding her husband to her ambitions. No woman, least of all his wife, would attempt to mould Sandy Clanroyden ... And the gods had given her tough material – not a docile piece of American manhood, but something exotic and unpredictable, something for which she had acquired a desperate affection, but of which she had only a dim understanding.

As for Francis, that shadow too was taking form. Leithen now had a picture of him in his mind, but it was not that of the portrait in the hall of the Park Avenue apartment. Oddly enough, it was of an older man, with a rough yellow beard. His eyes were different too, wilder, less assured, less benevolent. He told himself that he had reconstructed the physical appearance to match his conception of the character. For he had arrived at a provisional assessment of the man ... The chains of race and tradition are ill to undo, and Galliard, in his brilliant advance to success, had loosened, not broken them. Something had happened to tighten them again. The pull of an older world had jerked him out of his niche. But how? And whither?

# 11

The valley above the township was an ugly sight. The hillsides had been lumbered out and only scrub was left, and the shutes where the logs had been brought down were already tawny with young brushwood. In the bottom was a dam, which had stretched well up the slopes, for the lower scrub was bleached and muddied with water. But the sluices had been opened and the dam had shrunk to a few hundred yards in width, leaving the near hillsides a hideous waste of slime, the colour of a slag-heap. The place was like the environs of a town in the English Black Country.

Suddenly he was haunted by a recollection, a shadow at the back of his mind. The outline of the hills was familiar. Looking back, he realized that he had seen before the bluff which cut the view of the St Lawrence into a wedge of blue water. He had forgotten the details of that journey thirty years ago when he had tramped down from the mountains; but it must have been in this neighbourhood. There was a navvy on some job by the roadside, and he stopped the car and spoke to him.

The man shook his head. 'I'm a newcomer here. There's a guy up there – a Frenchie – maybe he'd tell you.'

Johnny Frizel went up the track in the bush to where a countryman was cutting stakes. He came back and reported.

'He says that before the dam was made there was a fine little river down there. The Clairefontaine was the name of it.'

Leithen's memory woke into vivid life. This valley had been his road down country long ago. He remembered its loveliness when Château-Gaillard had been innocent of pulp mills and no more than a hamlet of painted houses and a white church. There had been a strip of green meadow-land by the waterside grazed by old-fashioned French cattle, and the stream had swept through it in deep pools and glittering shallows, while above it pine and birch had climbed in virgin magnificence to the crests. Now all the loveliness had been butchered to enable some shoddy newspaper to debauch the public soul. He had only seen the place once long ago at the close of a blue autumn day, but the desecration beat on his mind like a blow. What had become of the little Clairefontaine farm at the river head, and that delicate place on the height of land which had of late been haunting him? ... He felt a curious nervousness and it brought on a fit of coughing.

At the end of the dam the road climbed the left side of the valley through patches of spruce and a burnt-out area of blackened stumps. A ridge separated it from the stream, and when it turned again to the water's edge the character of the valley had changed. The Clairefontaine rumbled in a deep gorge, and as the aged Ford wheezed its way up the dusty roads Château-Gaillard and its ugliness were shut off and Leithen found himself in a sanctuary of the hills. He could not link up the place with his memory of thirty years ago when he had descended it on foot in the gold and scarlet of autumn. Then it had been a pathway to the outer world; now it was the entry into a secret and strange land. There was no colour in the scene, except the hard blue of the sky. The hot noon had closed down like a lid on an oppressive dull green waste which offered no welcome.

His mind was full of Francis Galliard. Once this had been the seigneury of his family, running back from the tide-water some scores of miles into the wilderness. He felt the man here more vividly than ever before, but he could not affiliate him with the landscape, except that he also was a mystery ...

Why had his wife and his friends in New York been so oddly supine in looking for him? They had waited and left it for a stranger to take on the job. Fear of publicity, of course, in that over-public world. But was that the only reason? Was there not also fear of Galliard? He was not of their world, and they admired and loved him, but uncomprehendingly. Even Felicity. What did they fear? That they might wreck a subtle mechanism by a too heavy hand? They were all sensitive people and highly intelligent, and they would have not walked so delicately without a cause. Only now, when he was entering the cradle of Galliard's race, did he realize how intricate was the task to which he had set himself. And one to be performed against time. He remembered the young Ravelston's words. There was a time limit for Francis Galliard, as there was one for Edward Leithen.

The valley mounted by steps, each one marked by the thunder of a cataract in the gorge. Presently they rose above the woods, and came out on a stretch of open upland where the stream flowed among patches of crops and meadows of hay. Now his memory was clearer, for he remembered this place in exact detail. There was the farm of Clairefontaine, with its shingled, penthouse roof, its white-painted front, its tall weather-beaten barn, its jumble of decrepit outhouses. There was the little church of the parish, the usual white box, with a tin-coated spire now shining like silver in the sun, and beside it a hump-backed presbytery. And there was something beyond of which the memory was even sharper. For the valley seemed to come to an end, the wooded ranges closed in on it, but there was a crack through which the stream must flow from some distant upland. He knew what lay beyond that nick which was like the back-sight of a rifle.

'We won't stop here,' he told Johnny, who handled the Ford like an artist. 'Go on as far as the road will take us.'

It did not take them far. They bumped among stumps and roots over what was now a mere cart track, but at the beginning of the cleft the track died away into a woodland trail. They got out, and Leithen led the way up the Clairefontaine. There was something tonic in the air which gave him a temporary vigour, and he was surprised that he could climb the steep path without too great discomfort. When they rested on a mossy rock by the stream he found that he ate his sandwiches with some appetite. But after that it was heavy going, for there was the inevitable waterfall to surmount, and, weary and panting, he came out into the ultimate meadow of the Clairefontaine, which was fixed so clearly in his recollection.

It was a cup in the hills, floored not with wild hay, but with short, crisp pasture like an English down. From its sides descended the rivulets which made the Clairefontaine, and in the heart of it was a pool fringed with flags, so clear that through its six-foot depth the little stir in the sand could be seen where the water bubbled up from below. The place was so green and gracious that all sense of the wilds was lost, and it seemed like a garden in a long-settled land, a garden made centuries ago by the very good and the very wise.

But it was a watch-tower as well as a sanctuary. Looking south, the hills opened to show *Le Fleuve*, the great river of Canada, like a pool of colourless light. North were higher mountains, which seemed to draw together with a purpose, huddling to shepherd the streams towards a new goal. They were sending the waters, not to the familiar St Lawrence, but to untrodden Arctic wastes. That was the magic of the place. It was a frontier between the desert and the sown. To Leithen it was something more. He felt again the spell which had captured him here in his distant youth. It was the borderline between the prosaic world, where things went by rule and rote and were all fitted to the human scale, and the world as God first made it out of chaos, which had no care for humanity.

He stretched himself full length on the turf, his eyes feasting on the mystery of the northern hills. Almost he had a sense of physical well-being, for his breath was less troublesome. Then Johnny Frizel came into the picture, placidly smoking an old black pipe. He fitted in well, and Leithen began to reflect on his companion, who had docilely, at the order of his superiors, flown over half Canada to join him.

Johnny was a small man, about five feet six, with broad shoulders and sturdy, bandy legs. He wore an old pair of khaki breeches and a lumberman's laced boots, but the rest of his garb was conventional, for he had put on his best clothes, not knowing what his duties might be. He had a round bullet head covered with black hair cut very short, and his ears stuck out like the handles of a pitcher. His Indian mother showed in his even brown colouring, and his father in his mild, meditative blue eyes. So far Leithen had scarcely realized him, except to admire his speech, which was a wonderful blend of the dialect of the outlands, the slang of America, and literary idioms, for Johnny was a great reader – all spoken in the voice of a Scots shepherd, and with a broad Scots accent. When the War broke out Johnny had been in the Labrador and his brother Lew on the lower Mackenzie, and both, as soon as they got the news, had made a bee-line for France and the front. They had been notable snipers in the Canadian Corps, as the notches on the butts of their service rifles witnessed.

'You have been lent to me, Johnny,' Leithen said. 'Seconded for special service, as we used to say in the army. I had better tell you our job.' Briefly he sketched the story of Francis Galliard.

'This is the place where he was brought up,' he said. 'My notion is that he's in Canada now. I think he is with your brother – at any rate, I know that he was making inquiries about him in the early spring. You haven't heard from your brother lately?'

'Not since Christmas. Lew never troubles to put me wise about his doings. He may be anywhere on God's earth.'

'We want to find out if we can, from old Gaillard at the farm and the priest, if the young Galliard has been here. Or your brother. If my guess is right they won't be very willing to speak, but with luck they may give themselves away. If the young Galliard has been here it gives us a bit of a clue. They are a hospitable lot, so I propose that we quarter ourselves on them for the night to have the chance of a talk. You can put up at the farm, and I dare say I can get a shake-down at the presbytery.'

Johnny nodded approval. His blue eyes dwelt searchingly on Leithen's thin face, from which the flush of bodily exercise had gone, leaving a grey pallor.

They retraced their steps when the sun had sunk behind the hills and the evening glow was beginning, soft as the bloom on a peach. The Ford was turned, and rumbled down the valley until it was parked in the presbytery yard. The priest, Father Paradis, came out to greet them, a tall, lean old man much bent in the shoulders, who, like all Quebec clergy, wore the cassock. He had been gardening, and his lumberjack's boots were coated with soil.

To Leithen's relief Father Paradis spoke the French of France, for, though Canadian born, he had been trained in a seminary at Beauvais.

'But of a surety,' he cried. 'You shall sleep here, monsieur, and share my supper. I have a guest room, though it is as small as the Prophet's Chamber of the Scriptures.'

He would have Johnny stay also.

'No doubt Augustin can lodge Monsieur Frizel, but I fear he will have rough quarters.'

Leithen's kit was left at the presbytery and he and Johnny walked to the farm to pay their respects to the squire of Clairefontaine. He had ascertained that this Augustin Gaillard, to whom the farm had descended, was an uncle of Francis. The priest had given him a rapid sketch of the family history. The mother had died in bearing Francis; the father a year after Francis had left for the States. There had been an elder brother, Paul, who two years ago had disappeared into the north, leaving his uncle from Château-Gaillard in his place. There were also two sisters who were Grey Nuns serving somewhere in the west – the priest did not know where.

Augustin Gaillard was a man of perhaps sixty years, with a wisp of grey beard and a moist, wandering eye. Everything about him bespoke the drunkard. His loud-patterned shirt had a ragged collar and sleeves, his waistcoat was discoloured with the dribbling of food, his trousers had holes at the knees, and his bare feet were shod with *bottes-sauvages*. There was nothing in his features to suggest the good breeding which Leithen had noted in the picture of Francis. The house, which was more spacious than the ordinary farm, was in a condition of extreme dirt and disorder. Somewhere in the background Leithen had a glimpse of an ancient crone, who was doubtless the housekeeper.

But Augustin had the fine manners of his race. He placed his dwelling and all that was in it at their disposal. He pressed Leithen to remove himself from the presbytery.

'The good Father,' he said, 'has but a poor table. He will give you nothing to drink but cold water.'

Leaving Johnny deep in converse in the *habitant* patois, Leithen went back in the dusk to the presbytery. He was feeling acutely

49

the frailty of his body, as he was apt to do at nightfall. Had he chosen a different course he would be going back to delicate invalid food, to a soft chair and a cool bed; now he must make shift with coarse fare and the hard pallet of the guest room. He wondered for a moment if he had not been every kind of fool.

But no sick-nurse could have been more attentive than Father Paradis. He had killed and cooked a chicken with his own hands. For supper there was soup and the fowl, and coffee made by one who had learned the art in France. The little room was lit by a paraffin lamp, the smell of which brought back to Leithen faraway days in a Scots shooting box. The old man saw his guest's weakness, and after the meal he put a pillow in his chair and made him rest his legs on a stool.

'I see you are not in good health. monsieur,' he said. 'Do you travel to restore yourself? The air of these hills is well reputed.'

'Partly. And partly in hope of finding a friend. I am an Englishman, as you see, and am a stranger in Canada, though I have visited it once before. On that occasion I came to hunt, but my hunting days are over.'

Father Paradis screwed up his old eyes.

'At home you were perhaps a professor?'

'I have been a lawyer – and also a Member of our Parliament. But my working days are past, and I would make my soul.'

'You are wise. You are then in retreat? You are not, I think, of the Faith?'

Leithen smiled. 'I have my faith to find, and perhaps I have little time in which to find it.'

'There is little time for any of us,' said the old man. He looked at Leithen with eyes long experienced in life, and shook his head sadly.

'I spoke of a friend,' said Leithen. 'Have you had many visitors this summer?'

'Few come here nowadays. A pedlar or two, and a drover in the fall for the farm cattle. There is no logging, for our woods are bare. People used to come up from Château-Gaillard on holiday, but Château-Gaillard is for the moment stagnant. Except for you and Monsieur Frizel it is weeks since I have seen a stranger.'

'Had you no visitor from New York – perhaps in May? A man of the name of Francis Galliard?'

50

Leithen, from long practice in cross-examination, was accustomed to read faces. He saw the priest's eyes suddenly go blank, as if a shutter had been drawn over them, and his mouth tighten.

'No man of that name has visited us,' he said.

'Perhaps he did not give that name. The man I mean is still young,' and he described the figure as he had seen it in the New York portrait. 'He is a kinsman, I think, of the folk at the farm.'

Father Paradis shook his head.

'No, there has been no Francis Galliard here.'

But there was that in the old man's eyes which informed Leithen that he was not telling all he knew, and also that no cross-examination would elicit more. His face had the stony secrecy of the confessional.

'Well, I must look elsewhere,' Leithen said cheerfully. 'Tell me of the people at the farm. I understand they are one of the oldest families in Canada.'

Father Paradis's face lightened.

'Most ancient, but now, alas! pitifully decayed. The father was a good man, and a true son of the Church, but his farm failed, for he had little worldly wisdom. As for Augustin, he is, as you see, a drunkard. The son Paul was a gallant young man, but he was not happy on this soil. He was a wanderer, as his race was in the old days.'

'Wasn't there a second son?'

'Yes, but he left us long ago. He forsook his home and his faith. Let us not speak of him, for he is forgotten.'

'Tell me about Paul.'

'You must know, monsieur, that once the Gaillards were a stirring race. They fought with Frontenac against the Iroquois, and very fiercely against the English. Then, when peace came, they exercised their hardihood in distant ventures. Many of the house travelled far into the west and the north, and few of them returned. There was one, Aristide, who searched for the lost British sailor Frankolin – how do you call him? – and won fame. And only the other day there was Paul's uncle – also an Aristide – who found a new road to the Arctic shores and discovered a great river. Its name should be the Gaillard, but they tell me that the maps have the Indian word, the Ghost.'

Leithen, who had a passion for studying maps, remembered the river which flowed from north of the Thelon in the least-known corner of Canada.

'Is that where Paul went?' he asked.

'That is what we think. He was restless ever after his father died. He would go off for months to guide parties of hunters – even down to the Labrador, and in his dreams he had always his uncle Aristide; he was assured he was still alive and that if he went to the Ghost River he would find him. So one day he summons the other uncle, the worthless one, and bids him take over the farm of Clairefontaine.'

'You have heard nothing of him since?'

'Not a word has come. Why should it? He has no care for Clairefontaine ... Now, monsieur, it is imperative that you go to bed, for you are very weary. I will conduct you to the Prophet's Chamber.'

Leithen was in the habit of falling asleep at once – it was now his one bodily comfort – but this night he lay long awake. He thought that he had read himself into the soul of Francis Galliard, a summary and provisional reading, but enough to give him a starting point. He was convinced beyond doubt that he had come to Clairefontaine in the spring. He could not mistake the slight hesitation in the speech of Father Paradis, the tremor of the eyelids, the twitch of the mouth before it set – he had seen these things too often in the courts to be wrong. The priest had not lied, but he had equivocated, and had he been pressed would have taken refuge in obstinate silence. Francis had been here and had enjoined secrecy on the priest and no doubt on old Augustin. He was on a private errand and wanted to shut out the world.

He could picture the sequence of events. The man, out of tune with his environment, had fallen into the clutches of the past. He had come to Château-Gaillard and seen the ravaged valley – ravaged by himself and his associates – and thereby a bitter penitence had been awakened. His purpose now was to make his peace with the past – with his family, his birthplace, and his religion. No doubt he had confessed himself to the priest. Perhaps he had gone, as Leithen had gone, to the secret meadow at the river head, and, looking to the north, had had boyish memories and ambitions awakened. It was his business – so Leithen read his thoughts – to make restitution, to appease his offended household gods. He must shake off the bonds of an alien civilization, and, like his uncle and his brother and a hundred Gaillards of old, worship at the altars of the northern wilds.

Leithen fell asleep with so clear a picture in his mind that he might have been reading in black and white Francis's confession.

# 12

'We go back to Quebec,' he told Johnny next morning. 'But first I want to go up the stream again.'

The mountain meadow haunted his imagination. There, the afternoon before, he had had the first hour of bodily comfort he had known for months. The place, too, inspired him. It seemed to stiffen his purpose and to quicken his fancy.

Once again he lay on the warm turf beside the spring looking beyond the near forested hills to the blue dimness of the far mountains. It was that halcyon moment of the late Canadian summer when there are no flies, and even the midday is cool and scented, and the first hints of bright colour are stealing into the woods.

'I didn't get a great deal out of the old man,' said Johnny. 'He kept me up till three in the morning listenin' to his stuff. He was soused when he began, and well pickled before he left off, but he was never lit up – the liquor isn't brewed that could light up that old carcase. I guess he's got a grouse against the whole world. But I found out one thing. Brother Lew has been here this year.'

Leithen sat up. 'How do you know?'

'Why, he asked me if I was any relation to another man of my name – a fellow with half a thumb on his left hand and a scar above his right eyebrow. That's Lew to the life, for he got a bit chawed up at Vimy. When I asked more about the chap he felt he had said too much and shut up like a clam. But that means that Lew has been here all right, and that Augustin saw him, for to my certain knowledge Lew was never before east of Quebec, and yon old perisher has never stirred out of this valley. So I guess that Lew and your pal were here, for Lew wouldn't have come on his own.'

Leithen reflected for a moment.

'Was Lew ever at the Ghost River?' he asked. 'I mean the river half-way between Coronation Gulf and the top of Hudson's Bay.'

'Never heard of it. Nope. I'm pretty sure brother Lew was never within a thousand miles of it. It ain't his bailliewick.'

'Well, I fancy he's there now ... You and I are setting out for the Ghost River.'

# 13

Leithen spent two weary days in Montreal, mostly at the telephone, a business which in London he had always left to Cruddock or his clerk. He knew that the Northland was one vast whispering gallery, and that it was easier to track a man there than in the settled countries, so he hoped to get news by setting the machine of the R.C.M.P. to work. There was telephoning and telegraphing far and wide, but no result. No such travellers as Galliard and Lew Frizel had as yet been reported north of the railways. One thing he did ascertain. The two men had not flown to the Ghost River. That was the evidence of the Air Force and the private aeroplane companies. Leithen decided that this was what he had expected. If Galliard was on a mission of penitence he would travel as his uncle Aristide and his brother Paul had travelled – by canoe and trail. If he had started early in May he should just about have reached the Arctic shores.

The next task was to get a machine for himself. He hired an aeroplane from Air-Canada, a Baird-Sverisk of a recent pattern, and was lucky enough to get one of the best of the northern flyers, Job Teviot, for his pilot, and one Murchison as his mechanic. The contract was for a month, but with provision for an indefinite extension. All this meant bringing in his bankers, and cabling home, and the influence of Ravelstons had to be sought to complete the business. The barometer at Montreal stood above 100°, and there were times before he and Johnny took off when he thought that his next move would be to a hospital.

He felt stronger when they reached Winnipeg, and next day,

flying over the network of the Manitoba lakes, he found that he drew breath more easily. He had flown little before, and the air at first made him feel very sleepy. This passed, and, since there was no demand for activity, his mind turned in on itself. He felt like some disembodied creature, for already he seemed to have shed all ordinary interests. Aforetime on his travels and his holidays he had been acutely interested in what he saw and heard, and part of his success at the Bar had been due to the wide range of knowledge thus acquired. But now he had no thoughts except for the job on hand. He had meant deliberately to concentrate on it, in order to shut out fruitless meditations on his own case; but he found that this concentration had come about automatically. He simply was not concerned about other things. In New York he had listened to well-informed talk about politics and business and books, and it had woken no response in his mind. Here in Canada he did not care a jot about the present or future of a great British Dominion. The Canadian papers he glanced at were full of the perilous situation in Europe – any week there might be war. The news meant nothing to him, though a little while ago it would have sent him home by the next boat. The world had narrowed itself to Francis Galliard and the frail human creature that was following him.

By and by it was the latter that crowded in on his thoughts. Since he had nothing to do except watch a slowly moving landscape and the cloud shadows on lake and forest, he began to reflect on the atom, Edward Leithen, now hurrying above the world. The memory of Felicity kept returning – the sudden anguish in her eyes, her cry 'I love him! I love him!' and he realized how lonely his life had been. No woman had ever felt like that about him; he had never felt like that about any woman. Was it loss or gain? Gain, he told himself, for he implicated no one in his calamity. But had he not led a starved life? A misfit like Galliard had succeeded in gaining something which he, with all his social adaptability, had missed. He found himself in a mood almost of regret. He had made a niche for himself in the world, but it had been a chilly niche. With a start he awoke to the fact that he was very near the edge of self-pity, a thing forbidden.

In a blue windless twilight they descended for the night at a new mining centre on the Dog-Rib River. Johnny pitched a tent and cooked supper, while the pilot and the mechanic found quarters with other pilots who ran the daily air service to the south. There was a plague of black flies and mosquitoes, but Leithen was too tired to be troubled by them, and he had eight hours of heavy, unrefreshing sleep.

When he stood outside the tent next morning, looking over a shining lake and a turbulent river, he had a moment of sharp regret. How often he had stood like this on a lake shore – in Scotland, in Norway, in Canada long ago – and watched the world heave itself out of night into dawn! Like this – but how unlike! Then he had been exhilarated with the prospect of a day's sport, tingling from his cold plunge, ravenous as a hawk for breakfast, the blood brisk in his veins and every muscle in trim. Now he could face only a finger of bacon and a half-cup of tea, and he was weary before the day had begun.

'There's plenty here knows Lew,' Johnny reported. 'They haven't come this way. If they're at the Ghost River, my guess is that they've gone by the Planchette and the Old Man Falls.'

They crossed Great Slave Lake and all morning flew over those plains miscalled the Barrens, which, seen from above, are a delicate lace-work of lakes and streams criss-crossed by ridges of bald rock and banks of gravel, and with now and then in a hollow a patch of forest. They made camp early at the bend of a river, which Johnny called the Little Fish, for Murchison had some work to do on the engine. While Leithen rested by the fire Job went fishing and brought back three brace of Arctic char. He announced that there was another camp round the next bend – a white man in a canoe with two Crees – a sight in that lonely place as unexpected as the great auk. Somewhat refreshed by his supper, Leithen in the long-lighted evening walked upstream to see his neighbour.

He found a middle-aged American cleaning a brace of ptarmigan which he had shot, and doing it most expertly. He was a tall man, in breeches, puttees, and a faded yellow shirt, and Leithen took him for an ordinary trapper or prospector until he heard him speak.

'I saw you land,' the stranger said. 'I was coming round presently to pass the time of day. Apart from my own outfit you are the first man I've seen for a month.'

He prepared a bed of hot ashes, and with the help of rifle rods set the birds to roast. Then he straightened himself, filled a pipe, and had a look at Leithen.

'I'm an American,' he said. 'New York.'

Leithen nodded. He had already detected the unmistakable metropolitan pitch of the voice.

'You're English? Haven't I seen you before? I used to be a good deal in London ... Hold on a minute. I've got it. I've heard you speak in the British Parliament. That would be in —.' And he mentioned a year.

'Very likely,' said Leithen. 'I was in Parliament then. I was Attorney-General.'

'You don't say. Well, we're birds of the same flock. I'm a corporation lawyer. My name's Taverner. Yours – wait a minute – is Leven.'

'Leithen,' the other corrected.

'Odd we should meet here in about the wildest spot in North America. It's easy enough to come by air, like you, but Matthew and Mark and I have taken two blessed months canoeing and portaging from railhead, and it will take us about the same time to get back.'

'Can corporation lawyers like you take four months' holiday?'

Mr Taverner's serious face relaxed in a smile.

'Not usually. But I had to quit or smash. No, I wasn't sick. I was just tired of the dam' racket. I had to get away from the noise. The United States is getting to be a mighty noisy country.'

The cry of a loon broke the stillness, otherwise there was no sound but the gurgle of the river and the grunting of one of the Indians as he cleaned a gun.

'You get silence here,' said Leithen.

'I don't mean physical noise so much. The bustle in New York doesn't worry me more than a little. I mean noise in our minds. You can't get peace to think nowadays.' He broke off. 'You here for the same cause?'

'Partly,' said Leithen. 'But principally to meet a friend.'

'I hope you'll hit him off. It's a biggish country for an assignation. But you don't need an excuse for cutting loose and coming here. I pretend I come to fish and hunt, but I only fish and shoot for the pot. I'm no sort of sportsman. I'm just a poor devil that's been born in the wrong century. There's quite a lot of folk like me. You'd be surprised how many of us slip off here now and then to get a little quiet. I don't mean the hearty, husky sort of fellow who goes into the woods in a fancy mackinaw and spends his time there drinking whisky and playing poker. I mean quiet citizens like myself, who've simply got to breathe fresh air and get the din out of their ears. Canada is becoming to some of us like a medieval monastery to which we can retreat when things get past bearing.'

Taverner, having been without white society for so long, seemed to enjoy unburdening himself.

'I'm saying nothing against my country. I know it's the greatest on earth. But my God! I hate the mood it has fallen into. It seems to me there isn't one section of society that hasn't got some kind of jitters – big business, little business, politicians, the newspaper men, even the college professors. We can't talk except too loud. We're bitten by the exhibitionist bug. We're all boosters and high-powered salesmen and propagandists, and yet we don't know what we want to propagand, for we haven't got any kind of common creed. All we ask is that a thing should be colourful and confident and noisy. Our national industry is really the movies. We're one big movie show. And just as in the movies we worship languishing Wops and little blonde girls out of the gutter, so we pick the same bogus deities in other walks of life. You remember Emerson speaks about some nations as having guano in their destiny. Well, I some-times think that we have got celluloid in ours.'

There was that in Leithen's face which made Taverner pause and laugh.

'Forgive my rigmarole,' he said. 'It's a relief to get one's peeves off the chest, and I reckon I'm safe with you. You see, I come of New England stock, and I don't fit in too well with these times.'

'Do you know a man called Galliard?' Leithen asked. 'Francis Galliard – a partner in Ravelstons?'

'A little. He's a friend of Bronson Jane, and Bronson's my cousin. Funny you should mention him, for if I had to choose a fellow that fitted in perfectly to the modern machine, I should pick Galliard. He enjoys all that riles me. He's French, and that maybe explains it. I've too much of the Puritan in my blood. You came through New York, I suppose. Did you see Galliard? How is he? I've always had a liking for him.'

'No. He was out of town.'

Leithen got up to go. The long after-glow in the west was fading, and the heavens were taking on the shadowy violet which is all the northern summer darkness.

'When do you plan to end your trip?' Taverner asked as he shook hands.

'I don't know. I've no plans. I've been ill, as you see, and it will depend on my health.'

'This will set you up, never fear. I was a sick man three years ago and I came back from Great Bear Lake champing like a prize-fighter. But take my advice and don't put off your return too late. It don't do to be trapped up here in winter. The North can be a darn cruel place.'

# 14

Late next afternoon they reached the Ghost River delta, striking in upon it at an angle from the south-west. The clear skies had gone, and the 'ceiling' was not more than a thousand feet. Low hills rimmed the eastern side, but they were cloaked in a light fog, and the delta seemed to have no limits, but to be an immeasurable abscess of decay. Leithen had never imagined such an abomination of desolation. It was utterly silent, and the only colours were sickly greens and drabs. At first sight he thought he was looking down on a bit of provincial Surrey, broad tarmac roads lined with asphalt footpaths, and behind the trim hedges smooth suburban lawns. It took a little time to realize that the highways were channels of thick mud, and the lawns bottomless quagmires. He was now well inside the Circle, and had expected from the Arctic something cold, hard, and bleak, but also clean and tonic. Instead he found a horrid lushness – an infinity of mire and coarse vegetation, and a superfluity of obscene insect life. The place was one huge muskeg. It was like the no-man's-land between the trenches in the War – a colossal no-man's-land created in some campaign of demons, pitted and pocked with shell-holes from some infernal artillery.

They skirted the delta and came down at its western horn on the edge of the sea. Here there was no mist, and he could look far into the North over still waters eerily lit by the thin evening sunlight. It was like no ocean he had ever seen, for it seemed to be without form or reason. The tide licked the shore without purpose. It was simply water filling a void, a treacherous, deathly waste, pale like a snake's belly, a thing beyond humanity and beyond time. Delta and sea looked as if here the Demiurge had let His creative vigour slacken and ebb into nothingness. He had wearied of the world which He had made and left this end of it to ancient Chaos.

Next morning the scene had changed, and to his surprise he felt a lightening of both mind and body. Sky and sea were colourless, mere bowls of light. There seemed to be no tides, only a gentle ripple on the grey sand. Very far out there were blue gleams which he took to be ice. The sun was warm, but the body of the air was cold, and it had in it a tonic quality which seemed to make his breathing easier. He remembered hearing that there were no germs in the Arctic, that the place was one great sanatorium, but that did not concern one whose trouble was organic decay. Still, he was grateful for a momentary comfort, and he found that he wanted to stretch his legs. He walked to the highest point of land at the end of a little promontory.

It was a place like a Hebridean cape. The peaty soil was matted with berries, though a foot or two beneath was eternal ice. The breeding season was over and the migration not begun, so there was no bird life on the shore; the wild fowl were all in the swamps of the delta. The dead-level of land and sea made the arc of sky seem immense, the 'intense inane' of Shelley's poem. The slight recovery of bodily vigour quickened his imagination. This was a world not built on the human scale, a world made without thought of mankind, a world colourless and formless, but also timeless; a kind of eternity. It would be a good place to die in, he thought, for already the clinging ties of life were loosened and death would mean little since life had ceased.

To his surprise he saw a small schooner anchored at the edge of a sandbank, a startling thing in that empty place. Johnny had joined him, and they went down to inspect it. An Eskimo family was on board, merry, upstanding people from far-distant Gordans Land. The skipper was one Andersen, the son of a Danish whaling captain and an Eskimo mother, and he spoke good English. He had been to Herschell Island to lay in stores, and was now on his way home after a difficult passage through the ice of the western Arctic. The schooner was as clean as a new pin, and the instruments as well kept as on a man-o'-war. It had come in for fresh water, and Job was able to get from it a few tins of gasolene, for it was a long hop to the next fuelling stage. The visit to the Andersens altered Leithen's mood. Here was a snug life being lived in what had seemed a place of death. It switched his interest back to his task.

Presently he found what he had come to seek. On the way to the tent they came on an Eskimo cemetery. Once there had been a settlement here which years ago had been abandoned. There were half a dozen Eskimo graves, with skulls and bones showing through chinks in the piles of stone, and in one there was a complete skeleton stretched as if on a pyre. There was something more. At a little distance in a sheltered hollow were two crosses of driftwood. One was bent and weathered, with the inscription, done with a hot iron, almost obliterated, but it was possible to read ....TID. GAIL...D. There was a date too blurred to decipher. The other cross was new and it had not suffered the storms of more than a couple of winters. On it one could read clearly PAUL LOUIS GAILLARD and a date eighteen months back.

To Leithen there was an intolerable pathos about the two crosses. They told so much, and yet they told nothing. How had Aristide died? Had Paul found him alive? How had Paul died? Who had put up the memorials? There was a grim drama here at which he could not even guess. But the one question that mattered to him was, had Francis seen these crosses?

Johnny, who had been peering at the later monument, answered that question.

'Brother Lew has been here,' he said.

He pointed to a little St Andrew's cross freshly carved with a knife just below Paul's name. Its ends were funnily splayed out.

'That's Lew's mark,' he said. 'You might say it's a family mark. Long ago, when Dad was working for the Bay, there was a breed of Indians along the Liard, some sort of Slaveys, that had got into their heads that they were kind of Scots, and every St Andrew's Day they would bring Dad a present of a big St Andrew's Cross, very nicely carved, which he stuck above the door like a horse-shoe. So we all got into the way of using that cross as our trade mark, especially Lew, who's mighty particular. I've seen him carve it on a slab to stick above a dog's grave, and when he writes a letter he puts it in somewhere. So whenever you see it you can reckon Lew's ahead of you.'

'They can't be long gone,' said Leithen.

'I've been figuring that out, and I guess they might have gone a week ago – maybe ten days. Lew's pretty handy with a canoe. What puzzles me is where they've gone and how. There's no place hereaways to get supplies, and it's a good month's journey to the nearest post. Maybe they shot caribou and smoked 'em. I tell you what, if your pal's got money to burn, what about him hiring a plane to meet 'em here and pick 'em up? If that's their game it won't be easy to hit their trail. There's only one thing I'm pretty sure of, and that is they didn't go home. If we fossick about we'll maybe find out more.'

Johnny's forecast was right, for that afternoon they heard a shot a mile off, and, going out to inquire, found an Eskimo hunter. At the sight of them the man fled, and Johnny had some trouble rounding him up. When halted he stood like a sullen child, a true son of the Elder Ice, for he had a tattooed face and a bone stuck through his upper lip. Probably he had never seen a white man before. He had been hunting caribou before they migrated south from the shore, and had a pile of skins and high-smelling meat to show for his labours. He stubbornly refused to accompany them back to the tent, so Leithen left him with Johnny, who could make some shape at the speech of the central Arctic.

When Johnny came back Andersen and the schooner had sailed, and Ghost River had returned to its ancient solitude.

'Lew's been here right enough,' he said. 'He and his boss and a couple of Indians came in two canoes eleven days back – at least I reckoned eleven days as well as I could from yon Eskimo's talk. Two days later a plane arrived for them. The Eskimo has never seen a horse or an automobile, but he knows all about aeroplanes. They handed over the canoes and what was left of the stores to the Indians and shaped a course pretty well due west. They've gotten the start of us by a week or maybe more.'

That night after supper Johnny spoke for the first time at some length.

'I've been trying to figure this out,' he said, 'and here's what

I make of it. Mr Galliard comes here and sees the graves of his brother and uncle. So far so good. From what you tell me that's not going to content him. He wants to do something of his own on the same line by way of squarin' his conscience. What's he likely to do? Now, let's see just where brother Lew comes in. I must put you wise about Lew.'

Johnny removed his pipe from his mouth.

'He's a wee bit mad,' he said solemnly. 'He's a great man; the cutest hunter and trapper and guide between Alaska and Mexico, and the finest shot on this continent. But he's also mad – batty – loony – anything you like that's out of the usual. It's a special kind of madness, for in most things you won't find a sounder guy. Him and me was buck privates in the War until they made a sharp-shooter of him, and you wouldn't hit a better-behaved soldier than old Lew. I was a good deal in trouble, but Lew never was. He has just the one crazy spot in him, and it reminds me of them Gaillards you talk about. It's a kind of craziness you're apt to find in us Northerners. There's a bit of country he wants to explore, and the thought of it comes between him and his sleep and his grub. Say, did you ever hear of the Sick Heart River?'

Leithen shook his head.

'You would if you'd been raised in the North. It's a fancy place that old-timers dream about. Where is it? Well, that's not easy to say. You've heard maybe of the South Nahanni that comes in the north bank of the Liard about a hundred miles west of Fort Simpson? Dad had a post up the Liard and I was born there, and when I was a kid there was a great talk about the South Nahanni. There's a mighty big waterfall on it, so you can't make it a canoe trip. Some said the valley was full of gold, and some said that it was as hot as hell owing to warm springs, and everybody acknowledged that there was more game there to the square mile than in the whole of America. It had a bad name, too, for at least a dozen folk went in and never came out. Some said that was because of bad Indians, but that was punk, for there ain't no Indians in the valley. Our Indians said it was the home of devils, which sounds more reasonable.'

Johnny stopped to relight his pipe, and for a few minutes smoked meditatively.

'Do you get to the Sick Heart by the South Nahanni?' Leithen asked.

'No, you don't. Lew's been all over the South Nahanni, and barring the biggest grizzlies on earth and no end of sheep and goat and elk and caribou, he found nothing. Except the Sick Heart. He saw it from the top of a mountain, and it sort of laid a charm on him. He said that first of all you had snow mountains bigger than any he had ever seen, and then icefields like prairies, and then forests of tall trees, the same as you get on the coast. And then in the valley bottom, grass meadows and an elegant river. A Hare Indian that was with him gave him the name – the Sick Heart, called after an old-time chief that got homesick for the place and pined away. Lew had a try at getting into it and found it no good – there was precipices thousands of feet that end. But he come away with the Sick Heart firm in his mind, and he ain't going to forget it.'

'Which watershed is it on?' Leithen asked.

'That's what no man knows. Not on the South Nahanni's. And you can't get into it from the Yukon side, by the Pelly or the Peel or the Ross or Macmillan – Lew tried 'em all. So it looks as if it didn't flow that way. The last time I heard him talk about it he was kind of thinking that the best route was up from the Mackenzie, the way the Hare Indians go for their mountain hunting. There's a river there called the Big Hare. He thought that might be the road.'

'Do you think he's gone there now?'

'I don't think, but I suspicion. See here, mister. Lew's a strong character and mighty set on what he wants. He's also a bit mad, and mad folks have persuasive ways with them. He finds this Galliard man keen to get into the wilds, and the natural thing is that he persuades him to go to his particular wilds, which he hasn't had out of his mind for ten years.'

'I think you're probably right,' said Leithen. 'We will make a cast by way of the Sick Heart. What's the jumping-off ground?'

'Fort Bannerman on the Mackenzie,' said Johnny. 'Right, we'll start tomorrow morning. We can send back the planes from there and collect an outfit. We'll want canoes and a couple of Hares as guides.'

And then he fell silent and stared into the fire. Now and then he took a covert glance at Leithen. At last he spoke a little shyly.

'You're a sick man, I reckon. I can't help noticin' it, though you don't make much fuss about it. If Lew's on the Sick Heart and we follow him there it'll be a rough passage, and likely we'll have to go into camp for the winter. I'm wondering can you stand it? There ain't no medical comforts in the Mackenzie mountains.'

Leithen smiled. 'It doesn't matter whether I stand it or not. You're right. I'm a sick man. Indeed, I'm a dying man. The doctors in England did not give me more than a year to live, and that was weeks ago. But I want to find Galliard and send him home, and after that it doesn't matter what happens to me.'

'Is Galliard your best pal?'

'I scarcely know him. But I have taken on the job to please a friend, and I must make a success of it. I want to die on my feet, if you see what I mean.'

Johnny nodded.

'I get you. I'm mighty sorry, but I get you ... Once I had a retriever bitch, the best hunting dog I ever knew, and her and me had some great times on the hills. She could track a beast all day, and minded a blizzard no more than a spring shower. Well, she got something mortally wrong with her innards, and was dying all right. One morning I missed her from her bed beside the stove, and an Indian told me he'd seen her dragging herself up through the woods in the snow. I followed her trail and found her dead just above the tree line, the place she'd been happiest in when she was well. She wanted to die on her feet. I reckon that's the best way for men and hounds.'

# 15

For three days Leithen was in abject misery. They had no receiver in their plane and therefore no means of getting weather reports, and when they took off the next morning the only change was an increased chill in the air. By midday they had run into fog, and, since in that area Job was uncertain of his compass, they went north again to the Arctic coast, and followed it to the Coppermine. Here it began to blow from the north, and in a series of rainstorms they passed the Dismal Lakes and came to the shore of the Great

Bear Lake. Job had intended to pass the night at the Mines, but there was no going further that evening in the mist and drizzle.

Next day they struggled to the Mines with just enough gasolene. Leithen looked so ill that the kindly manager would have put him to bed, but he insisted on restarting in the afternoon. They had a difficult take-off from the yeasty lake – Job insisted on their getting into their life-jackets, for he said that the betting was that in three minutes they would be in the water. The lake was safely crossed, but Job failed to hit off the outlet of the Great Bear River, and with the low 'ceiling' he feared to try a compass course to the Mackenzie because of the Franklin mountains. It was midnight before they struck the outlet and they had another wretched bivouac in the rain.

After that things went better. The weather returned to bright sun, clear skies, and a gentle wind from the north-east. Presently they were above the Mackenzie and far in the west they saw the jumble of dark ridges which were the foothills of the Mackenzie mountains. In the afternoon the hills came closer to the river, and on the left bank appeared a cluster of little white shacks with the red flag of the Hudson's Bay flying from a post.

'Fort Bannerman,' said Johnny, as they circled down. 'That's the Big Hare, and somewhere at the back of it is the Sick Heart. Mighty rough country.'

The inhabitants of the fort were grouped at the mud bank where they went ashore – the Hudson's Bay postmaster, two Oblate Brothers, a fur trader, a trapper in for supplies, and several Indians. The trapper waved a hand to Johnny –

'Hullo, boy!' he said. 'How goes it? Lew's been here. He lit out for the mountains ten days ago.'

# PART II

There is a river, the streams whereof shall make glad
the city of God.

*Psalm XLVI*

# 1

It took three days to get the proper equipment together. Johnny was leaving little to chance.

'If we find Lew and his pal we may have to keep 'em company for months. It won't be easy to get to the Sick Heart, but it'll be a darn sight harder to get out. We've got to face the chance of a winter in the mountains. Lucky for us the Hares have a huntin' camp fifty miles up-river. We can dump some of our stuff there and call it our base.'

The first question was that of transport. Water was the easiest until the river became a mountain torrent. The common Indian craft was of moose hides tanned like vellum and stretched on poplar ribs; but Johnny managed to hire from a free-trader a solid oak thirty-foot boat with an outboard motor; and, as subsidiaries, a couple of canoes brought years ago from the south, whose seams had been sewn up with strips of tamarack root and caulked with resin. Two Indians were engaged, little men compared with the big Plains folk, but stalwart for the small-boned Hares. They had the slanting Mongol eyes of the Mackenzie River tribes, and had picked up some English at the Catholic mission school. Something at the back of Leithen's brain christened them Big Klaus and Little Klaus, but Johnny, who spoke their tongue, had other names for them.

Then the Hudson's Bay store laid open its resources, and Johnny was no niggardly outfitter. Leithen gave him a free hand, for they had brought nothing with them. There were clothes to be bought for the winter – parkas and fur-lined jerkins, and leather breeches, and lined boots; gloves and flapped caps, blankets and duffel bags. There were dog packs, each meant to carry twenty-five pounds. There was a light tent – only one, for the Hares would fend for themselves at the up-river camp, and Lew and Galliard were no doubt already well provided. There were a couple of shot-guns and a couple of rifles and ammunition, and there was a folding tin stove. Last came the provender: bacon and beans and flour, salt and sugar, tea and coffee, and a fancy assortment of tinned stuffs.

'Looks like we was goin' to start a store,' said Johnny, 'but we may need every ounce of it and a deal more. If it's a winter-long job we'll sure have to get busy with our guns. Don't look so scared, mister. We've not got to back-pack that junk. The boat'll carry it easy to the Hares' camp, and after that we'll cache the feck of it.'

Leithen's quarters during these days were in the spare room of the Bay postmaster. Fort Bannerman was a small metropolis, for besides the Bay store it had a Mounted Police post, a hospital run by the Grey Nuns, and an Indian school in charge of the Oblate Brothers. With one of the latter he made friends, finding that he had served in a French battalion which had been on the right of the Guards at Loos. Father Duplessis was from Picardy. Leithen had once been billeted in the shabby flat-chested château near Montreuil where his family had dwelt since the days of Henri Quatre. The Fathers had had a medical training and could at need perform straightforward operations, such as that on an appendix, or the amputation of a maimed limb. Leithen sat in his little room at the hospital, which smelt of ether and carbolic, and they talked like two old soldiers.

Once they walked together to where the Big Hare strained to the Mackenzie through an archipelago of sandy islets.

'I have been here seven years,' Father Duplessis told him. 'Before that I was three years in the eastern Arctic. That, if you like, was isolation, for there was one ship a year, but here we are in a thoroughfare. All through the winter the planes from the northern mines call weekly, and in summer we have many planes as well as the Hudson's Bay boats.'

Leithen looked round the wide circle of landscape – the huge drab Mackenzie two miles broad, to the east and south interminable wastes of scrub and spruce, to the west a chain of tawny mountains, stained red in parts with iron, and fantastically sculptured.

'Do you never feel crushed by this vastness?' he asked. 'This country is outsize.'

'No,' was the answer, 'for I live in a little world. I am always busy among little things. I skin a moose, or build a boat, or hammer a house together, or treat a patient, or cobble my boots or patch my coat – all little things. And then I have the offices of the Church, in a blessedly small space, for our chapel is a midget.'

'But outside all that,' said Leithen, 'you have an empty world and an empty sky.'

'Not empty,' said Father Duplessis, smiling, 'for it is filled with God. I cannot say, like Pascal, "*le silence éternel de ces espaces infinis m'effraie*". There is no silence here, for when I straighten my back and go out of doors the world is full of voices. When I was in my Picardy country there were little fields like a parterre, and crowded roads. There, indeed, I knew loneliness – but not here, where man is nothing and God is all.'

# 2

They left Fort Bannerman on a clear fresh morning when the sky was a pale Arctic blue, so pale as to be almost colourless, and a small cold wind, so tiny as to be little more than a shudder, blew from the north. The boat chugged laboriously up the last feeble rapids of the Big Hare, and then made good progress through long canal-like stretches in a waste of loess and sand. Here the land was almost desert, for the scrub pines had ceased to clothe the banks. These rose in shelves and mantelpieces to the spurs of the mountains, and one chain of low cliffs made a kind of bib round the edge of the range. There was no sound except the gurgle of the water and an occasional sandpiper's whistle. A selvedge of dwarf willow made the only green in the landscape, though in distant hollows there were glimpses of poplar and birch. The river was split into a dozen channels, and the Hares kept the boat adroitly in deep water, for there was never a moment when it grounded. It was an ugly country, dull as a lunar landscape, tilted and eroded ridges which were the approach to the granite of the high mountains.

The three days at Fort Bannerman had done Leithen good, and though he found his breathing troublesome and his limbs weak, the hours passed in comparative comfort, since there was no need for exertion. On the Arctic shore and in the journey thence he had realized only that he was in a bleak infinity of space, a natural place in which to await death. But now he was conscious of the details of his environment. He watched the drifting duck and puzzled over their breed, he noted the art with which the Hares kept the boat in slack and deep water, and as the mountains came nearer he felt a feeble admiration for one peak which had the shape of Milan cathedral. Especially he was aware of his companion. Hitherto there had been little conversation, but now Johnny came into the picture, sitting on the gunwale, one lean finger pressing down the tobacco in his pipe, his far-sighted eyes searching the shelves for game.

Johnny was very ready to talk. He had discovered that Leithen was Scots, and was eager to emphasize the Scottish side of his own ancestry. On the little finger of his left hand he wore a ring set with a small bloodstone. He took it off and passed it to Leithen.

'Dad left me that,' he said. 'Lew has a bigger and better one. Dad was mighty proud of the rings and he told us to stick to them, for he said they showed we come of good stock.'

Leithen examined it. The stone bore the three cinquefoils of Fraser. Then he remembered that Frizel had been the name for Fraser in the border parish where he had spent his youth. He remembered Adam Fraser, the blacksmith, the clang of his smithy on summer mornings, the smell of sizzling hooves and hot iron on summer afternoons. The recollection gave Johnny a new meaning for him; he was no longer a shadowy figure in this fantastic world of weakness; he was linked to the vanished world of real things, and thereby acquired a personality.

As they chugged upstream in the crisp afternoon, hourly drawing nearer to the gate of the mountains, Leithen enjoyed something which was almost ease, while Johnny in his slow drawling voice dug into his memory. That night, too, when they made camp at the bottom of a stone-shoot, and, since the weather was mild, kept the driftwood fire alight more for show than for warmth, Johnny expanded further. Since in his experience all sickness was stomachic, he had included invalid foods among the stores, and was surprised when Leithen told him that he need not fuss about his diet. This made him take a more cheerful view of his companion's health, and he did not trouble to see him early to bed. In his sleepingbag on a couch of Bay blankets Leithen listened to some chapters of Johnny's autobiography.

He heard of his childhood on Great Slave Lake and on the Liard, of his father (his mother had died at his birth), of his brother Lew – especially of Lew.

'We was brothers,' said Johnny, 'but also we was buddies, which ain't always according to rule.'

He spoke of his hunting, which had ranged from the Stikine to the Churchill, from the Clearwater to the Liard, and of his trapping, which had been done mostly about the upper waters of the Peace. Johnny as talker had one weak point – he was determined that his auditor should comprehend every detail, and he expounded in minutiae. He seemed resolved that Leithen should grasp the difference in method between the taking of mink and marten, the pen on the river bank and the trap up in the hills. He elaborated also the technique of the spearing of muskrats, and he was copious on the intricate subject of fox ... In every third sentence there was a mention of Lew, his brother, until the picture that emerged for Leithen from the talk was not that of wild animals but of a man.

It was a picture which kept dislimning, so that he could not see it clearly; but it impressed him strangely. Lew came into every phase of Johnny's recollections. He had said this or that; he had done this or that; he seemed to be taken as the ultimate authority on everything in heaven and earth. But Johnny's attitude was something more than the admiration for an elder brother, or the respect of one expert for a greater. There was uneasiness in it. He seemed to bring in Lew's name in a kind of ritual, as if to convince himself that Lew was secure and happy ... What was it that he had said on the Arctic shore? He had called Lew mad, meaning that he was possessed by a dream. Now Lew was hot on the trail of that dream, and Johnny was anxious about him. Of that there was no doubt.

Leithen laughed. He looked at Johnny's bat ears and bullet head. Here was he, one who had seen men and cities and had had a hand in great affairs, with his thoughts concentrated on an unknown brother of an Indian half-breed! Galliard had almost gone out of the picture; to Johnny he was only Lew's 'pal', the latest of a score or two of temporary employers. Even to Leithen himself the errant New Yorker, the husband of Blenkiron's niece, the pillar of Ravelstons, seemed a minor figure compared to the masterful guide who was on the quest for a mysterious river. Had Lew in-spired Galliard with his fancies? Or was the inspiration perhaps Galliard's? What crazy obsession would he find if and when he overtook the pair somewhere in that wild world behind which the sun was setting?

That night they made camp at the very doorstep of the mountains, where the river, after a string of box-canyons, emerged from the foothills. It was an eerie place, for the Big Hare, after some miles of rapids, drowsed in a dark lagoon beneath sheer walls of rock. Leithen's mind, having been back all day in the normal world, now reacted to a mood of black depression. What had seemed impressive a few hours before was now merely grotesque and cruel. His errand was ridiculous – almost certainly futile, and trivial even if it succeeded. What had he to do with the aberrations of American financiers and the whims of half-breeds? Somewhere in those bleak hills he would die – a poor ending for a not undignified life! ... But had his life been much of a thing after all? He had won a certain amount of repute and made a certain amount of money, but neither had meant much to him. He had had no wife, no child. Had his many friends been more, after all, than companions? In the retrospect his career seemed lonely, self-centred, and barren, and what was this last venture? A piece of dull stoicism at the best – or, more likely, a cheap bravado.

# 3

All next morning they smelt their way through the box-canyons, sometimes with the engine shut off and the Hares poling madly. There were two dangerous rapids, but navigation was made simpler by the fact that there were no split channels and no shallows. They were going through the limestone foothills, and the cliffs on either side were at least seven hundred feet high, sheer as a wall where they did not overhang. Johnny had a tale about the place. Once the Hares had been hunted by the Crees – he thought it was the Crees, his own people, but it might have been the Dog-Ribs. At that time the Big Hare River had come out of the mountains underground. The Hare boats were no match for the fleet Cree canoes, and the wretched tribe, fleeing upstream, looked for annihilation when they reached the end of the waterway. But to their amazement they found the mountains open before them and a passage through the canyons to the upper valley where was now the Hares' hunting camp. When they looked back there were no pursuing Crees, for the mountain wall had closed behind them. But some days later, when the disappointed enemy had gone back to their Athabaska swamps, the passage opened again, and the Hares could return when they pleased to the Mackenzie.

'Big magic,' said Johnny. 'I reckon them Hares got the story out of the Bible, when the missionaries had worked a bit on them, for it's mighty like the children of Israel and old Pharaoh.'

Suddenly the boat shot into a lake, the containing walls fell back, and they were in a valley something less than a mile wide, with high mountains, whose tops were already powdered with snow, ringing it and blocking it to the north. The shores were green with scrub-willow, and the lower slopes were dark with spruce and pine.

At the upper end of the lake, on a half-moon of sward between the woods and the water, was the Hares' encampment. Big Klaus and Little Klaus set up a howl as they came in sight of it, and they were answered by a furious barking of dogs.

The place was different from Leithen's expectation. He remembered from old days the birch-bark lodges of eastern Canada; but in this country, where the birches were small, he had looked for something like the tall teepees of the Plains, with their smoke-holes and their covering of skins. Instead he found little oblong cabins thatched with rush-mats or brushwood. They had a new look as if they had recently been got ready for the winter, and a few caribou-skin tents showed what had been the summer quarters. On the highest point of ground stood what looked like a chapel, a building of logs surmounted at one end by a rough cross. Penned near it was an assortment of half-starved dogs who filled the heavens with their clamour.

The place stank foully, and when they landed Leithen felt nausea stealing over him. His legs had cramped with the journey and he had to lean on Johnny's shoulder. They passed through a circle of silent Indians, and were greeted by their chief, who wore a medal like a soup plate. Then a little old man hobbled up who introduced himself as Father Wentzel, the Oblate who spent the summer here. He was about to return to Fort Bannerman, he said, when his place would be taken for the winter by Father Duplessis. He had a little presbytery behind the chapel, where he invited Leithen to rest while Johnny did his business with the Hares.

The priest opened the door which communicated with the chapel, lit two tapers on the altar, and displayed with pride a riot of barbaric colours. The walls were hung with cloths painted in bedlamite scarlets and purples and oranges – not the rude figures of men and animals common on the teepees, but a geometrical nightmare of interwoven cubes and circles. The altar cloth had the same byzantine exuberance.

'That is the work of our poor people,' said the priest. 'Helped by Brother Onesime, who had the artist's soul. To you, monsieur, it may seem too gaudy, but to our Indians it is a foretaste of the New Jerusalem.'

Leithen sat in the presbytery in a black depression. The smells of the encampment – unclean human flesh, half-dressed skins of animals, gobbets of putrefying food – were bad enough in that mild autumn noon. The stuffy little presbytery was not much better. But the real trouble was that suddenly everything seemed to have become little and common. The mountains were shapeless, mere unfinished bits of earth; the forest of pine and spruce had neither form nor colour; the river, choked with logs and jetsam, had none of the beauty of running water. In coming into the wilderness he had found not the majesty of Nature, but the trivial, the infinitely small – an illiterate half-breed, a rabble of degenerate Indians, a priest with the mind of a child. The pettiness culminated in the chapel, which was as garish as a Noah's Ark from a cheap toyshop ... He felt sick in mind and very sick in body.

Father Wentzel made him a cup of tea, which he could barely swallow. The little priest's eyes rested on him with commiseration in them, but he was too shy to ask questions. Presently Johnny arrived in a bustle. He would leave certain things, if he were permitted, in the presbytery cellar. He had arranged with the chief about dogs when they were wanted, but that was not yet, for it would be a fortnight at least before snow could be looked for, even in the high valleys, and, since they would travel light, they did not need dogs as pack animals. They would take the boat, for a stage or two was still possible by it; after that they would have the canoes, and he had kept the Hares as canoe-men – 'for the portagin' business would be too much for you, mister'.

He had news of Lew. The two men were not more than a week ahead, for a sudden flood in the Big Hare had delayed them. They had canoes, but no Indians, and had gone in the first instance to Lone Tree Lake. 'That's our road,' said Johnny. 'Maybe they've made a base camp there. Anyhow, we'll hit their trail.'

He had other news. It was the end of the seven years' cycle, and disease had fallen on the snow-shoe rabbit, upon which in the last resort all wild animals depend. Therefore the winter hunting and trapping of the Hares would be poor, and there might be a shortage of food in their camp. 'You tell Father Duplessis that when you get back to Fort Bannerman,' he told the priest. Their own camp, if they were compelled to make one, might run short. 'Lucky we brought what we did,' he told Leithen. 'If we catch up with Lew we'll be all right, for he'd get something to eat off an iceberg.'

They passed one night in the presbytery. While Johnny slept the deep, short sleep of the woodsman, Leithen had a word with Father Wentzel.

'The two men who have gone before?' he asked. 'One is the brother of my guide, and the other is a friend of my friends. How did they impress you?'

The child-like face of the priest took on a sudden gravity.

'The gentleman, he was of the Faith. He heard mass daily and made confession. He was a strange man. He looked unhappy and hungry and he spoke little. But the other, the guide, he was stranger. He had not our religion, but I think he had a kind of madness. He was in a furious haste, as if vengeance followed him, and he did not sleep much. When I rose before dawn he was lying with staring eyes. For his companion, the gentleman, he seemed to have no care – he was pursuing his own private errand. A strong man, but a difficult. When they left me I did not feel happy about the two messieurs.'

77

# 4

Out of the encumbered river by way of easy rapids the boat ran into reaches which were like a Scottish salmon stream on a big scale, long pools each with a riffle at its head. The valley altered its character, becoming narrower and grassier, with the forest only in patches on infrequent promontories. The weather, too, changed. The nights were colder, and a chill crept into even the noontide sunshine. But it was immensely invigorating, so that Johnny sang snatches of Scots songs instead of sucking his pipe, and Leithen had moments of energy which he knew to be deceptive. The air had a quality which he was unable to describe, and the scents were not less baffling. They were tonic and yet oddly sedative, for they moved the blood rather to quiescence than to action. They were aromatic, but there was nothing lush or exotic in them. They had on the senses the effect of a high violin note on the ear, as of something at the extreme edge of mortal apprehension.

But the biggest change was in Leithen's outlook. The gloomy apathy of the Oblate's presbytery disappeared, and its place was taken by a mood which was almost peace. The mountains were no longer untidy rock heaps, but the world which he had loved long ago, that happy upper world of birds and clouds and the last magic of sunset. He picked out ways of ascent by their ridges and gullies, and found himself noting with interest the riot of colour in the woods: the grey splashes of caribou moss, the reds of partridge-berry, cranberry, blueberry, and Saskatoon; the dull green interspaces where an old forest fire had brought forth acres of young spruces; above all the miracle of the hardwood trees. The scrub by the river, red-dog-willow, wolfberry willow, had every shade of yellow, and poplar and birch carried on the pageant of gold and umber far up the mountain sides. Birds were getting infrequent; he saw duck and geese high up in the heavens, but he could not identify them. Sometimes he saw a deer, and on bare places on the hills he thought he detected sheep. Black bears were plentiful, revelling among the berries or wetting their new winter coats in the river's shallows, and he saw a big grizzly lumbering across a stone shoot.

Three long portages took them out of the Big Hare valley to Lone Tree Lake, which, in shape like a scimitar, lay tucked in a mat of forest under the wall of what seemed to be a divide. They reached it in the twilight, and, since the place was a poor camping-ground, they launched the canoes and paddled half-way up till they found a dry spit, which some ancient conflagration had cleared of timber. The lake was lit from end to end with the fires of sunset, and later in the night the aurora borealis cast its spears across the northern end. The mountains had withdrawn, and only one far snow peak was visible, so that the feeling of confinement, inevitable in the high valleys, was gone, and Leithen had a sense of infinite space around him. He seemed to breathe more freely, and the chill of the night air refreshed him, for frost crisped the lake's edges. He fell asleep as soon as he got under his blankets.

He awoke after midnight to see above him a wonderful sky of stars, still shot with the vagrant shafts of the aurora. Suddenly he felt acutely his weakness, but with no regret in his mind, and indeed almost with comfort. He had been right in doing as he had done, coming out to meet death in a world where death and life were colleagues and not foes. He felt that in this strange place he was passing, while still in time, inside the bounds of eternity. He was learning to know himself, and with that might come the knowledge of God. A sentence of St Augustine came into his head as he turned over and went to sleep again: *'Deum et animam scire cupio. Nihil ne plus? Nihil omnino.'*

## 5

He woke to find himself sweating under his blankets. The weather had changed to a stuffy mildness, for a warm chinook wind was blowing from the south-west. Johnny was standing beside him with a grave face.

'Lew's been here,' he said. 'He's left his mark all right. Eat your breakfast and I'll show you.'

At the base of the promontory there was a stand of well-grown spruce. A dozen of the trees had been felled, stripped, cut into lengths, and notched at each end. An oblong had been traced on a flat piece of ground, and holes dug for end-posts. A hut had been prospected, begun – and relinquished.

'Lew's been on this job,' said Johnny. 'You can't mistake his axe-work.'

He stood looking with unquiet eyes at the pile of cut logs.

'Him and his pal put in a day's work here. And then they quit. What puzzles me is why Lew quit. It ain't like him.'

'Why shouldn't he change his mind?' Leithen asked. 'He must have decided that this was not the best place for a base camp.'

Johnny shook his head.

'It ain't like him. He never starts on a job until he has thought all round it and made sure that he's doin' right, and then hell fire wouldn't choke him off it. No, mister. There's something queer about this, and I don't like it. Something's happened to Lew.'

The mild blue eyes were cloudy with anxiety.

'They've back-packed their stuff and gone on. They've cached their canoe,' and he nodded to where a bulky object was lashed in the lower branches of a tall poplar. 'We've got to do the same. We'll cache most of our stuff, for when we catch up with Lew we can send back for it. We'll take the Indians, for you ain't fit to carry a load. Their trail won't be hard to follow. I've been over the first bit of it. Lew pushed on ahead, and the other was about fifty yards back of him and limping. Looks like they've quarrelled.'

# 6

The trail led away from the lake shore up a tributary stream towards what looked like the main wall of the divide. The berry-clad, ferny hillside made easy walking, and since the timber was small there were few troublesome windfalls. Johnny carried his .44 rifle, his axe, and a bag containing his own personal effects and most of Leithen's; the Hares, Big Klaus and Little Klaus, had the heavy stuff, tent, cooking utensils, portable stove, stores; while Leithen had no more than a light haversack about the weight which he had often carried in the Alps. The pattern of his day was now so familiar that he found it hard to fit into it the astounding novelties in his life – his quest for a man whom he had never seen, in the least-known corner of North America – the fact that presently some-where in this wilderness he must die.

New also in his experience were the weather and his own weakness. The sun was getting low and the days were shortening; each night frost crisped the edges of the streams, and the first hour of the morning march was through crackling pools and frozen herbage. But by noon the sun was warm and it set daily over their left shoulders in a haze of opal and pearl. The morning and evening chills were keenly felt, but the tonic air seemed to soothe his coughing. It was the very quintessence of air, quickening every sense so that he smelt more keenly, heard more clearly, saw things in sharper outline. He had never used spectacles, and he found that his eyes were fully the equal of Johnny's when he knew what to look for.

He might have had an appetite, too, had it not been for his fatigue. He was so tired when they made camp for the night that he could scarcely eat, and Johnny had to turn his beans and bacon into a kind of soup before he could swallow them. He would lie in a half-stupor drawing his breath painfully for the better part of an hour, while Johnny and the Hares built the fire. Johnny was merciful, and accommodated his pace to his dragging feet, but the easiest gait was too much for him, and soon he had to have hourly rests. The trail went in and out of the glens, rising slowly to the higher benches, and, but for a few patches of swamp and one laborious passage over a rockfall, it was a road a child could have walked. But except for a very few minutes in the day it was for Leithen one long purgatory.

He started out in the morning with wobbling legs. After a mile or so, when his blood moved more briskly, he had a short spell of comfort. Then his breath began to trouble him, and long before midday he was plodding like a conscientious drunkard. He made it a point of honour to continue until Johnny called a halt, and, though Johnny did this often, he found himself always near the limits of his strength, and would drop like a log when the word was given. He returned unconsciously to an old habit of his mountaineering days, when he had had a long dull course to complete, counting his steps up to a thousand and walking to the rhythm of 'Old Soldiers Never Die' . . .

At the head of a little pass Johnny halted, though the march had only been going for twenty minutes. The Hares, when they came up, set down their packs and broke into a dismal howling, which seemed to be meant for a chant. There was a big jack-pine with the lower branches lopped off, and some fifty feet from the ground a long bundle was lashed to the trunk, something wrapped in caribou skin tanned white.

Johnny removed his disreputable hat. 'That's a chief up there. Good old scout he was – name of Billy Whitefish ... Passed out last fall.'

# 7

One blue day succeeded another, and each was followed by a colder night. The earth was yawning before it turned to its winter sleep. Leithen, though the days tired him to desperation, yet found the nights tolerable, and could let his thoughts stray from his bodily discomfort. He listened to Johnny's talk.

Johnny talked much, for he had lost his shyness of Leithen, and this kind of trip was child's play to him.

'This is a pretty good land,' he said, 'to them that knows their way about. I guess a man could starve in the barrens, but not in the woods. Why, there's forty kinds of berries – and a whole lot of different sorts of mushrooms – and rock-tripe – and bark you can boil to make porridge. And there's all the animals that Noah had in the Ark. And there's nothing to hurt a body provided the body's got sense, and don't tackle a grizzly uphill.'

He had strong views on food. 'B'ar's right enough in the fall when he's fat. A young un's as good as mutton, but an old un's plain shoe leather.' He did not care for moose meat, preferring caribou or deer, and he liked best partridge or ptarmigan in half-plumage.

'What's here? Grizzly, black b'ar, brown b'ar, moose, caribou, three kinds of sheep – everything except goats. The Almighty left goats out when He stocked them mountains.'

It was clearly his purpose to picture the land as an easy place even for a sick man to travel in. 'Canadians,' he said (he used the word as the equivalent of strangers, embracing everybody except the men of the North-west), 'think we've got hell's own climate up here. They're wrong. We get milder winters than the Prairies. Besides, winter's a fine time to travel if you know the ways of it. You'll be snugger in a hole in the snow at forty below than in an apartment house in Winnipeg, and a darn lot healthier.

'But you've got to watch your step in the Northland,' he would add. He would tell experiences of his own to show the cruelty of the wilds, though he was always careful to explain that his misfortunes were due to his own folly. He was a white-water man, though not of Lew's class, and above all things he hated towing a boat with a long trackline. 'The thing's just waitin' to murder you,' he said, 'trip you over a cliff, or drown you, or get round your neck and saw your head off.' . . .

He had been near starvation. 'I can go three days without food and not feel it, and I've done it pretty often. I reckon Lew could go five. But there's never been no reason for it except my own dam' folly. Once I lost all my kit in a river, including my knife which I had in my teeth, and I had to make shift with flint-flakes to kill and skin. I once lived for a week on berries and one porcupine.'

He had had his accidents, too, as when a pine he was chopping down split with the cold and sent a sliver through his shoulder. He had once walked twenty miles to find a bottle of painkiller which he had cached, his throat choking with laryngitis. But his worst adventure – he seemed shy in telling it – was when he was caught without snow-shoes in an early fall blizzard, and crossed unknowingly a bottomless half-frozen sphagnum swamp which heaved under his tread and made him vomit up his soul.

He would talk, too, about the secret lore of the woods. He could make the crows speak to him, and the squirrels, but not the whisky-jacks, because they were fools with only a cry and no speech. Lew could make anything talk.

It was always Lew, the mentor, the magician. But he never spoke his brother's name, or so it seemed to Leithen, without an accent of disquiet. He followed unerringly Lew's blazing of the trail, and often the blazes were so small that only a skilled woodman could have noticed them. He studied carefully every bivouac. Sometimes in marshy places he found the moccasin tracks still fresh, and then his anxiety seemed to increase.

'Lew's settin' a terrible pace,' he said, 'and the other's laggin'. They're still messin' together at night, but the other must be getting in pretty late, and he can't be having much sleep, for each morning they starts together ... I don't like it somehow. I wonder what brother Lew's aiming at?'

# 8

The trail wound intricately along the slopes of deep parallel glens, now and then crossing from one to another by a low pass. Johnny had been over it before, and was puzzled. 'Them rivers run down to the Yukon,' he told Leithen. 'But Lew swears the Sick Heart don't do that, and we're over the divide from the Mackenzie. I reckon it can't have nothin' to do with the Peel, so it must disappear into the earth. That's my guess. Anyhow, this trail ain't going to get us nowhere except to the Yukon.'

The celestial weather continued, wintry in the small hours of the night, but in the sun as balmy as June. Leithen had fallen into a state which was neither ease nor mal-ease, but something neutral like his bodily condition at the end of a hard term at the Bar, when he was scarcely ill but assuredly not well. He could struggle through the day and have a slender margin for the interests of the road.

There was one new thing – the wild animals were beginning to show themselves, as if they were stretching their legs for the last time before the snows came. One morning he saw the first moose – well up the hillside in a patch of dwarf spruce, showing against the background like elephants.

'Them beasts ain't happy here,' Johnny said. 'They want the hardwood country, for they ain't like caribou that feed on moss – they likes the juicy underbrush. I guess they'll come down before the snow to the bottoms and stamp out a *ravage* so as to get to the shoots. I'll tell you a queer thing. The moose is pushin' further north. I mind the day when there wasn't one north of the Great Slave Lake, and now Lew has seen them on the Arctic shore east of the Mackenzie. I wonder what's bitin' them?'

The caribou had not yet appeared, being still on the tundras, but there were birds – ptarmigan and willow grouse – and big Arctic hares just getting into their winter coats. Also there were wolves, both the little grey wolves and the great timber wolves. They did not howl, but Johnny – and Leithen also – could hear them padding at night in the forest. Sometimes dim shapes slipped across a glade among the trees. One night, too, when Leithen could not sleep, he got up and watched the northern heavens where the aurora flickered like a curtain of delicate lace wrought in every tint of the rainbow. It lit up the foreground across which stalked a procession of black forms like some frieze on a Greek urn.

He found Johnny at his side. 'That's the North,' he said solemnly. 'The wolves and the Aurory. God send us a kind winter.'

## 9

One day the trail took an odd turn, for it left the parallel ridges and bore away to the east to higher ground. Johnny shook his head. 'This is new country for me,' he said. 'Here's where Lew has taken the big chance.'

Mountains prematurely snow-covered had been visible from the Hares' settlement, and Leithen at Lone Tree Camp had seen one sharp white peak in a gap very far off. Ever since then they had been moving among wooded ridges at the most two thousand feet high. But now they suddenly came out on a stony plateau, the trees fell away, and they looked on a new world.

The sedimentary rocks had given place to some kind of igneous formation. In front were cliffs and towers as fantastic as the Dolomites, black and sinister against a background of great snowfields, sweeping upward to ice arêtes and couloirs which reminded Leithen of Dauphiné. In the foreground the land dropped steeply into gorges which seemed to converge in a deep central trough, but they were very unlike the mild glens through which they had been ascending. These were rifts in the black rock, their edges feathered with dwarf pines, and from their inky darkness in the sunlight they must be deep. The rock towers were not white and shining like the gracious pinnacles above Cortina, but as black as if they had been hewn out of coal by a savage Creator.

But it was not the foreground that held the eye, but the immense airy sweep of the snowfields and ice pinnacles up to a central point, where a tall peak soared into the blue. Leithen had seen many snow mountains in his time, but this was something new to him – new to the world. The icefield was gigantic, the descending glaciers were on the grand scale, the central mountain must compete with the chief summits of the southern Rockies. But unlike the Rockies the scene was composed as if by a great artist – nothing untidy and shapeless, but everything harmonized into an exquisite unity of line and colour.

His eyes dropped from the skyline to the foreground and the middle distance. He shivered. Somewhere down in that labyrinth was Galliard. Somewhere down there he would leave his own bones.

Johnny was staring at the scene without speaking a word, without even an exclamation. At last he drew a long breath.

'God!' he said. 'Them's the biggest mountains in the Northland and only you and me and Lew and his pal has seen 'em, and some Indians that don't count. But it's going to be a blasted country to travel. See that black gash? I reckon that's where the Sick Heart River flows, and it'll be hell's own job to get down to it.'

'D'you think Lew and Galliard are there?' Leithen asked.

'Sure. I got their trail a piece back on the sand of that little pond we passed. We'll pick it up soon on them shale slides.'

'Is the road possible?'

'Lew thinks it is. I told you he'd seen the Sick Heart once but couldn't get down the precipices. It couldn't have been this place or he wouldn't have gone on, for he don't try impossibilities. He sure knows there's a way down.'

Leithen, sitting on the mountain gravel, had a sudden sharp pang of hopelessness, almost of fear. He realized that this spectacle of a new mountain-land would once have sent him wild with excitement, the excitement both of the geographer and the mountaineer. But now he could only look at it with despair. It might have been a Pisgah-sight of a promised land; but now it was only a cruel reminder of his frailty. He had still to find Galliard, but Galliard had gone into this perilous labyrinth. Could he follow? Could he reach him? ... But did it matter after all? The finding of Galliard was a task he had set himself, thinking less of success than of the task. It was to tide away the time manfully before his end so that he could die standing. A comforting phrase of Walt Whitman's came back to him, 'the delicious nearby assurance of death'.

Sometimes lately he had been surprised at himself. He had not thought that he possessed this one-idea'd stoicism which enabled him to climb the bleak staircase of his duty with scarcely a look behind ... But perhaps this was the way in which most men faced death. Had his health lasted he would be doing the same thing a dozen or a score of years ahead. Soon his friends would be doing it – Hannay and Lamancha and Clanroyden – if they were fated to end in their beds. It was the lot of everyone sooner or later to reach the bleak bag's-end of life into which they must creep to die.

# 10

They soon picked up the tracks of their forerunners in the long spouts of gravel, and as they slowly zigzagged downhill to the tree line the weather changed. The cold blue sky beyond the mountains dulled to a colder grey and all light went out of the landscape. It was like the coming of the Polar Night of which he had read, the inexorable drawing down of a curtain upon the glory of the world. The snow began to fall in big flakes, not driven by any wind, but like the gentle emptying of a giant celestial bin. Soon there was nothing but white round them, except the tops of the little gnarled firs.

Luckily they had reached the tree line before the snow began, for otherwise they might have lost the trail. As it was, Johnny soon picked it up from the blazes on the diminutive trunks. It led them down a slope so steep that it was marvellous that any roots could cling to it. They had to ford many ice-cold streams, and before they reached flat ground in the evening Leithen was tottering on the very outside edge of his strength. He scarcely heard Johnny's mutter, 'Looks like Lew has lost his pal. Here's where he camped and there's just the one set of tracks.' He was repeating to himself Whitman's words like a prayer.

Johnny saw his weariness and mercifully said no more, contenting himself with making camp and cooking supper. Leithen fell asleep as soon as he had finished his meal, and did not wake until he heard the crackling of the breakfast fire. The air was mild and most of the snow had gone, for the wind had shifted to the south-west. Every limb ached after the long march of yesterday, but his chest was easier and there seemed more pith in his bones.

Johnny wore an anxious face. 'We've made up on 'em,' he said. 'I reckon Lew's not two days ahead.'

Leithen asked how he knew this, but Johnny said he knew but could not explain – it would take too long and a stranger to the wilds would not understand.

'He's gone on alone,' he repeated. 'This was his camping-ground three nights back, and the other wasn't here. They parted company some time that day, for we had the trail of both of 'em on the shale slides. What in God's name has happened? Lew has shook off his pal, and that pal is somewhere around here, and, being new to the job, he'll die. Maybe he's dead already.'

'Has Lew gone on?'

'Lew's gone on. I've been over a bit of his trail. He's not wastin' time.'

'But the other – my friend – won't he have followed Lew's blazes?'

'He wouldn't notice 'em, being raw. Lew's blazed a trail for his use on the way back, not for any pal to follow.'

So this was journey's end for him – to have traced Galliard to the uttermost parts of the earth only to find him dead. Remembrance of his errand and his original purpose awoke exasperation, and exasperation stirred the dying embers of his vitality.

'Our job is to find Mr Galliard,' he said. 'We stay here until we get him dead or alive.'

Johnny nodded. 'I guess that's right, but I'm mighty anxious about brother Lew. Looks like he's gone haywire.'

The snow was the trouble, Johnny said. It was disappearing fast under sun and wind, and its melting would obliterate all tracks on soft ground, almost as completely as if it still covered them. He thought that the Hares were better trackers than himself and they might find what he missed. He proposed that Leithen should lie up in camp while he and the Indians went back on yesterday's trail in the hope of finding the place where the two men had parted.

Johnny packed some food and in half an hour he and the Hares were climbing the steep side of the glen. Leithen carried his blankets out to a patch which the sun had already dried, and basked in the thin winter sunshine. Oddly enough, Johnny's news had not made him restless, though it threatened disaster to his journey. He had wanted that journey to succeed, but the mere finding of Galliard would not spell success, or the loss of him failure. Success lay in his own spirit. A slight increase of bodily comfort had given him also a certain spiritual ease. This sun was good, though soon for him it would not rise again.

The search-party did not return until the brief twilight. Johnny, as he entered the tent, shook his head dolefully.

'No good, mister. We've found where the other feller quit the trail – them Hares are demons at that game. Just what I expected – up on the barrens where there ain't no trees to blaze and brother Lew had got out of sight. But after that we couldn't pick up no trail. He might have gone left or he might have gone right, but anyhow he must have gone down into the woods. So we started to beat out the woods, each of us takin' a line, but we've struck nothin'. Tomorrow we'll have another try. I reckon he can't have gone far, for he's dead lame. He must be lyin' up somewhere and starvin'.'

Johnny counted on his fingers.

'Say, look! He's been three days quit of Lew – he's dead lame, and I reckon he wasn't carryin' more'n his own weight – if he didn't catch up with Lew at night he didn't have no food – maybe he wasn't able to make fire – maybe he didn't carry more'n one blanket – if he's alive he's mighty cold and mighty hungry.'

He was silent until he went to bed, a certain proof of anxiety.

'This sure is one hell of a business,' he said as he turned in. 'Lew kind of mad and streakin' off into space, and his pal aimin' to be a corpse. It's enough to put a man off his feed.'

# 11

Johnny and the Hares were off at dawn next morning. The weather was mild, almost stuffy, and there had been little frost in the night. Leithen sat outside the tent, but there was no sun to warm him, only a grey misty sky which bent low on the hills. He was feeling his weakness again, and with it came a deep depression of spirit. The wilds were brutal, inhuman, the abode of horrid cruelty. They had driven one man mad and would be the death of another. Not much comfort for Felicity Galliard in his report – 'Discovered where your man had gone. Followed him and found him dead.' That report would be carried by Johnny some time down into the civilized places, and cabled to New York, signed with the name of Leithen. But he would not see Felicity's grief, for long before then he would be out of the world.

In the afternoon the weather changed. The heavens darkened and suddenly burst into a lace-work of lightning. It was almost like the aurora, only it covered the whole expanse of sky. From far away there was a kind of muttering, but there were no loud thunder peals. After an hour it ceased and a little cold wind came out of the west. This was followed by a torrential rain, the heaviest Leithen had ever seen, which fell not in sheets but with the solid three dimensions of a cataract. In five minutes the hillside was running with water and the floor of the tent was a bog. In half an hour the brook below was a raving torrent. The downpour ceased and was followed by a burst of sunshine from a pale lemon sky, and a sudden sharpening of the air. Johnny had spoken of this; he had said that the winter would not properly be on them until they had the father and mother of a thunderstorm and the last rains.

Leithen pulled on his gum-boots and went out for a breath of air. The hill was melting under him, and only by walking in the thicker patches of fern and berries could he find decent foothold. Somehow his depression had lifted with the passing of the storm, and in the sharp air his breath came easier. It was arduous work walking in that tangle. 'I had better not go far,' he told himself, 'or I'll never get home. Not much chance for Johnny and the Indians after such a downpour.'

He turned to look back . . . There seemed to be a lumbering body at the door of the tent trying to crawl inside. A bear, no doubt. If the brute got at the food there would be trouble. Leithen started to slither along the hillside, falling often, and feeling his breath run short.

The thing was inside. He had closed the door-flap before leaving, and now he tore it back to let in the light. The beast was there, crouching on its knees on the muddy floor. It was a sick beast, for it seemed to nuzzle the ground and emit feeble groans and gasps of pain. A bear! Its hinder parts were one clot of mud, but something like a ragged blanket seemed to be round its middle. The head! The head looked like black fur, and then he saw that this was a cap and that beneath it was shaggy human hair.

The thing moaned, and then from it came a sound which, though made by dry lips, was articulate speech.

'Frizelle!' it said. 'Oh, Frizelle! . . . pour l'amour de Dieu!'

# 12

It took all Leithen's strength to move Galliard from the floor to his bed. He folded a blanket and put it under his head. Then he undid the muffler at his throat and unbuttoned the shirt. The man's lips were blue and sore, and his cheeks were shrunk with hunger and fatigue. He seemed to be in pain, for as he lay on his back he moaned and screwed up his eyes. His wits were dulled in a stupor, and, apart from his first muttered words, he seemed to be unconscious of his environment.

Leithen mixed a little brandy and tinned milk and forced it between his lips. It was swallowed and immediately vomited. So he lit the stove and put on the kettle to boil, fetching water from the nearby spring. The moaning continued as if the man were in pain, and he remembered that Johnny had guessed at a wounded foot. The sight of another mortal suffering seemed to give Leithen a certain access of strength. He found himself able to undo Galliard's boots, and it was no light task, for they were crusted thick with mud. The left one had been sliced open like a gouty man's shoe, to give ease to a wound in his shin, a raw, ragged gash which looked like an axe cut. Before the boot could be removed the moaning had several times changed to a gasp of pain. Leithen made an attempt to wash the wound, and bound it up with a handkerchief, which was all he had in the way of a bandage. That seemed to give Galliard relief, and the moaning ceased.

The kettle was boiling and he made tea. Galliard tried to take the pannikin, but his hands were shaking so that Leithen had to feed him like a child. He swallowed all that he did not spill and seemed to want more. So Leithen tried him again with brandy and milk, the milk this time thinned and heated. Now two brown eyes were staring at him, eyes in which consciousness was slowly dawning. The milk was drunk and Galliard lay for a little blinking at the tent wall. Then his eyes closed and he slept.

Leithen laid himself down on Johnny's mattress and looked at the shapeless heap which had been the object of his quest. There was the tawny beard which he had come to expect, but for the rest – it was unfamiliar wreckage. Little in common had it with the gracious portrait in the Park Avenue hall, or the Nattier, or the Aubusson carpet, or Felicity's rose-and-silver drawing-room. This man had chosen the wilderness, and now the wilderness had taken him and tossed him up like the jetsam of a flood.

There was no satisfaction for Leithen in the fact that he had been successful in his search. By an amazing piece of luck he had found Galliard and in so doing had achieved his purpose. But now the purpose seemed trivial. Was this derelict of so great importance after all? The unaccustomed bending in his handling of Galliard had given him a pain in his back, and the smell of the retched brandy and milk sickened him. He felt a desperate emptiness in his body, in his soul, and in the world.

It was almost dark when Johnny and the Hares returned. Leithen jerked his thumb towards the sleeping Galliard. Johnny nodded.

'I sort of suspicioned he'd be here. We got his tracks, but lost them in the mud. The whole darned hill is a mud-slide.' He spoke slowly and flatly, as if he were very tired.

But his return set the little camp going, and Leithen realized what a blundering amateur he was compared with Johnny and the Indians. In a few minutes a fire was crackling before the tent door. Galliard, still in a coma, was lifted and partly unclothed, and his damaged leg was washed and rebandaged by Johnny with the neatness of a hospital nurse. The tent was tidied up and supper was set cooking – coffee on the stove and caribou steaks on the fire. Johnny concocted a dish of his own for the sick man, for he made a kind of chicken broth from a brace of willow grouse he had shot.

'You'd better eat,' he said. 'We'll feed the soup to that feller when he wakes. Best let him sleep a little longer. How you feelin' yourself? When I come in you looked mighty bad.'

'I found Galliard more than I could manage; but never mind me. What about him?'

Johnny's bat's ears seemed to prick up as he bent over the sleeping figure. He was like a gnome in a fairy-tale; but he was human enough when he turned to Leithen, and the glow of the fire showed his troubled blue eyes.

'He'll come through a' right,' he said. 'He's been a healthy man and he ain't bottomed his strength yet. But he's plumb weary. He can't have fed proper for three days, and I reckon he can't have slept proper for a week.'

'The wound?'

'Nasty cut he's got, and he'll have to watch his self if he don't want to go lame all his days. He can't move for a good spell.'

'How long?'

'Ten days – a fortnight – maybe more.'

Leithen had the appetite of a bird, but Johnny was ordinarily a good trencherman. Tonight, however, he ate little, though he emptied the coffee-pot. His mind was clearly on his brother, but Leithen asked no questions. At last, after half an hour's sucking at his pipe, he spoke.

'I figure that him' – and he nodded towards Galliard – 'and brother Lew has been agreein' about as well as a carcajou and a sick b'ar. Lew'd gotten into a bad mood and this poor soul didn't know what the matter was, and got no answer when he asked questions. But he was bound to hang on to Lew or get lost and perish. Pretty nasty time he's been havin'. Lew's been actin' mighty mean, I'd say. But you can't just blame Lew, for, as I figure it, he don't know what he's doin'. He ain't seein' his pal, he ain't seein' nothin' except the trail he's blazin' and somethin' at the end of it.'

'What's that?'

'The old Sick Heart River.'

'Then he's gone mad?'

'You might say so. And yet Lew for ordinar' is as sane as you, mister, and a darn lot saner than me. He's gotten a vision and he's bound to go after it.'

'What's to be done?'

'Our first job is to get this feller right. That was the reason you come down North, wasn't it? Every man's got to skin his own skunk. But I don't mind tellin' you I'm worried to death about brother Lew.'

The attention of both was suddenly diverted to Galliard, who had woke up, turned on his side, and was looking at them with wide-awake eyes – pained eyes, too, as if he had awakened to suffering. Johnny took the pannikin of soup which had been heating on the stove, and began to feed the sick man, feeding him far more skilfully than Leithen had done, so that little was spilt. The food seemed to revive him and ease his discomfort. He lay back for a little, staring upward, and then he spoke.

His voice was hoarse, little above a croak. Johnny bent over him to catch his words. He shook his head.

'It's French, but Godamighty knows what he means. It don't sound sense to me.'

Leithen dragged himself nearer. The man was repeating some form of words like a litany, repeating it again and again, so that the same phrase kept recurring. To his amazement he recognized it as a quotation from Chateaubriand, which had impressed him long ago and which had stuck to his fly-paper memory.

'*S'il est parmi les anges,*' the voice said, '*comme parmi des hommes, des campagnes habitées et des lieux déserts.*'

There was a pause. Certain phrases followed, '*Solitudes de la terre*', '*Solitudes célestes*'. Then the first sentence was repeated. Galliard spoke the words in the slurred patois of Quebec, sounding harshly the final consonants.

'He is quoting a French writer who lived a century ago,' Leithen told Johnny. 'It's nonsense. Something about the solitary places of heaven.'

Galliard was speaking again. It was a torrent of *habitant* French and his voice rose to a pitch which was almost a scream. The man was under a sudden terror, and he held out imploring hands which Johnny grasped. The latter could follow the babble better than Leithen, but there was no need of an interpreter, for the pain and fear in the voice told their own tale. Then the fit passed, the eyes closed, and Galliard seemed to be asleep again.

Johnny shook his head. 'Haywire,' he said. 'Daft – and I reckon I know the kind of daftness. He's mortal scared of them woods. You might say the North's gotten on his mind.'

'But it was a craze for the North that dragged him here.'

'Yep, but having gotten here he's scared of it. His mind's screwed right round. It's a queer thing, the North, and you need to watch your step for fear it does you down. This feller was crazy for it till he poked his head a wee bit inside, and now he's scared out of his life, and would give his soul to quit. I've known it happen before. Folks come down here thinking the North's a pretty lady, and find that she can be a cruel, bloody-minded old bitch, and they scurry away from her like jack-rabbits from a forest fire. I've seen them as had had a taste of her ugly side, and ever after the stink of smoke-dried Indian moccasins, and even the smell of burning logs, would turn out their insides ... I reckon this feller's had a pretty purifyin' taste of it. Ever been lost?'

'Never.'

'Well, it ain't nice, and it tests a man's guts.'

The air sharpened in the night and the little tent with its three occupants was not too stuffy. Galliard never stirred. Johnny had the short sound slumbers of a woodman, waking and rising before dawn; but Leithen slept badly. He had found his man, but he was a lunatic – for the time being. His task now was to piece together the broken wits. It seemed to him a formidable and unwelcome business. Could a dying man minister to a mind diseased? He would have preferred his old job – to go on spending his bodily strength till he had reached the end of it. That would, at any rate, have given him peace to make his soul.

Johnny set the camp stirring and was everywhere at once, like a good housewife. Galliard was washed and fed and his wound dressed. Leithen found that he had more power in his legs, and was able to make a short promenade of the shelf on which the camp stood, breathing air which was chilly as ice and scented with a thousand miles of pines. Johnny and the Hares were busy with measurements.

Leithen, huddled in the lee of the fire, watched the men at work. They were laying out the ground plan of a hut. It was to be built against the hillside, the gravel of which, when cut away, would make its back wall, and it seemed to be about twenty feet square. The Hares did the levelling of the shelf, and presently came the sound of Johnny's axe from the woods. In a couple of hours the four corner posts were cut, trimmed, and set up, and until the midday meal all three were busy felling well-grown spruce and pine.

Johnny's heavy preoccupation lightened a little as they ate.

'We need a hut whatever happens,' he said. 'The feller' – that was how he referred to Galliard – 'will want something snugger than a tent when the cold sets in, for he ain't goin' to get well fast. Then there's you, a mighty sick man. And please God, there'll be brother Lew.'

'Is there no way of getting back to the Hares' camp?'

'For Lew and me – not for you and the feller. We got to plan to spend the winter here, or hereabouts. We can send the Indians back for stores and dog-teams, and maybe we could get out in February when the good snows come. But we got to plan for the winter. I can fix up a tidy hut, and when we get the joints nicely chinked up with mud, and plenty of moss and sods on the roof, we'll be as snug as an old b'ar in its hole. I'm aimin' to fix a proper fireplace inside, for there's the right kind of clay in the creek for puddlin'.'

'Let me help.'

'You can't do nothin' yet, so long as we're on the heavy jobs, but I'll be glad of you when it comes to the inside fixin'. You get into the tent beside the feller and sleep a bit. I'm all right if I wasn't worried about Lew.'

Johnny was attending to the bodily needs of the sick man like a hospital nurse, feeding him gruel and chicken broth and weak tea. Galliard slept most of the time, and even his waking hours were a sort of coma. He was asleep when Leithen entered the tent, and presently, to the accompaniment of Johnny's axe in the woods, Leithen himself drowsed off, for by this time of the day he was very weary. But sleep was for him the thinnest of films over the waking world and presently he was roused by Galliard's voice. This time it sounded familiar, something he had heard before, and not the animal croak of yesterday.

Two dull brown eyes were staring at him, eyes in which there was only the faintest spark of intelligence. They moved over his person, lingering some time at his boots, and then fastened on his face. There was bewilderment in them, but also curiosity. Their owner seemed to struggle for words, and he passed his tongue over his dry lips several times before he spoke.

'You are – what?'

He spoke in English, but his hold on the language seemed to slip away, for when Leithen replied in the same tongue the opaque eyes showed no comprehension.

'I am a friend of your friends,' he said. 'We have come to help you. I have the brother of Lew Frizel with me.'

After a pause he repeated the last sentence in French. Some word in it caught Galliard's attention. His face suddenly became twisted with anxiety, and he tried to raise himself on his bed. Words poured from him, words tumbling over each other, the French of Quebec. He seemed to be imploring someone to wait for him – to let him rest a little and then he would go on – an appeal couched in queer childish language, much of which Leithen could not understand. And always, like the keynote of a threnody, came the word *Rivière* – and *Rivière* again – and once *Rivière du Cœur Malade*.

The partner of Ravelstons had suffered a strange transformation. Leithen realized that it would be idle to try to link this man's memory with his New York life. He had gone back into a very old world, the world of his childhood and his ancestors, and though it might terrify him, it was for the moment his only world.

The babbling continued. As Leithen listened to it the word that seemed to emerge from the confusion was Lew's name. It was on Lew that Galliard's world was now centred. If he was to be brought back to his normal self Lew must be the chief instrument ... And Lew was mad himself, raving mad, far away in the mountains on a crazy hunt for a mystic river! A sudden sense of the lunatic inconsequence of the whole business came over Leithen and forced from him a bitter laugh. That laugh had an odd effect upon Galliard for it seemed to frighten him into silence. It was as if he had got an answer to his appeals, an answer which slammed the door.

Next day the cold was again extreme, but the sun was out for six hours, and the shelf in the forest was not uncomfortable. Johnny, after sniffing the air, pronounced on the weather. The first snow had fallen; there would be three days of heavy frost; then for maybe ten days there would be a mild, bright spell; then a few weeks before Christmas would come the big snows and the fierce cold. The fine spell would enable him to finish the hut. A little drove of snow-buntings had passed yesterday; that meant, he said, since the birds were late in migrating, that winter would be late.

'You call it the Indian Summer?'

'The Hares call it the White Goose Summer. It ends when the last white goose has started south.'

That day Leithen made an experiment. Galliard was mending well, the wound in the leg was healing, he could eat better, only his mind was still sick. It was important to find out whether the time had come to link his memory up with his recent past, to get him on the first stage on the road back to the sphere to which he belonged.

He chose the afternoon, when his own fatigue compelled him to rest, and Galliard was likely to be wakeful after the bustle of the midday meal. He had reached certain conclusions. Galliard had lost all touch with his recent life. He had reverted to the traditions of his family, and now worshipped at ancestral shrines, and he had been mortally scared by the sight of the goddess. These fears did not impel him to mere flight, for he did not know where to flee to. It drove him to seek a refuge, and that refuge was Lew. He was as much under the spell of Lew as Lew was under the spell of his crazy river. Could this spell be lifted?

So far Galliard had been a mere automaton. He had spoken like a waxwork managed by a ventriloquist. It was hardly possible to recognize a personality in that vacant face, muffled in a shaggy beard, and unlit by the expressionless eyes. Yet the man was regaining his health, his wound was healing fast, his cheeks had lost their famished leanness. As Leithen looked at him he found it hard to refrain from bitterness. He was giving the poor remnants of his strength to the service of a healthy animal with years of vigour before him.

He crushed the thought down and set himself to draw Galliard out of his cave. But the man's wits seemed to be still wandering. Leithen plied him with discreet questions but got an answer to neither French nor English. He refrained from speaking his wife's name, and the names of his American friends, even of Ravelstons itself, woke no response. He tried to link up with Château-Gaillard, and Clairefontaine – with Father Paradis – with Uncle Augustin – with the Gaillards, Aristide and Paul Louis, who had died on the Arctic shores. But he might have been shouting at a cenotaph, for the man never answered, nor did any gleam of recognition show in his face. It was only when Leithen spoke again of Lew that there was a flicker of interest; more than a flicker, indeed, for the name seemed to stir some secret fear; the pupils of the opaque eyes narrowed, the lean cheeks twitched, and Galliard whimpered like a lost dog.

Leithen felt wretchedly ill all that day, but after supper, according to the strange fashion of his disease, he had a sudden access of strength. He found that he could think clearly ahead and take stock of the position. Johnny, who was labouring hard all day, should have tumbled into bed after supper and slept the sleep of the just. But it was plain that there was too much on his mind for easy slumber. He sucked at his pipe, kept his eyes on the fire outside the open door, and spoke scarcely a word.

'How is he getting on?' Leithen asked.

'Him? The feller? Fine, I guess. He's a mighty tough body, for he ha'n't taken no scaith, barrin' the loss of weight. He'll be a' right.'

'But his mind is gone. He remembers nothing but what happened in the last weeks. A shutter has come down between him and his past life. He's a child again.'

'Aye. I've known it happen. You see he was scared out of his skin by something – it may have been Lew, or it may have been jest loneliness. He's got no sense in him and it's goin' to take quite a time to get it back. That's why I'm fixin' this hut. He wants nursin' and quiet, and a sort of feel that he's safe, and for that you need four walls, even though they're only raw lumber. If you was to take him out in the woods you'd have him plumb ravin' and maybe he'd never get better. I've seen the like before. It don't do to play tricks with them wild places.'

'I don't understand,' said Leithen. 'Lew goes mad and terrifies Galliard and lets him lag behind so that he nearly perishes. Galliard has the horror of the wilds on him, but no horror of Lew. He seems to be crying for him like a child for his nurse.'

'That's so. That's the way it works. The feller don't know that his troubles was all Lew's doin'. He's gotten scared of loneliness in this darned great wild country, and he claws on to anything human. The only human thing near at hand is brother Lew. But that ain't all. If it was all you and me might take Lew's place, for I guess we're human enough. But, as I figure it, Lew has let him in on his Sick Heart daftness, and kind of enthused him about it, and, the feller bein' sick anyhow, it has got possession of his mind. You told me back in Quebec that he'd a notion, which runs in his family, of pushing north, and we seen the two graves at Ghost River.'

'Still I don't understand,' said Leithen. 'He's frightened of the wilds and yet he hankers to get deeper into them, right to a place where nobody's ever been.'

Johnny shook out his pipe.

'He's not thinkin' of the Sick Heart as part of the woods. He's thinkin' of it the same as Lew, as a sort of Noo Jerusalem – the kind of place where everything'll be a' right. He and Lew ain't thinkin' of it with sane minds, and if Lew's there now he won't be lookin' at it with sane eyes. Sick Heart is a mighty good name for it.'

'What sort of place do you think it is?'

'An ordinary creek, I guess. It's hard to get near, and that's maybe why Lew's crazy about it. My father used to have a sayin' that he got out of Scotland, "Far-away hills is always shiny." '

'Then how is Galliard to be cured of this madness?'

'We've got to get Lew back to him – and Lew in his right mind. At least, that's how I figure it. I mind once I was huntin' with the Caribou-Eaters in the Thelon, east of Great Slave Lake. There was an Indian boy – Two-sticks, his name was – and he come under the spell of my Chipewyan hunter, him they called White Partridge. Well, the trip came to an end and we all went home, but next year I heard that Two-sticks had been queer all winter. He wasn't cured until they fetched old White Partridge to him. And that meant a three-hundred-mile trip from Nelson Forks to the Snowdrift River.'

'How can we get Lew back?'

'Godamighty knows! If I was here on my own I'd be on his trail like a timber wolf. Maybe he's sick in body as well as mind. Anyhow, he's alone, and it ain't good to be alone down North, and he's all that's left to me in the family line. But I can't leave here. I took on a job with you and I've got to go through with it. There's the feller, too, to nurse, and he'll want a tidy bit o' nursin'. And there's you, mister. You're a pretty sick man.'

'Go after Lew and fetch him back and I'll stay here.'

Johnny shook his head.

'Nothin' doin'. You can't finish this hut. The Hares are willin' enough, but they've got to be told what to do. And soon there'll be need of huntin' for fresh supplies, for so far we've been livin' mostly on what we back-packed in. And we've got to send out to the Hares' camp for some things. Besides, you ain't used to the woods, and what's easy for me would be one big trouble for you. But most of all you're sick – god-awful sick – a whole lot sicker than the feller. So I say Nothin' doin', though I'm sure obliged to you. We've got to carry on with our job and trust to God to keep an eye on brother Lew.'

Leithen did not reply. There was a stubborn sagacious dutifulness in that bullet head, that kindly Scots face, and those steadfast blue eyes which was beyond argument.

# 14

He spent a restless night, for he felt that the situation was slipping out of his control. He had come here to expend the last remnants of his bodily strength in a task on which his mind could dwell, and so escape the morbidity of passively awaiting death. He had fulfilled part of that task, but he was as yet a long way from success. Galliard's mind had still to be restored to its normal groove. This could only be done – at least so Johnny said – by fetching and restoring to sanity the man who was the key to its vagaries. Johnny could not be spared, so why should he not go himself on Lew's trail, with one of the Hares to help him? It was misery to hang about this camp, feeling his strength ebbing and getting no further on with his job. That would be dying like a rat in a hole. If it had to be, far better to have found a hole among the comforts of home. If he followed Lew, he would at any rate die in his boots, and whether he succeeded or failed, the end would come while he was fighting.

He told Johnny of his decision and at first was derided. He would not last two days; a Hare might be a good enough tracker, but he wanted a white man to guide him, one who was no novice. The road to the Sick Heart was admittedly difficult and could only be traversed, if at all, by a fit man; there might be storms and mountains made impassable. Moreover, what would he say to Lew, to whom he was a stranger? If Lew was found he would for certain resent any intrusion in his lair. This was the point to which Johnny always returned.

'You've heard of mad trappers and the trouble they give the Mounties. If Lew's mad he'll shoot, and he don't miss.'

'I know all that,' said Leithen, 'and I've made my book for it. You must understand that anyhow I am going to die pretty soon. If I hurry on my death a little in an honest way, I won't be the loser. That's how I look at it. If I never get to Lew, and perish on the road, why, that's that. If I find Lew and his gun finds me, well, that's that. There is just the odd chance that I may persuade him to be reasonable and bring him back here, and that is a chance I'm bound to take. Don't you worry about me, for I tell you I'm taking the easiest way. Since I've got to die, I want to die standing.'

Johnny held out his hand. 'You got me beat, mister. Lew and myself ain't reckoned timid folk, but for real sand there's not your like on this darned continent.'

# 15

Leithen found the ascent of the first ridge from the valley bottom a stern business, for Lew had not zigzagged for ease, but had cut his blazes in the straight line of a crow's flight. But once at the top the road led westerly along a crest, the trees thinned out, and he had a prospect over an immense shining world.

The taller of the Hares, the one he called Big Klaus, was his companion. He himself travelled light, carrying little except a blanket and extra clothing, but the Indian had a monstrous pack which seemed in no way to incommode him. He had the light tent (the hut being now far enough advanced to move Galliard into it), a rifle and shot-gun, axes, billy-can, kamiks to replace moccasins, and two pairs of snow-shoes. The last were of a type new to Leithen – not the round 'bear-paws' of eastern Canada made for the deep snow of the woods, but long, narrow things, very light, constructed of two separate rods joined by a toe-piece, and raised in front at a sharp angle. The centres were of coarse babiche with a large mesh, so as to pick up the least amount of snow, and since the meshing entered the frame by holes and was not whipped round it, the wooden surface was as smooth as skis. On such shoes, Johnny said, an active man could travel forty miles in a day.

Once the ridge had been gained, Leithen found that his breath came a little more easily. He seemed to have entered a world where the purity of the air was a positive thing, not the mere absence of impure matter, but the quintessence of all that was vital in Nature. The Indian Summer forecast by Johnny had begun. There was a shuddering undercurrent of cold, but the sun shone, and though it gave light rather than warmth, it took much of the bleakness out of the landscape. Also there was no wind. The huge amphitheatre, from the icy summit of the central peak to the gullies deep-cut in the black volcanic rock, was as quiet as a summer millpond. Yet there was nothing kindly in this peace; it seemed unnatural, as if the place were destined for strife. On the scarps the little spruces were bent and ragged with the winds, and the many bald patches were bleached by storms. This cold, raw hill-top world was not made for peace; its temporary gentleness was a trap to lure the unwary into its toils.

It was not difficult to follow Lew's blazes, and in a little swamp they found his tracks. He must be a bigger man than Johnny, Leithen thought, or else heavily laden, for the footprints went deep.

The Hare plodded steadily on with his queer in-toed stride. He could talk some English, and would answer questions, but he never opened a conversation. He was a merciful man, and kept turning in his tracks to look at Leithen, and when he thought he seemed weary, promptly dropped his pack and squatted on the ground. His methods of cooking and camping were not Johnny's, but in their way they were efficient. At the midday and evening meals he had a fire going at miraculous speed with his flint and steel and punk-box, and he could make a good bed even of comfortless spruce boughs. His weapon was a cheap breech-loader obtained from some trader, and with it he managed to shoot an occasional partridge or ptarmigan, so that Leithen had his bowl of soup. The second night out he made a kind of Dutch oven and roasted a porcupine, after parboiling it, and he cooked ash-cakes which were nearly as palatable as the pease-meal bannocks which Leithen had eaten in his youth.

That second night he talked. It had been a melancholy summer, for it had been foretold that many of the Hare people would presently die, and the whole tribe had fasted and prepared for their end. The manner of death had not been predicted – it might be famine, or disaster, or a stupendous storm. They had been scolded for this notion by Father Duplessis at Fort Bannerman and by Father Wentzel at the mountain camp, and before the end of the summer the spirits of the tribe had risen, and most believed that the danger had passed. But not all; some wise men thought that bad trouble was coming in the winter.

'It is not good to wait too long on death,' said Big Klaus. 'Better that it should come suddenly when it is not expected.' He looked reflectively at Leithen as if he knew that here was one who was in the same case as the Hares.

For three days they followed the network of ridges according to Lew's blazing. They seemed rarely to lose elevation, for they passed gullies and glens by the scarps at their head waters. But nevertheless they had been steadily descending, for the great rift where the Sick Heart was believed to flow was no longer in the prospect, and the hanging glaciers, the ice couloirs and arêtes, and the poised avalanches of the central peak now overhung and dominated the landscape.

It was a strange world through which Leithen stumbled, conserving his strength greedily and doling it out like a miser. There was sun, light, no great cold, no wind; but with all these things there was no kindness. Something had gone out of the air and that something was hope. Night was closing down, a long night from which there would be a slow awakening. Scarcely a bird could be seen, and there were no small innocent frightened beasts to scurry into hiding. Everything that could move had gone to sanctuary against the coming wrath. The tattered pines, the bald, blanched pastures, were no more a home for life than the pinnacles of intense ice that glittered in mid-heaven. Dawn came punctually, and noon, and nightfall, and yet the feeling was of a perpetual twilight.

In these last weeks Leithen's memory seemed to have become a closed book. He never thought of his past, and no pictures from it came to cheer or torture him. He might have been like the Hare, knowing no other world than this of laborious days and leaden nights. A new discomfort scarcely added to his misery, and food and fine weather did not lighten it. Every hour he was looking at marvels of natural beauty and magnificence, but they did not affect him. Life now awoke no response in him, and he remembered that some wise man had thus defined death. The thought gave him a queer comfort. He was already dead; there only remained the simple snapping of the physical cord.

# 16

They came on it suddenly in the afternoon of the third day. The scraggy forest of jack-pines, which seemed to stretch to the very edge of the snows, suddenly gave place to empty air, and Leithen found himself staring breathlessly not up, but down – down into a chasm nearly a mile wide and two thousand feet deep. From his feet the ground fell away in screes to a horizontal rib of black rock, below which, in a blue mist very far down, were the links of a river. Beyond it were meadows and woods, and the woods were not of scrub pine, but of tall timber – from one or two trees in scattered clumps he judged them to be a hundred feet high. Beyond them again the opposite wall rose sheer to fantastic aiguilles of dark rock. He was looking at some mighty volcanic rift which made a moat to the impregnable castle of the snows.

The strength seemed to go from his limbs, and he collapsed among the crowberries and pine cones. He fumbled in a pocket to find his single Zeiss glass, but gave up the search when he realized the weakness of his hands. This sudden vision had drained the power from his body by intense quickening of his senses and mind. It seemed to him that he was looking at the most marvellous spectacle ever vouchsafed to man. The elements were commonplace – stone and wood, water and earth – but so had been the pigments of a Raphael. The celestial Demiurge had combined them into a masterpiece.

He lay full in the pale sun and the air was mild and mellow. As his eyes thirstily drank in the detail he saw that there was little colour in the scene. Nearly all was subfusc, monochrome, and yet so exquisite was the modelling that there was nothing bleak in it; the impression rather was of a chaste, docile luxuriance. The valley bottom, so far as he could see it, seemed to be as orderly as a garden. The Sick Heart was like a Highland salmon river, looping itself among pools and streams with wide beaches of pebbles, beaches not black like the enclosing cliffs, but shining white. Along its course, and between the woods were meadows of wild hay, now a pale russet against the ripple of the stream and the evergreen of the trees ... Something from his past awoke in Leithen. He was far up in the Arctic north; winter had begun, and even in this false summer the undercurrent of cold was stinging his fingers through his mitts. But it was not loneliness or savagery that was the keynote of this valley. Pastoral breathed from it; it was comforting and habitable. He could picture it in its summer pride, a symphony of mild airs and singing waters. Stripped and blanched as it was, it had a preposterous suggestion of green meadows and Herrick and sheep.

'We'll camp here,' he told Big Klaus. 'There's nothing to show us the road down. It'll take some finding.'

He found the Zeiss glass at last and tried to make out further details. There must be hot springs, he thought, natural in a volcanic country; that would explain the richness of the herbage. The place, too, was cunningly sheltered from the prevailing winds, and probably most of the river that he could see never froze. That would mean wildfowl and fish, even in the depths of winter ... He pocketed his glass, for he did not want to learn more. He was content with what he saw. No wonder the valley had cast its spell on the old Indian chief and on Lew Frizel. It was one of those sacred places on which Nature had so lavished her art that it had the magic of a shrine.

Big Klaus made camp in a little half-moon of shingle on the verge of the cliffs, with trees to shelter it on north and east. He built an enormous fire on a basis of split wood, piled like a little wigwam, and felled two spruces so that they met in the centre of the heap, and as their ends burned away would slip further down and keep alight without tending until morning.

'It will be very cold,' said the Hare, sniffing towards the north like a pointer dog.

Leithen ate little at supper, for his mind was in a fever. He had won a kind of success as he was nearing the brink of death, for he had found something which other men had longed to find and about which the world knew nothing. Some day there would be books of travel and guide-books, and inevitably it would be written that among the discoverers of the secret valley was one Edward Leithen, who had once been His Majesty's Attorney-General in England, and who had died soon afterwards ... This unexpected feat obscured the fact that he had also found Galliard, for, setting out on one task he had incidentally accomplished a greater, like Saul the son of Kish who, seeking his father's asses, stumbled upon a kingdom.

The big fire roared and crackled at the mouth of the little tent, and beyond it was a blue immensity, sapphire in the mid-heaven, but of a milky turquoise above the mountains where the moon was rising.

He fell asleep early, and awoke after midnight to a changing world. The fire had sunk, but it was still fierce around the point where the spruce trunks intersected. The moon had set and the sky was hung with stars and planets – not inlaid, but hung, for the globes of sheer light were patently suspended in the heavens, and it seemed as if the eye could see behind them into aboriginal darkness. The air had suddenly become bitterly cold, cold almost beyond bearing. The shudder which had for some days lurked behind the sunlight had sharpened to an icy rigour. Frost like a black concrete was settling over everything, gumming the eyes and lips together. He buried his head under his blankets but could not get warm again ...

Some time towards dawn he fell into an uneasy sleep. When he awoke Big Klaus was tending the fire, white as an icicle and bent double against the fury of the north-west wind. Snow was drifting in flakes like pigeons' eggs. With a bound winter had come up on them.

Movement was impossible, and the two men lay all day in the tent, Leithen half in a stupor, for the sudden onrush of cold seemed to have drained the remnants of his strength. With the snow the first rigour abated, and presently the wind sank, and the smoke of the fire no longer choked the tent. The Hare split wood and rose every hour or so to tend the fire; for the rest he dozed, but he had a clock in his brain and he was never behindhand in his stoking. There was no fresh meat, so he cooked bacon and camp biscuit for luncheon, and for supper made a wonderful stew of tinned bully-beef and beans.

At twilight the snow ceased, and with the dark the cold deepened. The silence deepened, too, except for trees cracking in the fierce stricture of the frost. Leithen had regained some vitality during the day, enough to let him plan ahead. It was his business to get down into the valley where, beyond question, Lew had preceded him. It would be hard to find Lew's route, for there were no trees to blaze, and the weather of the past week would have obliterated his trail. To a mountaineer's eye it seemed an ugly place to descend, for the rock did not fissure well into footholds and hand-grips. But the snow might solve the problem. The wind from the north-west had plastered it against the eastern side of the valley, the side on which they had made camp. It must have filled the couloirs and made it possible to get down by step-cutting or glissade. He had only two fears – whether his body was not too feeble, and whether the Hare was sufficient of a mountaineer for the attempt.

Morning brought no fresh snow, and the extreme cold seemed

to slacken. Leithen thought that it could not be more than ten degrees below zero. Having an immediate practical task before him, he found himself possessed of a certain energy. He ate his meagre breakfast almost with relish, and immediately after was on his feet. There must be no delay in getting down into the valley.

With Big Klaus he explored the rim of the cliffs, following the valley downward, as he was certain Lew had done. Mercifully it was easy going, for with the trees withdrawn from the scarp there was no tangle of undergrowth, and what normally might have been loose screes was now firm snow.

For a little the cliffs overhung or fell sheer. Then came fissures by which, in open weather, a trained mountaineer might have descended, but which now were ice-choked and impossible. Leithen had walked more than a mile and come very near the limit of his strength before he found what he sought. The rocks fell back into a V-shaped bay, and down the bay to the valley floor swept a great wave of snow, narrow at the top and spreading out fanwise beneath. The angle was not more than thirty or thirty-five degrees. This must have been Lew's route, and no doubt he had had to face awkward rock falls and overhangs which now were obliterated in one great smooth white swirl. Leithen got out his glass and searched the lower slopes. No, there seemed to be no snags there; a good skier would tackle the descent without a thought.

'We must shift our stuff here,' he told the Hare. 'But first make a fire or I will freeze.'

He cowered beside the blaze until Big Klaus had brought up the camp baggage. They cooked the midday meal, and then ransacked the stores. There was rope, but not enough of it. First they must pack their kit so that it would be kept together in the descent, for Leithen knew what a sepulchre snowdrifts could be for a man's belongings. Then he would have liked another hundred feet of rope for the Hare and himself. He meant to go down slowly and carefully, feeling his way and humouring his wretched body.

The baggage took up every inch of rope. Leithen had the gun and rifle lashed on his own back, and the rest made up a huge bundle which was attached to Big Klaus and himself by short lengths of cord. It was the best he could do, but it was an unwieldy contraption, and he prayed that there might be no boulders or pockets in the imperfectly seen lower reaches, for it would be impossible to steer a course. The Hare was sent into the wood to cut two long poles. He did not seem to realize the purpose until he returned and Leithen explained what must be done.

'The snow is firm enough,' he said. 'It will give good footholds. One step at a time, remember, and we must never move together. I stand still when you move. For God's sake keep your balance. If you slip, turn on your face and dig in your hands and feet. Don't let the kit pull you out of your steps. You understand?'

He repeated the instructions several times, but Big Klaus stared at him dully. When at last he realized that it was proposed to descend the shoot, he shook his head violently. He patted his stomach and made the motions of one about to be sick. Twice he went to the edge and peered down, and each time there was something like panic in his heavy eyes.

'Come on! There's no time to be lost. Even if we roll all the way it won't kill us.'

Leithen took two steps down, leaning inward as he moved.

'Come on, you fool!'

The Hare put out a foot, like a timid bather in cold water. He was a brave man, for, though he was mortally afraid, he kept his eyes away from the void and imitated Leithen in hugging the slope.

At first all went well. The grade was steeper than had appeared above, but not much, and, though the baggage wobbled and swayed, they managed to keep their balance.

They had emerged from the throat of the couloir, and were out on the fan of the lower and easier slopes when disaster overtook them. The Hare miscalculated a foothold at a place where there was glazed ice on the snow, and shot downward on his back. He, and the weight of the baggage, plucked Leithen from his stance, and the next second the whole outfit had started a mad glissade. The rope round Leithen's middle choked the breath out of him. He cannoned into the baggage and ricocheted off; he cannoned into Big Klaus; his mouth and eyes were choked with snow; some rib of rock or ice caught his thigh and hurt him ... Once, climbing at Courmayeur alone, he had slipped on a snowfield and been whirled to what he believed to be his end in a *bergschrund* (which happened to be nearly full of snow into which he had dropped comfortably). Now once again, before his senses left him, he had the same certainty of death and the same apathy . . .

# 17

He recovered consciousness to find the Hare attempting a kind of rough massage of his chest. For a minute or two he lay comatose, breathing•heavily, but not suffering pain except for his bruised thigh. Slowly, with immense difficulty, he tested his body for damage. There seemed to be little – no concussion – the bruise – the breath knocked out of him but returning under the Hare's ministrations. It was not until he tried to get to his feet that he realized how much the glissade had taken toll of his strength.

The valley bottom was like a new creation, for the whole flavour of the landscape was changed. It was no longer the roof of the world where the mind and eye were inured to far horizons, but a place enclosed, muffled, defended by great rock bastions from the blank upper air. Against the eastern wall the snow lay piled in big drifts, but there was no snow on the western side and very little in the intervening meadows. In these same meadows there was what looked like frozen pools, but the rigour of the frost had not touched the whole river, for below one of the patches of forest there was a gleam of running water. There was not a breath of wind, the slanting sunlight gilded the russet grasses and snow patches, the air was unbelievably mild. Here in this fantastic sanctuary was nothing of North America. Apart from the sheer containing walls, the scene might have been a Northumbrian pasture in an English December.

But all the pith had gone out of him. It seemed as if the strain of the descent had damaged some nerve control, for his weakness was worse than pain. He struggled to his feet and clutched at the Hare to keep himself from falling. The latter had got the baggage straightened out and was restrapping the guns. He nodded down the valley –

'He has gone that way,' he said. But how he had guessed Lew's route he did not tell, nor did the other inquire.

For to Leithen it looked as if in this strange place he had got very near his journey's end. He toiled in the wake of the Hare for something less than a mile, counting each step, utterly oblivious of anything but the dun herbage under foot. He tried to step in the Indian's prints, but found them too long for his enfeebled legs. He who had once had the stride of a mountaineer now teetered like an affected woman. He made little bets with himself – how many steps until he fell? – would Big Klaus turn back, see his distress, and stop of his own accord? . . . The latter guess was right. The Indian, turning, saw a face like death, and promptly flung down his pack and announced that he would make camp.

There was a patch of gravel where the stream made a sharp bend, and there, in the lee of a tall coppice, a fire was lit. The Hare had to loosen the light pack from Leithen's shoulders, for he had lost all muscular power. His fingers seemed to bend back on him if he tried to lift a blanket. Also his breath was so troublesome that in that open place he panted like a man suffocating in a hole. The fit passed and by the time the tent was up and the beds laid his main trouble was his desperate weakness. Big Klaus fed him for supper with gruel and strong tea, but he was able to swallow little. His throat was as impotent as his hands and legs.

But his mind was no longer wholly apathetic, for he had stumbled on a queer corner of recollection. He had been conscious of the apathy of his memory, for, had he been able to choose, he would have been glad in those evil days to 'count his mercies', to remember with a wry satisfaction the many pleasant things in his life. No present misery could kill his gratitude for past joys. But the past had remained a closed book to him, and he had had no thoughts except for the moment.

Now suddenly, with blinding clearness, he saw a picture. Outside his bedroom door in a passage on the upper floor of the old Scots country house of his boyhood, there had hung a print. It was a Munich photogravure called *Die Toten-Insel*, and showed an island of tall cliffs, and within their angle a grove of cypresses, while a barge full of bent and shrouded figures approached this home of the dead. The place was Sick Heart Valley – the same sheer cliffs, the same dark, evergreen trees; the Hare and he, bowed and muffled figures, were approaching the graveyard ... As a boy he had been puzzled by the thing, but had rather liked it. As he dashed out on a spring morning its sombreness had pleased him by its contrast with his own sunlit world ... Now, though he saw the picture of those April days, he could not recapture the faintest flavour of that spring rapture. He saw only the dark photogravure on the distempered passage wall, and his interest was faintly touched by its likeness to his present environment ... Surely he was already dead, for he had ceased to react to life!

Through the open tent door he could see the northern heavens ablaze with the aurora. The frost was closing down again, for the Dancers seemed to give out a crackling sound as if the sky were the back-cloth of a stage with the painted canvas strained to cracking-point. The spectacle did not stir his apathy. This blanched world was rioting in colour, but it was still blanched and bleached, the enemy of all life.

As he lay wakeful, scarcely conscious of the dull pain in his chest or of the spasms in his breathing, but desperately aware of his weakness, he felt the shadow of eternity deepening over him. Like Job, the last calamities had come on him. Thank Heaven he was free from loquacious friends. Like Job he bowed his head and had no impulse to rebel. The majesty of God filled his universe. He was coming face to face with his religion.

He had always been in his own way a religious man. Brought up under the Calvinistic shadow, he had accepted a simple evangel which, as he grew older, had mellowed and broadened. At Oxford he had rationalized it in his philosophical studies, but he had never troubled to make it a self-sufficing logical creed. Certain facts were the buttresses of his faith, and the chief of them was the omnipotence and omnipresence of God. He had always detested the glib little humanism of most of his contemporaries.

But his creed had remained something aloof from his life. He had no communion with the omnipotent God and no craving for it. It rarely impinged on his daily experience. When things went well he felt a dim gratitude to Omnipotence; when badly, it was a comfort to tell himself that it was God's will and to take misfortune cheerfully. In the War it had been different. Then he felt a relation so close as to be almost communion – that he was not only under God's ultimate command, but under His direct care. That was why his nerves had been so steady. It was foolish to worry about what was pre-ordained.

Then had come long years of spiritual sloth. The world had been too much with him. But certain habits had continued. Still in his heart he had praised God for the pleasures of life, and had taken disappointments with meekness, as part of a divine plan. Always, when he reflected, he had been conscious of being a puppet in almighty hands. So he had never been much cast down or much puffed up. He had passed as a modest man – a pose, some said; a congenital habit, said others. His friends had told him that if he had only pushed himself he might have been Prime Minister. Foolish! These things were ordained.

Now his castles had been tumbled down. Pleasant things they had been, even if made of paste-board; in his heart he had always known that they were paste-board. Here was no continuing city. God had seen fit to change the sunlight for a very dark shadow. Well, under the shadow he must not quail but keep his head high, not in revolt or in defiance, but because He, who had made him in His image, expected such courage. 'Though Thou slay me, yet will I trust in Thee.'

There was no shade of grievance in Leithen's mind, still less self-pity. There was almost a grim kind of gratitude. He was now alone with God. In these bleak immensities the world of man had fallen away to an infinite distance, and the chill of eternity was already on him. He had no views about an after-life. That was for God's providence to decree. He was an atom in infinite space, the humblest of slaves waiting on the command of an august master.

He remembered a phrase of Cromwell's about putting his mouth in the dust. That was his mood now, for he felt above everything his abjectness. In his old bustling world there were the works of man's hands all around to give a false impression of man's power. But here the hand of God had blotted out life for millions of miles and made a great tract of the inconsiderable ball which was the earth, like the infinite interstellar spaces which had never heard of man.

## 18

He woke to a cold which seemed to sear that part of his face which the blanket left exposed. There was a great rosy light all about the tent which the frost particles turned into a sparkling mist.

The Hare stood above him.

'There is a man,' he said, 'beyond the river under the rocks. I have seen a smoke.'

The news gave Leithen the extra incentive that made it possible for him to rise. He hung on to the Hare's shoulder, and it was in that posture that he drank some strong tea and swallowed a mouthful of biscuit. The smoke, he was told, was perhaps a mile distant in a nook of the cliffs. The long pool of the river was frozen hard, and beyond it was open ground.

Leithen's strength seemed suddenly to wax. A fever had taken him, a fever to be up and doing, to finish off his business once for all. His weakness was almost a physical anguish, and there was a horrid background of nausea ... But what did it all matter? He was very near his journey's end. One way or another in a few hours he would be quit of his misery.

The Hare guided him – indeed, half carried him – over the frozen hummocks of the pool. Beyond was a slight rise, and from that a thin spire of smoke could be seen in an angle of the cliffs. In the shelter of the rise Leithen halted.

'You must stay here,' he told the Indian, 'and see what happens to me. If I am killed you will go back to where we came from and tell my friend what has happened. He may want to come here, and in that case you will show him the road. If I do not die now you will make camp for yourself a little way off and at dawn to-morrow you will come where the smoke is. If I am alive you may help me. If I am dead, you must return to my friend. Do you understand?'

The Hare shook his head. The orders seemed to be unacceptable, and Leithen had to repeat them again before he nodded in acquiescence.

'Good-bye,' he said. 'God bless you for an honest man.'

The turf was frozen hard, but it was as level as a croquet lawn and made easy walking. All Leithen's attention was concentrated on his crazy legs. They wobbled and shambled and sprawled, and each step was a separate movement which had to be artfully engineered. He took to counting them – ten, twenty, thirty, one hundred. He seemed to have made no progress. Two hundred, three hundred – here he had to scramble in and out of a small watercourse – four hundred, five hundred.

A cry made him lift his eyes, and he saw a man perhaps two hundred yards distant.

The man was shouting, but he could not hear what he said. A horrid nausea was beginning to afflict him – the overpowering sickness which comes to men who reach the extreme limits of their strength. Then there was a sound which was not the human voice, and something sang not far from his left shoulder. He had taken perhaps six further steps when the same something passed somewhere on his right.

His dulled brain told him the meaning of it. 'He must be bracketing,' he said to himself. 'The third shot will get me in the heart or the head, and then all will be over.' He found himself longing for it as a sick man longs for the morning. But it did not come. Instead came the nausea and the extremity of weakness. The world swam in a black mist, and strength fled from his limbs, like air from a slit bladder.

# 19

When Leithen's weakness overpowered him he might lose consciousness, but when he regained it there was no half-way house of dim perception to return to. He alternated between a prospect of acid clarity and no prospect at all ... Now he took in every detail of the scene, though he was puzzled at first to interpret them.

At first he thought that it was night and that he was lying out of doors, for he seemed to be looking up to a dark sky. Then a splash of light on his left side caught his attention, and he saw that it outlined some kind of ceiling. But it was a ceiling which lacked at least one supporting wall, for there was a great blue vagueness pricked out with points of light, and ruddy in the centre with what looked like flames. It took him some time to piece together the puzzle ... He was in a cave, and towards the left he was looking to the open where a big fire was burning ... There was another light, another fire it seemed. This was directly in front of him, but he could not see the flames, only the glow on floor and roof, so that it must be burning beyond a projecting rib of rock. There must be a natural flue there, he thought, an opening in the roof, for there was no smoke to make his eyes smart.

He was lying on a pile of spruce boughs covered with a Hudson's Bay blanket. There was a bitter taste on his lips as he passed his tongue over them – brandy or whisky it seemed; anyhow some kind of spirit. Somebody, too, had been attending to him, for the collar of his dicky had been loosened, and he was wearing an extra sweater which was not his own. Also his moccasins had been re-moved and his feet rolled snugly in a fold of the blanket ...

Presently a man came into the light of the inner fire. The sight of him awoke Leithen to memory of the past days. This could only be Lew Frizel, whom he had come to find – a man who had gone mad, according to his brother's view, for he had left Galliard to perish; one who a few hours back had beyond doubt shot at himself. Then he had marched forward without a tremor, expecting a third bullet to find his heart, for it would have been a joyful release. Now, freed from the extreme misery of weakness, he found himself nervous about this brother of Johnny's – why, he did not know, for his own fate was beyond caring about. Lew's madness, whatever it was, could not be wholly malevolent, for he had taken some pains to make comfortable the man he had shot at. Besides, he was the key to Galliard's sanity, and Galliard was the purpose of his quest.

He was a far bigger man than Johnny, not less, it appeared, than six feet two; a lean man, and made leaner by his dress, which was deer-skin breeches, a tanned caribou shirt worn above a jersey, and a lumberman's laced boots. His hair, as flaxen as a girl's, had been self-cut into a bunch and left a ridiculous fringe on his fore-head. It was only the figure he saw, a figure apparently of immense power and activity, for every movement was like the releasing of a spring.

The man glanced towards him and saw that he was awake. He lit a lantern with a splinter from the fire, and came forward so that Leithen could see his face. Plainly he was Johnny's brother, for there was the same shape of head and the same bat's ears. But his eyes were a world apart. Johnny's were honest, featureless pools of that indistinct colour which is commonly called blue or grey, but Lew's were as brilliant as jewels, pale, but with the pallor of intense delicate colour, the hue of a turquoise, but clear as a sapphire, and with an adamantine brilliance. They were masterful, compelling eyes, wild, but to Leithen not mad – at least it was the madness of a poet and not of a maniac.

He bent his big shoulders and peered into Leithen's face. There was nothing of the Indian in him, except the round head and the bat's ears. The man was more Viking, with his great high-bridged nose, his straight, bushy eyebrows, his long upper lip, and his iron chin. He was clean-shaven, too, unlike his brother, who was as shaggy as a bear. The eyes devoured Leithen, puzzled, in a way contemptuous, but not hostile.

'Who are you? Where do you come from?'

The voice was the next surprise. It was of exceptional beauty, soft, rich, and musical, and the accent was not Johnny's *lingua-franca* of all North America. It was a gentle, soothing Scots, like the speech of a Border shepherd.

'I came with Johnny – your brother. He's in camp three days' journey back. We've found Galliard, the man who was with you. He was pretty sick and wanted nursing.'

'Galliard!' The man rubbed his eyes. 'I lost him – he lost himself. Come to think of it, he wasn't much of a pal. Too darned slow. I had to hurry on.'

He lowered his blazing splinter and scanned Leithen's thin face and hollow eyes and temples. He looked at the almost transparent wrist. He lifted the blanket and put his head close to his chest so that he could hear his breathing.

'What brought you here?' he asked fiercely. 'You haven't got no right here.'

'I came to find you. Galliard needs you. And Johnny.'

'You took a big risk.'

'I'm a dying man, so risk doesn't matter.'

'You're over Jordan now. The Sick Heart is where you come to when you're at the end of your road ... I had a notion it was the River of the Water of Life, same as in *Revelation*.'

The man's eyes seemed to have lost their glitter and become pools of melancholy.

'Well, it ain't. It's the River of the Water of Death. The Indians know that and they only come here to die. Some, at least; but it isn't many that gets here, it being a damn rough road.'

He took Leithen's hand in his gigantic paw.

'You're sick. Terrible sick. You've got what the Hares call *tfitsiki* and white folk T.B. We don't suffer from it anything to signify, but it's terrible bad among the Indians. It's poor feeding with them; but that's not what's hunting you. Where d'you come from? Edmonton way, or New York like the man Galliard?'

'I come from England. I'm Scots, same as you.'

'That's mighty queer. You've come down north to look for Galliard? He's a sick man, too, sick in his mind, but he'll cure. You're another matter. You've a long hill to climb and I doubt if you'll win to the top of it.'

'I know. I'm dying. I made my book for that before I left England.'

'And you're facing up to it! There's guts left in the old land. What's your name? Leithen! That's south country. We Frizels come from the north.'

'I've seen Johnny's ring with the Fraser arms.'

'What's brother John thinking about me?'

'He's badly scared. He had to stay to attend to Galliard, and it's partly to ease his mind that I pushed on here.'

'I guess his mind wanted some easing. Johnny's thinking about mad trappers. Well, maybe he's right. I was as mad as a loon until this morning ... I've been looking for the Sick Heart River since I was a halfling, and Galliard come along and gave me my chance at last. God knows what *he* was looking for, but he fell in with me all right, and I treated him mighty selfish. I was mad and I don't mind telling you. That's the way the Sick Heart takes people. I thought when I found it I'd find a New Jerusalem with all my sins washed away, and the angels waiting for me ... Then you come along. I shot at you, not to kill, but to halt you – when I shoot to kill I reckon I don't miss. And you came on quite regardless, and that shook me. Here, I says, is someone set on the Sick Heart, and he's going to get there. And then you tumbled down in a heap, and I reckoned you were going to die anyway.'

Lew was speaking more quietly and the light had gone from his eyes.

'Something sort of clicked inside my head,' he went on, 'and I began to look differently at things. The sight of you cleared my mind. One thing I know – this is the River of the Water of Death. You can't live in this valley. There's no life here. Not a bird or beast, not a squirrel in the woods, not a rabbit in the grass, let alone bear or deer.'

'There are warm springs,' Leithen said. 'There must be duck there.'

'Devil a duck! I looked to find the sedges full of them, geese and ducks that the Eskimos and Indians had hurt and that couldn't move south. Devil a feather! And devil a fish in the river! When God made this place He wasn't figuring on humans taking up lots in it ... I got a little provender, but if you and I don't shift we'll be dead in a week.'

'What have you got?'

'A hindquarter of caribou – lean, stringy meat – a couple of bags of flour – maybe five pounds of tea.'

'There's an Indian with me,' said Leithen. 'He's gone to earth a mile or so back. I told him to wait to see what happened to me. He'll be hanging about tomorrow morning, and he's got some food.'

Lew rapped outa dozen questions, directed to identifying the Hare. Finally he settled who he was and gave him a name.

'What's he got?' he demanded.

'Flour and oatmeal and bacon and tea, and some stuff in tins. Enough for a week or so.'

'That's no good,' said Lew bitterly. 'We've got to winter here or perish. Man, d'you not see we're in a trap? Nothing that hasn't wings could get out of this valley.'

'How did you get in?'

Lew smiled grimly. 'God knows! I was mad, as I told you. I found a kind of crack in the rocks and crawled down it like a squirrel, helping myself with tree roots and creepers. The snow hadn't come yet. I fell the last forty feet, but by God's mercy it was into a clump of scrub cedar. I lost nothing except half my kit and the skin of my face. But now the snow is here and that door is shut.'

'The Hare and I came down by the snow, and it's the snow that's going to help us out again.'

Lew looked at him with unbelief in his eyes.

'You're a sick man – sick in the head, too. Likewise you're tireder than a flightin' woodcock. You've got to sleep. I'm goin' to shift your bed further out. Frost won't be bad tonight, and you want the air round you. See, I'll give you another blanket.'

Leithen saw that Lew was robbing his own bed, but he was too feeble to protest. He dropped straight away into the fathomless depths of exhausted sleep.

When he woke, with rime on his blankets and sunlight in his eyes, he saw that the Hare had been retrieved and was now attending to the breakfast fire. For a little he lay motionless, puzzling over what had happened to him. As always now at the start of a day, he felt wretchedly ill, and this morning had been no exception. But his eyes were seeing things differently ... Hitherto the world had seemed to him an etching without colour, a flat two-dimensional thing which stirred no feeling in his mind of either repulsion or liking. He had ceased to respond to life. A landscape was a map to him which his mind grasped, but which left his interest untouched ...

Now he suddenly saw the valley of the Sick Heart as a marvellous thing. This gash in the earth, full of cold, pure sunlight, was a secret devised by the great Artificer and revealed to him and to him only. There was no place for life in it – there could not be – but neither was there room for death. This peace was beyond living and dying. He had a sudden vision of it under a summer sun – green lawns, green forests, a blue singing stream, and cliffs of serrated darkness. A classic loveliness, Tempe, Phaeacic. But no bird wing or bird song, no ripple of fish, no beast in the thicket – a silence rather of the world as God first created it, before He permitted the coarse welter of life.

Lew boiled water, gave Leithen his breakfast, and helped him to wash and dress.

'You lie there in the sun,' he said. 'It's good for you. And listen to what I've got to say. How you feeling?'

'Pretty bad.'

Lew shook his head. 'But I've seen a sicker man get better.'

'I've had the best advice in the world, so I don't delude myself. I haven't got the shadow of a chance.'

Lew strode up and down before the cave like a sentry.

'You haven't a chance down here, living in a stuffy hole and eating the sweepings of a store. You want strong air, it don't matter how cold, and you want fresh-killed meat cooked rare. I've seen that work miracles with your complaint. But God help you! there's no hope for you here. You're in your grave already – and so are all of us. The Hare knows. He's squatting down by the water and starting on the dirges of his tribe.'

Then he took himself off, apparently on some futile foraging errand, and Leithen, half in the sun, half in the glow of the fire, felt his weakness changing to an apathy which was almost ease. This was the place to die in – to slip quietly away with no last convulsive attempt to live. He had reacted for a moment to life, but only to the afterglow of it. The thought of further effort frightened him, for there could be no misery like the struggle against such weakness as his. It looked as if the fates which had given him so much, and had also robbed him so harshly, had relented and would permit a quiet end. Whitman's phrase was like a sweetmeat on his tongue: 'the delicious nearby assurance of death'.

Lew and the Indian spent a day of furious activity. They cut huge quantities of wood and kept both fires blazing. Fire-tending seemed to give Lew some comfort, as if it spelled life in a dead place. He wandered round the outer fire like a gigantic pixie, then, as the evening drew on, he carried Leithen into the cave, and, having arranged a couch for him, stood over him like an angry schoolmaster.

'D'you believe in God?' he demanded.

'I believe in God.'

'I was brought up that way too. My father was bed-rock Presbyterian, and I took after him – not like brother Johnny, who was always light-minded. There was times when my sins fair bowed me down, and I was like old Christian in The Pilgrim's Progress – I'd have gone through fire and water to get quit of 'em. Then I got the notion of this Sick Heart as the kind of place where there was no more trouble, a bit of the Garden of Eden that God had kept private for them as could find it. I'd been thinking about it for years, and suddenly I saw a chance of gettin' to it and findin' peace for ever more. Not dying – I wasn't thinking of dying – but living happily ever after, as the story books say. That was my aim, fool that I was!'

His voice rose to a shout.

'I was mad! It was the temptation of the Devil and not a promise of God. The Sick Heart is not the Land-of-Beulah but the Byroad-to-Hell, same as in Bunyan. It don't rise like a proper river out of little springs – it comes full-born out of the rock and slinks back into it like a ghost. I tell you the place is no' canny. You'd say it had the best grazing in all America, and yet there's nothing can live here. There's a curse on this valley when I thought there was a blessing. So there's just the one thing to do if we're to save our souls, and that's to get out of it though we break our necks in the job.'

The man's voice had become shrill with passion, and even in the shadow Leithen could see the fire in his eyes.

'You're maybe thinking different,' he went on. 'You think you're dying and that this is a nice quiet place to die in. But you'll be damned for it. There's a chance of salvation for you if you pass out up on the cold tops, but there's none if your end comes in this cursed hole.'

Leithen turned wearily on his side to face the speaker.

'You'd better count me out. I'm finished. I'd only be a burden to you. A couple of days here should see me through, and then you can do what you like.'

'By God I won't! I can't leave you – I'd never hold up my head again if I did. And I can't stay here with Hell waitin' to grab me. Me and the Hare will help you along, for our kit will be light. Besides, you could show us the road out. The Hare says you know how to get along on steep snow.'

'Have you any rope?' Leithen asked.

Lew's wild face sobered. 'It's about all I have. I've got two hundred feet of light rope. Brought it along with the notion it might come in handy and I can make some more out of caribou skin.'

Leithen had asked the question involuntarily, for the thing did not interest him. The deep fatigue which commonly ended his day had dropped on him like a mountain of lead. Death was very near, and where could he meet it better than in this gentle place, remote alike from the turmoil of Nature and of man?

But after his meagre supper, as he watched Lew and the Indian repack their kit, the power of thought returned to him. This was the last lap in the race; was he to fail in it? Why had he come here when at home he might have had a cushioned death-bed among friends? Was it not to die standing, to go out in his boots? And that meant that he must have a purpose to fill his mind, and let that purpose exclude foolish meditations on death. Well, he had half-finished his job – he had found Galliard; but before he could get Galliard back to his old world he must bring to him the strange man who had obsessed his mind and who, having been mad, was now sane. Therefore he must get Lew out of the Sick Heart valley. He did not believe that Lew could find his way out alone. The long spout of snow was ice in parts, and Lew knew nothing of step-cutting. Leithen remembered the terror of the Hare in the descent. Mountaineering to men like Lew was a desperate venture. Could he guide them up the spout? It would have been child's play in the old days, but now! ... He bent his knees and elbows. Great God! his limbs were as flaccid as india-rubber. What kind of a figure would he cut on an ice slope?

And yet what was the alternative? To lie here dying by inches – by feet and yards, perhaps, but still slowly – with Lew in a panic and restrained from leaving him only by the iron camaraderie of the North. His own utter weakness made him crave for immobility, but something at the back of his mind cried out against it. Why had he left England if he was to cower in a ditch and not stride on to the end? That had always been his philosophy. He remembered that long ago in his youth he had written bad verses on the subject, demanding that he meet death 'with the wind in his teeth and the rain in his face'. It was no false stoicism, but the creed of a lifetime.

By and by he fell asleep, and – a rare thing for one whose slumbers seemed drugged – woke in the small hours. Lew could be heard snoring, but he must have been recently awake, for he had stoked both fires. A queer impulse seized Leithen to get up. With some difficulty he crawled out of his sleeping-bag and stumbled to his feet, wrapping a blanket round him ...

It was a marvellous night, cold, but not bitterly cold, and the flames of the outer fire were crimson against a sky of burnished gold. Moonshine filled the valley and brimmed over the edge of the cliffs. Those cliffs caught no reflection of light, but were more dark and jagged than by day; except that on the eastern side, where lay the snowdrifts, there was a wave of misty saffron.

Moonlight is a soothing thing, softening the raw corners of the world, but suddenly to Leithen this moonlight seemed monstrous and unearthly. The valley was a great golden mausoleum with ebony walls, a mausoleum, not a kindly grave for a common mortal. Kings might die here and lie here, but not Edward Leithen. There was a tremor in his steady nerves, a fluttering in his sober brain. He knew now what Lew meant . . . With difficulty he got back into his sleeping-bag and covered his head so that he could not see the moon. He must get out of this damned place though he used the last pennyweight of his strength.

## 20

Lew and the Indian had Leithen between them, steadying himself with a hand on each of their huge back-packs. The Hare's rope had gone to the cording of the dunnage, and Lew's was in a coil on Leithen's shoulder. The journey to the snow shoot was made in many short stages, across a frozen pool of the river, and then in the snow-sprinkled herbage below the eastern crags. The weather was changing, for a yellow film was creeping from the north over the sky.

'There'll be big snow on the tops,' said Lew, 'and maybe a god-awful wind.'

It was midday before they reached the foot of the couloir. The lower slopes, down which Leithen and the Hare had rolled, were set at a gentle angle, and the firm snow made easy going; it was up in the narrows of the cleft that it changed to a ribbon of ice. The problem before him stirred some forgotten chord in Leithen's mind, and he found himself ready to take command. First he sent Lew and the Hare with the kit up to the edge of the ice, and bade them anchor the packs there to poles driven into the last soft snow. That done he made the two men virtually carry him up the easy slopes. He had a meagre remnant of bodily strength, and he would need it all for the task before him.

In an hour's time the three were at the foot of the sunless narrows where the snow was hard ice. There he gave Lew his orders.

'I will cut steps, deep ones with plenty of standing room. Keep looking before you, and not down. I'll rope, so that if I fall you can hold me. If I get to the top I'll try to make the rope fast, and the Hare must follow in the steps. He will haul up the kit after him; then he will drop the rope for you, and you must tie it on. If you slip he will be able to hold you.'

Leithen chose the Hare to go second, for the Indian seemed less likely than Lew to suffer from vertigo. He had come up the lower slopes impassively while Lew had had the face of one in torment.

Lew's hatchet was a poor substitute for an ice axe. Leithen's old technique of step-cutting had to be abandoned, and the notches he hacked would have disgusted a Swiss guide. He had to make them deep and sloping inward for the sake of Lew's big moccasined feet. Also he had often to cut hand-holds for himself so that he could rest plastered flat against the ice when his knees shook and his wrists ached and his head swam with weariness.

It was a mortal slow business, and one long agony. Presently he was past the throat of the gully and in snow again, soft snow with a hard crust, but easier to work than the ice of the narrows. Here the wind, which Lew had foretold, swirled down from the summit, and he almost fell. The last stage was a black nightmare. Soon it would be all over, he told himself – soon, soon, there would be the blessed sleep of death.

He reached the top with a dozen feet of rope to spare, and straightaway tumbled into deep snow. There he might have perished, drifting into a sleep from which there would be no awakening, had not tugs on the rope from Lew beneath forced him back into consciousness. With infinite labour he untied the rope from his middle. With frail, fumbling, chilled hands he made the end fast to a jack-pine which grew conveniently near the brink. He gave the rope the three jerks which was the agreed signal that he was at the summit and anchored. Then a red mist of giddiness overtook him, and he dropped limply into the snow at the tree roots.

## 21

When Leithen came to his senses he found it hard to link the present with the past. His last strong sensation had been that of extreme cold; now it was as warm as if he were in bed at home, and he found that his outer garments had been removed and that he was wearing only underclothes and a jersey. It was night, and he was looking up at a sky of dark velvet, hung with stars like great coloured lamps. By and by, as his eyes took in the foreground, he found that he was in a kind of pit scooped in deep snow with a high rampart of snow around it. The floor was spread with spruce boughs, but a space had been left in the middle for a fire, which had for its fuel the butt-ends of two trees which met in the middle and slipped down as they smouldered.

He did not stay long awake, but in those minutes he was aware of something new in his condition. The fit of utter apathy had passed. He was conscious of the strangeness of this cache in the snow, this midwinter refuge in a world inimical to man. The bitter diamond air, like some harsh acid, had stung him back to a kind of life – at any rate to a feeble response to life.

Next day he started out in a state of abject decrepitude. Lew put snow-shoes on him, but he found that he had lost the trick of them, and kept on tangling up his feet and stumbling. The snow lay deep, and under the stricture of the frost was as dry and powdery as sand, so that his feet sank into it. Lew went first to break the trail, but all his efforts did not make a firm track, so that the stages had to be short, and by the midday meal Leithen was at the end of his tether. The glow of a fire and some ptarmigan broth slightly revived him, but his fatigue was such that Lew made camp an hour before nightfall.

That night, in his hole in the snow, Leithen's thoughts took a new turn. For long his mind had been sluggish, cognizant of walls but of no windows. Now suddenly it began to move and he saw things . . .

Lew was taking shape in his thoughts as a man and not as a portent. At first he had been a mystery figure, an inexplicable Providence which dominated Johnny's mind, and which had loomed big on Leithen's own horizon. Then he had changed to a disturbing force which had mastered Galliard and seemed to be an incarnation of the secret madness of the North. And then in the Sick Heart valley he had become a Saul whose crazy fit was passing, a man who was seeking something that he had lost and had reached his desired goal only to find that it was not there. Lew and Galliard were in the same boat, sufferers from the same spell.

But Lew had returned by way of panic to normal life. For a moment this strong child of Nature had been pathetic, begging help and drawing courage from Leithen himself, a dying man. The splendid being had been a suppliant to one whose body was in decay. The irony of it induced in Leithen a flicker of affection. He seemed, too, to draw a transitory vigour from a creature so instinct with life. His numb stoicism was shot with a momentary warmth and colour. Lew on the trail, shouting oddments of Scots songs in his rich voice, and verses of the metrical Psalms of his youth, engaged in thunderous discourse with the Hare in his own tongue, seemed to dominate the snowdrifts and the blizzards and the spells of paralysing cold. Leithen found that he had won a faint warmth of spirit from the proximity of Lew's gusto. And the man was as gentle as a woman. His eyes were never off Leithen; he arranged the halts to suit his feebleness, and at each of them tended him like a mother. At night he made his bed and fed him with the care of a hospital nurse.

'This ain't the food for you,' he declared. 'You want fresh meat. It's time we were at Johnny's camp where I can get it for you.'

Half a gale was blowing. He detected the scepticism in Leithen's eye and laughed.

'It don't look good for hunting weather, says you. Maybe not, but I'll get you what you need. We're not in the barrens to depend on wandering caribou. There's beasts in these mountains all the year round, and I reckon I know where to find 'em. There's caribou, the big woods kind, and there's more moose than anyone kens, except the Hares. They'll have stamped out their yards and we've got to look for 'em.'

'What's that?'

'Stamping the snow to get at the shoots. Yards they call 'em down east. But the Hares call 'em *ravages*. Got the name from the French missionaries.'

Next day the stages were short and difficult. There was a cruel north-east wind, and the snow was like kitchen salt and refused to pack. The Hare broke the trail, but Leithen, who followed, often sank to his knees in spite of his snow-shoes. ('We need bear-paws like they use down East,' Lew proclaimed. 'These northern kind are too narrow to spread the weight.') An hour's march brought him to utter exhaustion, and there were moments when he thought that that day would be his last.

At the midday meal he heard what stung his sense of irony into life. Lew had placed him in the lee of a low-growing spruce which broke the wind, and had forgotten his presence, for while he and the Indian collected wood for the fire they talked loudly, shouting against the blast. The Hare chose to speak English, in which he liked to practise himself.

'Him lung sick,' he said. There could be no doubt about his reference.

'Yeah,' Lew grunted.

'Him soon die, like my brother and my uncles.'

The reply was an angry shout.

'No, by God, he won't! You chew on that, you bloody-minded heathen. He's going to cheat old man Death and get well.'

Leithen smiled wryly. It was Uncle Toby's oath, but Uncle Toby's efforts had failed, and so would Lew's.

That night, since the day's journey had been short, his fatigue was a little less than usual, and after supper, instead of falling at once into a heavy sleep, he found himself watching Lew, who, wrapped in his blankets, was smoking his short pipe, and now and then stirring the logs with the spruce pole which he used as a poker. His eyes were half-closed, and he seemed to be in a not unpleasant reverie. Leithen – to his surprise, for he had resolved that his mind was dead to all mundane interests – found his curiosity roused. This was one of the most famous guides in the North. The country fitted him as a bearskin fitted the bear. Never, surely, was man better adapted to his environment. What had shaken him loose from his normal life and sent him on a crazy pilgrimage to a legendary river? It could not have been only a craving to explore, to find out what lay far away over the hills. There had been an almost mystical exaltation in the quest, for it had caused him to forget all his traditions, and desert Galliard.

and this exaltation had ended in a panicky rebound. When he had met him he had found a strong man in terror, shrinking from something which he could not name. It must have been a strange dream which resulted in so cruel an awakening.

He asked Lew the question point-blank. The man came out of his absorption and turned his bright eyes on the questioner.

'I've been trying to figure that out myself,' he said. 'All my life since I was a callant I've been looking for things and never findin' 'em.'

He stopped in some embarrassment.

'I don't know that I can rightly explain, for you see I'm not used to talking. When I was about eighteen I got kinda sick of my life, and wanted to get away south, to the cities. Johnny was never that way, nor Dad neither. But I reckon there were Frizels far back that had been restless too. Anyway, I was mighty restless. Then Dad died, and I had to take on some of his jobs, and before I knew I was deep in the business of guiding and feeling good about it. I wanted nothing except to know more about pelts than any trapper, and more about training than any Indian, and to keep my body as hard as whinstone, and my hearing like a timber wolf's, and my eyesight like a fishhawk's.'

'That was before the War?'

Lew nodded. 'Before the War. The War came and Johnny and me went overseas. We made a bit of a name as snipers, Johnny pretty useful and me a wee bit better. I enjoyed it right enough, and barring my feet, for I wasn't used to wearing army boots, I was never sick or sorry. But I was god-awful homesick, and when I smelt a muskeg again and saw the pointed sticks I could have grat with pleasure.'

Lew shook out his pipe.

'But the man that came back wasn't the same as him that crossed the sea. I was daft about the North, and never wanted to leave it, but I got a notion that the North was full of things that I didn't know nothing about – and that it was up to me to find 'em. I took to talking a lot with Indians and listening to their stories. And then I heard about the Sick Heart and couldn't forget it.'

Lew's embarrassment had returned. His words came slowly, and he kept his eyes on the hot ashes.

'It happened that I'd a lot of travelling to do by my lone – one trail took three months when I was looking for some lost gold-diggers. For two years I hadn't much guiding.'

'You were with Mr Walter Derwent, weren't you?'

'Yeah. Mr Derwent's a fine little man and my very good friend. But mostly I was alone and I was thinkin' a lot. Dad brought us up well, for he was mighty religious, and I got to puzzling about my soul. I had always lived decent, but I reckoned decent living wasn't enough. Out in the bush you feel a pretty small thing in the hands of God. There was a book of Dad's I had a fancy for, *The Pilgrim's Progress*, and I got to thinking of myself as the Pilgrim, and looking for the same kind of thing to happen to me. I can see now it wasn't sense, but at the time it seemed to me I was looking at a map of my own road. At the end there was the River for the Pilgrim to cross, and I got to imagining that the River was the Sick Heart. I guess I was a bit loony, but I thought I was the only sensible man, for what did it matter what the other folks were doing, running about and making money, and marrying and breeding, when there was this big business of saving your soul?

'Then Mr Galliard got hold of me. He was likewise a bit loony, but his daftness and mine was different, for he was looking for something in this world and, strictly speaking, I was looking for something outside the world. He didn't know what I wanted, and I didn't worry about him. But as it fell out he gave me the chance I'd been looking for, and we took the trail together. I behaved darned badly, for I wasn't sane, and by the mercy of God you and Johnny found the man I deserted . . . I pushed on like a madman and found the Sick Heart, and then, praise God, my daftness left me.

'I don't know what I'd expected. A land flowing with milk and honey, and angels to pass the time of day! What opened my eyes was when I found there was no living thing in that valley. That was uncanny, and gave me the horrors. And then I considered that that great hole in the earth was a grave, a place to die in but not to live in, and not a place either for an honest man to die in. I'm like you, I'm sworn to die on my feet.'

Lew checked himself with a glance of apology.

'I had to get out,' he said, 'and I had to get you out, for there's no road to Heaven from the Sick Heart. What did I call it? – a byroad to Hell!'

'You are cured?' Leithen asked.

'Sure I am. I'm like a man getting better of a fever. I see things in their proper shape and size now, and not big as mountains and dancing in the air. I've got to save my soul, and that's to be done by a sane man, and not by a loony, and in a man's job. I'm the opposite to King David, for God's goodness to me has been to get me away from yon green pastures and still waters, back among the rocks and the jack-pines.'

## 22

In two days, said Lew, they should make Johnny's camp and Galliard. But he would not talk about Galliard. He left that problem to the Omnipotence who had solved his own.

The man was having a curious effect on Leithen, the same effect on his spirit that food had on his body, nourishing it and waking it to a faint semblance of life. The blizzard died away, and there followed days of sun, when a rosy haze fell on the hills, and the air sparkled with frost crystals. That night Leithen was aware that another thought had stabbed his dull mind into wakefulness.

When he left England he had reasoned himself into a grim resignation. Life had been very good to him, and, now that it was ending, he made no complaint. But he could only show his gratitude to life by maintaining a stout front to death. He was content to be a pawn in the hands of the Almighty, but he was also a man, and, as Lew put it, must die standing. So he had assumed a task which interested him not at all, but which would keep him on his feet. That task he must conscientiously pursue, but success in it mattered little, provided always he relaxed no effort.

Looking back over the past months, he realized that his interest in it, which at first had been a question of mere self-coercion, was now a real thing. He wanted to succeed, partly because of his liking for a completed job, and partly because the human element had asserted itself. Galliard was no longer a mathematical symbol, a cipher in a game, but a human being and Felicity's husband, and Lew was something more, a benefactor, a friend.

It was the remembrance of Lew that convinced Leithen that a change had come over his world of thought. He had welcomed the North because it matched his dull stoicism. Here in this iron and icy world man was a pigmy and God was all in all. Like Job, he was abashed by the divine majesty and could put his face in the dust. It was the temper in which he wished to pass out of life. He asked for nothing – 'nut in the husk, nor dawn in the dusk, nor life beyond death'. He had already much more than his deserts! And what Omnipotence proposed to do with him was the business of Omnipotence; he was too sick and weary to dream or hope. He lay passive in all-potent hands.

Now there suddenly broke in on him like a sunrise a sense of God's mercy – deeper than the fore-ordination of things, like a great mercifulness ... Out of the cruel North most of the birds had flown south from ancient instinct, and would return to keep the wheel of life moving. Merciful! But some remained, snatching safety by cunning ways from the winter of death. Merciful! Under the fetters of ice and snow there were little animals lying snug in holes, and fish under the frozen streams, and bears asleep in their lie-ups, and moose stamping out their yards, and caribou rooting for their grey moss. Merciful! And human beings, men, women, and children, fending off winter and sustaining life by an instinct old as that of the migrating birds. Lew nursing like a child one whom he had known less than a week – the Hares stolidly doing their jobs, as well fitted as Lew for this harsh world – Johnny tormented by anxiety for his brother, but uncomplainingly sticking to the main road of his duty ... Surely, surely, behind the reign of law and the coercion of power there was a deep purpose of mercy.

The thought induced in Leithen a tenderness to which he had been long a stranger. He had put life away from him, and it had come back to him in a final reconciliation. He had always hoped to die in April weather when the surge of returning life would be a kind of earnest of immortality. Now, when presently death came to him, it would be like dying in the spring.

## 23

That night he spoke of plans. The laborious days had brought his bodily strength very low, but some dregs of energy had been stirring in his mind. His breath troubled him sorely, and his voice had failed, so that Lew had to come close to hear him.

'I cannot live long,' he said.

Lew received the news with a stony poker face.

'Something must be settled about Galliard,' he went on. 'You know I came here to find him. I know his wife and his friends, and I wanted a job to carry me on to the end ... We must get him back to his own people.'

'And who might they be?' Lew asked.

'His wife ... His business associates. He has made a big place for himself in New York.'

'He didn't talk like that. I never heard him mention 'em. He hasn't been thinkin' much of anythin' except his old-time French forebears, especially them as went North.'

'You went to Clairefontaine with him?'

'Yeah. I wasn't supposed to tell, but you've been there and you've guessed it. It was like coming home for him, and yet not comin' home. We went to a nice place up the stream and he sat down and grat. Looked like it had once been his home, but that his home had shifted and he'd still to find it. After that he was in a kind of fever – all the way to the Arctic and then on here. He found that his brother and his uncle had died up there by the Ghost River.'

'I know. I saw the graves.'

Lew's eyes opened. 'You and Johnny went there? You stuck mighty close to our trail ... Well, up to then Galliard had been the daft one. I could get no sense out of him, and most of the time he'd sit dreaming like an old squaw by the fire. After Fort Bannerman it was my turn. I don't rightly remember anything he said after that, for I wasn't worryin' about him, only about myself and that damned Sick Heart ... What was he like when you found him?'

'He was an ill man, but his body was mending. His mind – well, he'd been lost for three days and had the horrors on him. But I won't say he was cured. You can have the terror of the North on you and still be under its spell.'

'That's so. It's the worst kind.'

'He kept crying out for you. It looks as though you were the only one that could release him. Your madness mastered his, and now that you are sane again he might catch the infection of your sanity.'

Lew pondered. 'It might be,' he said shortly.

'Well, I'm going out, and it's for you to finish the job. You must get him down country and back to his friends. I've written out the details and left them with Johnny. You must promise, so that I can die with an easy mind.'

For a little Lew did not speak.

'You're not going to die,' he said fiercely.

'The best authorities in the world have told me that I haven't the ghost of a chance.'

'They're wrong, and by God we'll prove them wrong!' The blue eyes had a frosty sternness.

'Promise me, anyhow. Promise that you'll see Galliard back among his friends. You could get him out, even in winter?'

'Yeah. We can get a dog-team from the Hares' camp if he isn't fit for the trail. And once at Fort Bannerman we can send word to Edmonton for a plane ... If it's to do you any good I promise to plant the feller back where he belongs. But you've got to take count of one thing. He must be cured right here in the bush. If he isn't cured before he goes out he'll never be cured. It's only the North can mend what the North breaks.'


# 24

Next day Leithen collapsed utterly, for the strength went from his legs, and his difficult breathing became almost suffocation. The business of filling the lungs with air, to a healthy man an unconscious function, had become for him a desperate enterprise where every moment brought the terror of failure. He felt every part of his decrepit frame involved, not lungs and larynx only, but every muscle and nerve from his brain to his feet. The combined effort of all that was left of him to feed the dying fires of life. A rough sledge was made and Lew and the Hare dragged him laboriously through the drifts. Fortunately they had reached the windswept ridges, where the going was easier. Twenty-four hours later there was delivered at Johnny's camp a man who looked to be in the very article of death.

# PART III

I had a singular feeling at being in his company. For I could hardly believe that I was present at the death of a friend, and therefore I did not pity him.

PLATO, Phaedo 58

# 1

In the middle of January there was a pause in the sub-zero weather, and a mild wind from the west made the snow pack like cheese, and cleared the spruce boughs of their burden. In front of the hut some square yards of flat ground had been paved by Johnny with stones from the brook, and, since the melting snow drained fast from it, it was dry enough for Leithen to sit there. There was now a short spell of sun at midday, and though it had no warmth it had light, and that light gave him an access of comfort.

He reminded himself for the thousandth time that a miracle had happened, and that he was not in pain. His breath was short, but not difficult. He was still frail, but the utter overwhelming weakness had gone.

As yet he scarcely dared even to hint to himself that he might get well. His reason had been convinced that that was impossible. There had been no doubts in the minds of Acton Croke and young Ravelston ... Yet Croke had refused to be too dogmatic. He had said, 'in the present position of our knowledge'. He had admitted that medical science was only beginning to understand the type of tuberculosis induced by gas-poisoning. Technicalities had begun to recur to Leithen's memory: Croke's talk of 'chronic fibrous infection', and 'broncho-pulmonary lesions'. Sinister-sounding phrases, but he remembered, too, reading or hearing somewhere that fibrous areas in the lungs could be walled off and rendered inert. That meant some sort of cure, at any rate a postponement of death.

Lew and the Hares had no doubt about it. 'You're getting well,' the former repeated several times a day. 'Soon you'll be the huskiest of the lot of us.' And the Indians had ceased to look at him furtively like something stricken. They ignored him, which was a good sign, for they knew better than most the signs of the disease which had decimated their people.

Lew's nursing had been drastic and tireless. Leithen's recollections of his arrival in camp from the Sick Heart River were vague, for he had been in a stupor of weakness. He remembered his first realization that he was under a roof – the smoke from the fire which nearly choked him – alternate overdoses of heat and cold – food which he could not swallow – horrid hours of nausea. And then his memories were less of pain and weakness than of grim discomfort. Lew's tyrannical hand had been laid on him every hour. He was made to eat food when he was retching, or at any rate to absorb the juices of it. His tongue was like a stick, and he longed for cold water, but he was never allowed it. He was wrapped in blankets like a mummy and kept in the open air when frost gummed his lips like glue, and every breath was like swallowing ice, and the air smote on his exposed face like a buffet.

He bore it dumbly, wretched but submissive. He might have been in a clinic, for he had surrendered his soul – not to a parcel of doctors and nurses, but to one fierce backwoodsman. Lew was life incarnate, and the living triumphed over what was half dead. The conscious effort involved in every hour of his past journey was at an end. He was not called on for decisions; these were made for him, and his mind sank into a stagnation which was almost painless.

Then strange things began to happen. He was stirred out of his apathy by little stabs of feeling which were remotely akin to pleasure. The half-raw meat seemed to acquire a flavour; he discovered the ghost of an appetite; he actually welcomed his morning cup of tea. He turned on his side to sleep without dismal forebodings about his condition when he woke ... His beard worried him, for in his old expeditions he had always shaved regularly, and one morning, to his immense surprise, he demanded his razor, and with Lew's approval shaved himself clean. He made a messy business of it, and took a long time over it, but the achievement pleased him. Surely the face that he looked at in the mirror was less cadaverous, the eyes less leaden, the lips less pallid, the texture of the skin more wholesome!

There was one memorable morning when, the intense cold having slackened, Lew stripped him to the buff, and he lay on a pile of skins before the fire while one of the Hares massaged his legs and arms. After that he took tottering walks about the hut, and one midday ventured out to the little platform. Presently Lew made him take daily exercise and in all weathers.

He was becoming conscious, too, of his surroundings. First came the hut. Assuredly Johnny was no slouch at hut-making. The earthen floor had been beaten flat and smooth by the Hares, whose quarters were a little annexe at one end. The building was some sixty feet square, but the floor space within was oblong, since four bunks had been built into one side. The walls were untrimmed spruce logs, and the roof was the same, but interwoven and overlaid with green boughs. Every chink in both walls and roof was filled with moss or mud. Johnny had constructed a fireplace of stones, with a bottle-shaped flue made of willow saplings puddled with clay. The fire was the special charge of the smaller Hare, and was kept going night and day to supplement the stove.

Warmth was a simple matter, but, though Leithen did not know it, food soon became a problem. Lew and Galliard had had scanty supplies, for they had set out on their journey with fevered brains. Johnny and the Hares had back-packed a fair amount, but the bulk of what they had brought from Fort Bannerman was cached at the Hares' camp or at Lone Tree Lake. It had been Johnny's intention to send the Hares back to bring up the reserves with a dog-team, and in the meantime to supplement the commissariat by hunting. He was a good shot, Lew was a famous shot, and the Indians were skilled trappers. That was well enough for the first weeks after Lew and Leithen joined them. There were ptarmigan and willow grouse to be got in the bush, and the woodland caribou, still plump from his autumn guzzling, whence came beef tea and under-done steaks for Leithen, and full meals of flesh for all.

But in the tail-end of December for ten days a blizzard blew. It came out of the north-east and found some alleyway into the mountains, for these gave no protection, so that it raged as fiercely as in the open barrens. The cold was not great, and it was therefore possible to keep the fire low and prevent the back smoke from choking the hut. But there was little fresh air for Leithen, though in the gaps of the storm Lew carried him out of doors and brought him back plastered like a snow man. There were three days when a heavy weight of snow fell, but for the rest it was rather a carnival of the winds, which blew sometimes out of a clear sky, swirling the fallen snow in a *tourmente*, and sometimes filled every aisle of the woods with thick twisting vapours.

Hunting was all but impossible – whether in the driving snow or in the Scots-mist type of weather the visibility was nil. Leithen was aware that the men were out, for often he was left alone, and in the few light hours there was never more than one at home, but his mind was still dull and he had no curiosity about what they were doing. It was as well, for he did not notice the glum faces and the anxious eyes of the others. But he did notice the change in his food.

He had come to like the fresh, bitter flavour of the half-raw caribou meat. That was his staple fare, that and his carefully measured daily dose of tomato juice; he rarely tasted Johnny's flapjacks. Now there was little fresh meat, and instead he was given pemmican, which he swallowed with difficulty, or the contents of one of the few remaining tins.

Johnny was getting very grave about supplies. As soon as the weather cleared an attempt must be made to get up the reserves from the Hares' camp. They were out of sugar, almost out of tea and coffee, and their skins would give trouble unless they had fruit juice. But, above all, the hunting must be resumed. That was their main source of supply, and since Christmas the caribou had been harder to get, and February might bring savage weather.

Of these anxieties Leithen knew nothing. He was overwhelmed with the miracle of vigour creeping back into his moribund body. On the road from the Sick Heart River he had found himself responding again to life, and had welcomed the change as the proper mood in which to die. But this was different – it was not the recognition of life, but life itself, which had returned to him.

At night in the pit in the snow with Lew and the Hare he had become suddenly conscious of the mercifulness of things. There was a purpose of pity and tenderness in the iron compulsion of fate. Now this thought was always with him – the mercy as well as the omnipotence of God. His memory could range over the past and dwell lovingly and thankfully on its modest pleasures. A little while ago such memories, if he could have revived them, would have been a torment.

His mind ran up and down the panorama of his life, selecting capriciously. Oddly enough, it settled on none of the highlights. There had been moments of drama in his career – an adventure in the Aegean island of Plakos, for example, and more than one episode in the War. And there had been hours of special satisfaction – when he won the mile at school and college, his first big success at the Bar, his maiden speech in the House, his capture of the salmon when he and Lamancha and Palliser-Yeates poached in the Highlands. But though his memory passed these things in review, it did not dwell on them. Three scenes seemed to attract it especially, and he found that he could spend hours contentedly in reconstructing them and tasting their flavour.

The first belonged to his childhood. One morning in spring he had left his Border home determined to find what lay beyond the head of a certain glen. He had his rod with him, for he was an ardent fisherman, and lunch in his pocket – two jam sandwiches, a dainty known as a currant scone, two bread-and-butter sandwiches, a hard-boiled egg, and an apple – lovingly he remembered every detail. His short legs had crossed the head of the glen beyond the well-eye of the burn, and had climbed to the tableland of peat haggs and gravel, which was the watershed. Here he encountered an April hailstorm, and had to shelter in a hagg, where he ate his luncheon with intense relish. The hail passed, and a mild blue afternoon succeeded, with the Cheviots clear on the southern sky-line.

He had struggled across the peat bog, into the head of the glen beyond the watershed, where another burn fell in delectable pools among rowans and birches, and in these pools he had caught trout whose bellies were more golden and whose spots were brighter than the familiar fish in his own stream. Late in the evening he had made for home, and had crossed the hills in an April sunset of rose and saffron. He remembered the exultation in his small heart, the sense of being an explorer and an adventurer, which competed with a passionate desire for food.

Everything that day had gone exactly right. No one had upbraided him for being late. The trout had been justly admired. He had sat down to a comfortable supper, and had fallen asleep and rolled off his chair in the middle of it. Assuredly a day to be marked with a white stone. He could recall the sounds that accompanied it – the tinkle of the burn in its tiny pools, the perpetual wail of curlews, the sudden cackle of a nesting grouse. And the scents, too – peat, wood smoke, crushed mountain fern, miles of dry bent, the pure, clean odour of icy water.

This memory came chiefly in the mornings. In the afternoons, when he was not asleep, he was back at Oxford. The scene was always the same – supper in the college hall, a few lights burning, the twilight ebbing in the lancet windows, the old portraits dim as a tapestry. There was no dinner in hall in the summer term, only supper, when you could order what you pleased. The memory of the fare almost made him hungry – fried eggs, cold lamb and mint sauce and salad, stewed gooseberries and cream, cheese and wheaten bread, and great mugs of home-brewed beer ... He had been in the open air most of the day, riding over Shotover or the Cumnor hills, or canoeing on the upper Thames in the grassy meadows above Godstow, or adventuring on a bicycle to fish the dry-fly in the Cotswold streams. His body had been bathed in the sun and wind and fully exercised, so his appetite was immense. But it was not the mere physical comfort which made him dwell on the picture. It was the mood which he remembered, and could almost recapture, the mood which saw the world as a place of long sunlit avenues leading to marvellous horizons. That was his twentieth year, he told himself, which mankind is always longing to find again.

The third memory was the most freakish. It belonged to his early days at the Bar, when he lived in small ugly rooms in one of the Temple courts, and had very little money to spend. It was the first day of the Easter vacation, and he was going to Devonshire with Palliser-Yeates to fish the Exmoor hill streams. The cheapest way was to drive with his luggage direct to Paddington, after the meagre breakfast which his landlady provided. But it seemed an occasion to celebrate, so he had broken his journey at his club in St James's Street, a cheerful, undistinguished young man's establishment, and had breakfasted there with his friend. It had been a fresh April morning; gulls had been clamorous as he drove along the Embankment, and a west wind had been stirring the dust in Pall Mall ... He remembered the breakfast in the shabby old coffee room, and Palliser-Yeates' fly-book which he spilt all over the table. Above all he remembered his own boyish anticipations. In twenty-four hours he would be in a farmhouse which smelt of paraffin and beeswax and good cooking, looking out on a green valley with a shallow brown stream tumbling in riffles and drowsing in pools under banks of yellow bent. The larch plantations would be a pale mist on the hillsides, the hazel coverts would be budding, plovers

144

would be everywhere, and water ouzels would be flashing their white breasts among the stones ... The picture was so dear and home-like that he found himself continually returning to it. It was like a fire at which he could warm his hands.

But there came a time when this pleasant picture-making ceased, and his mind turned back on itself. He had lost the hard stoical mood in which he had left London, but he was not clear as to what had replaced it. What was he doing here in a hut inside the Arctic Circle, among mountains which had never been explored and scarcely visited, in the company of Indians and half-breeds? ... And then he slowly became conscious of Galliard.

All these weeks he had not noticed Galliard's presence or inquired what had happened to him. This man, the original purpose of his journey, had simply dropped out of his line of vision. He pondered on the queer tricks which the mind can play. The Frizels and the Indians were the human background to his life, but it was a background undifferentiated, for he never troubled to distinguish between the two Hares, and Lew, who was his daily ministrant, seemed to have absorbed the personality of Johnny. Galliard had sunk also into this background. One evening, when he saw what appeared to be three Frizels in the hut, he thought his mind wandering.

Moreover, the broken man, bedridden, half crazy, whom he had left behind when he set out for the Sick Heart River, had disappeared. What he saw now was a big fellow, dressed in the same winter kit as Lew and Johnny, and busy apparently on the same jobs. He cut down young spruces and poplars for fuel, he looked after the big fire which burned outside and was used chiefly for melting snow and ice into water, and sometimes he hunted and brought back game. Slowly his figure disentangled itself from its background and was recognized. It had followed Leithen's example and shaved its beard, and the face was very much like that of the picture in the Park Avenue apartment.

Leithen's vitality had sunk so low that he had spoken little during his early recovery, and afterwards had been too much engaged with his own thoughts. This detachment had prevented him listening to the talk in the hut. His attention was only engaged when he was directly addressed, and that was done chiefly by Lew. But now, while he did not attempt to overhear, he was conscious of the drone of conversation after supper in the evening, and began to distinguish the different notes in it. There was no mistaking Lew's beautiful rich tones with their subtle Scots cadences, and Johnny's harsher and more drawling voice. Then he became aware of a third note, soft like Lew's, but more nasal, and one afternoon, at the tail-end of a blizzard, when Leithen lay abed in the firelight and the others were getting kindlings from the wind-felled trees, this voice addressed him.

'Can we talk now?' it said. 'I've been waiting for this chance now that you're mending. I think we have much to say to each other.'

Leithen was startled. This was what he had not heard for months, an educated voice, a voice from his own world. A stone had been thrown into the pool of his memory and the ripples stretched to the furthest shore. This was Galliard; he remembered everything about Galliard, reaching back to Blenkiron's first mention of him in his Down Street rooms.

'Tell me who you are,' the voice continued.

Leithen did not answer. He was wondering how to begin an explanation of a purpose which must seem wholly fantastic. He, the shell of a creature, had set out to rescue this smiling frontiersman who seemed to fit perfectly into his environment.

'Johnny says that you know some of my friends. Do you mind telling me your name? I don't trust Johnny's ear, but I think he said "Leven".'

'Not quite. Leithen.'

Galliard repeated the word, boggling, like all his countrymen, at the 'th'. 'Scotch, aren't you?'

'Yes, but I live in England.'

'You've been a pretty sick man, I gather, but you're mending fast. I wonder what brought a sick man to this outlandish place in midwinter? These mountains are not exactly a sanatorium ... You don't mind my asking questions? You see, we come out of the same world, and we're alone here – the only people of our kind for a thousand miles.'

'I want you to ask questions. It's the easiest way for me to tell you my story ... I crossed the Atlantic last summer thinking that I was a dying man. The best English authority said so, and the best American authority confirmed his view. I'm unmarried, and I didn't want to die in a nursing-home. I've always been an active man, and I proposed to keep going until I dropped. So I came out here.'

Galliard nodded. His brown eyes had a smiling, comprehending friendliness.

'That I understand – and admire. But why to America? – Why just here? – And on a trip like this?'

'I had to have a job. I must be working under orders, for it was the only way to keep going. And this was the job that offered itself.'

'Yes, but please tell me. How did it happen that a sick Englishman was ordered to the Arctic Circle? What kind of job?'

Leithen smiled. 'You will think it fantastic. The idea came from a kinsman of yours – a kinsman by marriage. His name is Blenkiron.'

Galliard's face passed from an amused inquisitiveness to an extreme gravity.

'Our Uncle John! Tell me, what job did he give you?'

'To find out where you had gone, and join you, and, if possible, bring you back. No, not *bring* you – for I expected to be dead before that – but to persuade you.'

'You were in New York? You saw our Uncle John there?'

'No. In London. I know his other niece, Lady Clanroyden – Clanroyden was at school and college with me – and I had some business once with Blenkiron. He came to my rooms one morning last summer, and told me about you.'

Galliard's eyes were on the ground. He seemed to have been overcome by a sudden shyness, and for a moment he said nothing. Then he asked –

'You took on the job because you liked Blenkiron? Or perhaps Lady Clanroyden?'

'No. I happen to like Lady Clanroyden very much – and old Blenkiron, too. But my motive was purely selfish. I wasn't interested in you – I didn't want to do a kindness to anybody – I wanted something that would keep me on my feet until I died. It wouldn't have mattered if I had never heard the name of any of the people concerned. I was thinking only of myself, and the job suited me.'

'You saved my life. If you and Johnny hadn't followed our trail

I would long ago have been a heap of bones under the snow.' Galliard spoke very softly, as if he were talking to himself.

Leithen felt acutely uncomfortable.

'Perhaps,' he said. 'But that was an accident, and there's no gratitude due, any more than to the policeman who calls an ambulance in a street accident.'

Galliard raised his head.

'You were in New York? Whom did you meet there? My wife?'

'Yes. The Ravelstons, of course. And some of your friends like Bronson Jane, and Derwent, and Savory. But principally your wife.'

'Can you' – the man stuttered – 'can you tell me about her?'

'She is a brave woman, but I need not tell you that. Anxious and miserable, of course, but one would never guess it. She keeps a stiff face to the world. She tells people that you are in South America inquiring into a business proposition. She won't have any fuss made, for she thinks it might annoy you when you come back.'

'Come back! She believes I will come back?'

'Implicitly. She thinks you had reached a cross-roads in your mind and had to go away and think it out and decide which one to take. When you have decided, she thinks you will come back.'

'Then why did she want you to go to look for me?'

'Because there was always a chance you might be dead – or sick. I sent her a message from Fort Bannerman saying that I had ascertained you were alive and well up to a week before.'

'How did you find me?'

'I guessed that you had gone first to Clairefontaine. I got no news of you there, but some little things convinced me that you had been there. Then I guessed you had gone North where your brother and your uncle had gone. So I followed. I saw their graves, and then Johnny told me about Lew's craze for the Sick Heart River, and I guessed again that he had taken you there. It was simply a series of lucky guesses. If you like, you can call them deductions from scanty evidence. I was lucky, but that was because I had made a guess at what was passing in your mind, and I think I guessed correctly.'

'You didn't know me – never met me. What data had you?'

'Little things picked up in New York and at Clairefontaine. You see I am accustomed to weighing evidence.'

'And what did you make of my psychology?'

'I thought you were a man who had got into a wrong groove and wanted to get out before it was too late ... No, that isn't the right way to put it. If it had been that way, there was no hope of getting you back. I thought you were a man who thought he had sold his birthright and was tortured by his conscience and wanted to buy it back.'

'You think that a more hopeful state of affairs?'

'Yes. For it is possible to keep your birthright and live in a new world. Many men have done it.'

Galliard got up and pulled on his parka and mitts. 'I'm going out,' he said, 'for I want to think. You're a wizard, Mr Leithen. You've discovered what was wrong with me; but you're not quite right about the cure I was aiming at ... I was like Lew, looking for a Sick Heart River ... I was seeking the waters of atonement.'

For a moment Leithen was alarmed. Galliard had seemed the sanest of men, all the saner because he had divested himself of his urban trappings and had yet kept the accent of civilization. But his last words seemed an echo of Lew – Lew before his cure. But a glance at the steady eyes and grave face reassured him.

'I mean what I say,' Galliard continued. 'I had been faithless to a trust and had to do penance for it. I had forgotten God and had to find Him ... We have each of us to travel to his own Sick Heart River.'

# 2

In the days of short commons Lew was a tower of strength. He ran the camp in an orderly bustle, the Indians jumped to his orders, and Johnny worked with him like an extra right hand. His friendly gusto kept up everyone's spirits, and Leithen was never aware of the scarcity of rations.

It was a moment when he seemed to have reached the turning-point of his disease. Most of his worst discomforts had gone, and only weakness vexed him and an occasional scantiness of breath. The night sweats had ceased, and the nausea, and he could eat his meals with a certain relish. Above all, power was creeping back into his limbs. He could put on his clothes without having to stop and pant, and something of his old striding vigour was returning to his legs. He felt himself fit for longer walks than the weather and the narrow camp platform permitted.

Lew watched him with an approving eye. As he passed he would stop and pat him on his shoulder.

'You're doing fine,' he would say. 'Soon you'll be fit to go huntin'. You much of a shot?'

'Fair.'

Lew laughed. 'If an Old Countryman 'lows he's a fair shot, it means he's darned good.'

One evening just before supper when the others were splitting firewood, Lew sat himself down before Leithen and tapped him on the knee.

'Mr Galliard,' he said – 'I'd like to say something about Mr Galliard. You know I acted mighty bad to him, but then I was out of my senses, and he wasn't too firm in his. Well, I'm all right now, but I'm not so sure that he is. His health's fine, and he can stand a long day in the bush. But he ain't happy – no happier than when he first hired me way back last spring. I mean he's got his wits back, and he's as sensible as you and me, but there's a lot worryin' him.' Lew spoke as if he found it difficult to say what he wanted.

'I feel kindo' responsible for Mr Galliard,' he said, 'seeing that he's my master and is paying me pretty high. And you must feel kindo' responsible for him or you wouldn't have come five thousand miles looking for him ... I see you've started talking to him. I'd feel easier in my mind if you had a good long pow-wow and got out of him what's biting him. You don't happen to know?'

Leithen shook his head.

'Only that he wasn't happy and thought he might feel better if he went North. But the plan doesn't seem to have come off.'

The conversation, as it fell out, was delayed until early in February, when, in a spell of fine weather, Johnny and the smaller Indian had set off to the Hares' camp to bring back supplies by dog-team. It was about three o'clock in the afternoon, and the sun was beginning to go down in a sea of gold and crimson. Leithen sat at the hut door, facing the big fire on the platform which Galliard had been stoking. The latter pulled out a batch of skins and squatted on them opposite him.

'Can we talk?' he said. 'I've kept away from you, for I've been trying to think out what to say. Maybe you could help me. I'd like to tell you just how I was feeling a year ago.'

Then words seemed to fail him. He was overcome with extreme shyness, his face flushed, and he averted his eyes.

'I have no business to trouble you with my affairs,' he stammered. 'I apologize ... I am a bore.'

'Get on, man,' said Leithen. 'I have crossed half the world to hear about your affairs. They interest me more than anything on earth.'

But Galliard's tongue still halted, and he seemed to find it impossible to start.

'Very well,' said Leithen ... 'I will begin by telling you what I know about you. You come from the Clairefontaine valley in Quebec, which Glaubsteins have now made hideous with a dam and a pulp mill. I believe your own firm had a share in that sacrilege. You belong to an ancient family, now impoverished, and your father farmed a little corner of the old seigneury ... When you were nineteen or so you got sick of your narrow prospects and went down to the States to try your luck. After a roughish time you found your feet, and are now a partner in Ravelstons, and one of the chief figures in American finance ... Meantime your father died, soon after you left him. Your brother Paul carried on the farm, and then he also got restless, and a year or two ago went off to the North, pretending he was going to look for your uncle Aristide, who disappeared there years before. Paul got to the river which Aristide discovered, and died there – the graves of both are there, and you saw them last summer ... At the other end something happened to *you*. You started out for Clairefontaine with Lew, and then you were at Ghost River, and then came on here. Is that sketch correct?'

Galliard nodded. His eyes were abstracted, as if he were in the throes of a new idea.

'Well, you must fill out the sketch. But let me tell you two other things. I went to Clairefontaine after you, and after you to the Ghost River, and I saw the crosses in the graveyard. Also, long ago, when I was a young man, I went hunting in Quebec, and I came out by way of Clairefontaine. I found the little meadow at the head of the stream, and I have never forgotten it. When I knew

I had to die, my first thought was to go there, for it seemed the place to find peace.'

Galliard's face woke to a sudden animation.

'By God! that's a queer thing. I went to that meadow – the first thing I did after I left New York. There's a fate in this! . . . I think now I can get on with my story . . .'

It was a tale which took long in the telling, and it filled several of the short winter twilights. There were times when the narrative lagged, and times when it came fast and confusedly. Galliard had curious tricks of speech; sometimes elaborate, the product of wide reading, and sometimes halting, amateurish, almost childlike, as if he were dragging his thoughts from a deep well.

From the village school of Château-Gaillard, he said, he had gone to the University of Laval. He was intended for the law, and his first courses were in classics and philosophy. He enjoyed them, and for a little even toyed with the notion of giving his life to those studies and looking for a university post. What switched his thoughts to another line was a slow revolt against the poverty-stricken life at Clairefontaine. He saw his father and brother bowed down with toil, for no purpose except to win a bare living. In the city he had occasional glimpses of comfort and luxury, and of a wide coloured world, and these put him wholly out of temper with his home. He did a good deal of solid thinking. If he succeeded as a lawyer he would exchange the narrow world of a country farm for the narrow world of a provincial city – more ease, certainly, but something far short of his dreams. He must make money, and money could only be made in big business. In Canada his own French people did little in business, having always left that to the English, and in Canada he might have to fight against prejudice. So he determined to go to the country where he believed there was no prejudice, where business was exalted above all callings, and where the only thing required of a man was to be good at his job.

He left Laval and went to a technical college, where he acquired the rudiments of accounting and a smattering of engineering science. The trouble came when his father discovered the change. The elder Gaillard had something of the seigneur left in him. There was a duty owed to gentle birth. A gentleman might be a farmer who laboured from dawn to dusk in the fields; he could be a priest; he could be a lawyer; but if he touched trade he forfeited his gentility. Moreover, the father hated the very word America. So when the son frankly announced his intention there was a violent family quarrel. Next day he left for Boston and he never saw his father again.

Galliard scarcely mentioned his early struggles. They had to be taken for granted like infantile ailments. He took up the tale when he had come to New York and had met Felicity Dasent.

To Leithen's surprise he spoke of Felicity without emotion. He seemed to be keeping his mind fixed on the need to make his story perfectly clear – an intellectual purpose which must exclude sentiment.

He had fallen deeply in love with her after a few meetings. To him she represented a new world very different from the tough world of buying and selling in which he had found his feet. It was a world which satisfied all the dreams of his boyhood and youth, a happy, gracious place with, as its centre, the most miraculous of beings. It was still more different from Clairefontaine with its poverty and monotony and back-breaking toil. Felicity seemed far further removed from Clairefontaine than from the grubbiest side of Wall Street. The old petty world of Mass and market was infinitely remote from her gracious and civilized life. It was a profanation to think of the two together. Only the meadow at the head of the stream seemed to harmonize with his thoughts about her.

Then came their marriage, and Galliard's entry into society, and his conspicuous social success. After that the trouble began in his soul . . .

He was not very clear about its beginnings. He found things in which he had had an acute interest suddenly go stale for him. He found himself in revolt against what he had once joyfully accepted, and when he probed for the reason he discovered, to his surprise, that it was because it clashed with some memory which he thought he had buried. At first he believed that it was only regret for his departing youth. Boyish recollections came back to him gilded by time and distance. But presently he realized that the trouble was not nostalgia for his dead boyhood, but regret for a world which was still living and which he had forsaken. Not exactly regret, either; rather remorse, a sense that he had behaved badly, had been guilty in some sense of a betrayal.

He fought against the feeling. It was childish, with no basis of reason. He was a rich man, and, if he liked, could have a country house in Quebec, which would offer all the enchantments of his youth without its poverty ... But he realized miserably that this was no solution. It was not Quebec that he wanted, but a different world of thought, which was hopelessly antagonistic to that in which he now dwelt. To his consternation he discovered that distaste for his environment was growing fast. What had been the pleasures of his life became its boredoms; high matters of business were only a fuss about trifles; men whom he had once reverenced seemed now trivial and wearisome. A lost world kept crowding in on him; he could not recover it, but he felt that without it there was no peace for him in life. There was only one stable thing, Felicity, who moved in a happy sphere of her own, from which he daily felt more estranged.

Ridiculous little things tormented him – a tune which reminded him of a French *chanson*, the smell of a particular tobacco which suggested the coarse stuff grown at Clairefontaine. He dared not go shooting or fishing because of their associations; golf, which belonged wholly to his new world, he came to loathe.

'It was like a cancer,' he said. 'A doctor once told me that cancer was a growth of certain cells at a wild pace – the pace at which a child grows in the womb – a sort of crazy resurgence of youth. It begins by being quite innocent, but soon it starts pressing in on other cells and checking their growth, and the thing becomes pathological. That was what happened to me. The old world came to bulk so big in my life that it choked the rest of me like a cancer in the mind.'

He had another trouble, the worst of all. He had been brought up a strict Catholic, but since he left home he had let his religion fall from him. He had never been to Mass. Felicity was an Episcopalian who took her creed lightly, and they had been married in a fashionable New York church. Now all the fears and repressions of his youth came back to him. He had forgotten something of desperate importance, his eternal welfare. He had never thought much about religion, but had simply taken it for granted till he began to neglect it, so he had no sceptical apparatus to support him. His conduct had not been the result of enlighten-ment, but flat treason.

'I came to realize that I had forgotten God,' he said simply.

The breaking-point came because of his love for Felicity. The further he moved away from her and her world, the dearer she became. The one thing he was resolved should not happen was a slow decline in their affection. Either he would recover what he had lost and harmonize it with what he had gained, or a clean cut would be made, with no raw edges to fester ... So on a spring morning, with a breaking heart, he walked out of Felicity's life ...

'You have guessed most of this?' he asked.

'Most of it,' said Leithen. 'What I want to know is the sequel. You have been nearly a year looking for your youth. What luck?'

'None. But you don't put it quite right, for I was willing enough to grow old decently. What I had to recover was the proper touch with the world which I had grown out of and could no more reject than my own skin. Also I had to make restitution. I had betrayed something ancient and noble, and had to do penance for my sins.'

'Well?' Leithen had to repeat the question, for words seemed to have failed Galliard.

'I did both,' he said slowly. 'To that extent I succeeded. I got into touch with my people's life, and I think I have done penance. But I found that more was needed. I belong to the North, and to go on living I had to master the North ... But it mastered me.'

Leithen waited for Galliard to expound this saying, but he waited a long time. The other's face had darkened, and he seemed to be wrestling with difficult thoughts. At last he asked a question.

'I cannot explain,' said Galliard, 'for I don't quite know what happened ... I thought that if I found my brother, or at least found out what had become of him, that I should have done the right thing – done the kind of thing my family have always been doing – defied the North, scored off it. It didn't work out like that. Up there on the Ghost River I was like a haunted man – something kept crushing me down. Yes, by God! I was afraid. Naked fear! – I had never known it before ... I had to go on or give up altogether. Then Lew started in about his Sick Heart River. He was pretty haywire, but I thought he was on the track of something wonderful.

He said it was a kind of Paradise where a man left his sins behind him. It wasn't sense, if I'd stopped to think, but I was beyond thinking. Here was a place where one could be reconciled to the North – where the North ceased to be a master and became a comforter. I can tell you I got as mad about the thing as Lew.

'But Lew was no good to me,' he went on. 'He forgot all about me. Being mad, he was thinking only of himself. I hurt my foot and had a difficult time keeping up with him. Pretty bad days they were – I don't want to go through anything of the sort again. Then I lost him and would have perished if you hadn't found me. You know the rest. Johnny nursed me back to bodily health, and partly to sanity, for he is the sanest thing ever made. But not quite. Lew has come back cured, but not me, though I dare say I look all right.'

He turned his weather-beaten, wholesome face to Leithen, and in his eyes there was an uncertainty which belied the strong lines of mouth and jaw.

'I will tell you the truth,' he said. 'I'm afraid, black afraid of this damned country. But I can't leave it until I've got on terms with it. And God knows how that is to be managed.'

3

Leithen found that his slowly mending health was having a marked effect upon his mind. It was like a stream released from the bondage of frost. Before, he had been plodding along in a rut with no inclination to look aside; now he was looking about him and the rut was growing broad and shallow. Before, he had stopped thinking about his body, for it was enough to endure what came to it; now he took to watching his sensations closely, eager to find symptoms of returning strength. This must mean, he thought, a breakdown of his stoicism, and he dreaded that, for it might be followed by the timidity which he despised.

But this new mental elasticity enabled him to reflect on the problem of Gaillard – on Galliard himself, who was ceasing to be a mere problem and becoming flesh and blood. For months Leithen had been insensitive to human relationships. Even his friends at home, who had warmed and lit his life, had sunk into the background, and the memory of them when it revived was scarcely an extra pang. His mind had assessed the people he met in New York, but they might have been ninepins for all he cared about them, though for Felicity he had felt a certain dim tenderness. But the return journey from Sick Heart River had wrought a change. His sudden realization of the mercifulness behind the rigour of Nature had made him warm towards common humanity. He saw the quality of Lew and Johnny, and thanked God for it. Now he was discovering Galliard, and was both puzzled and attracted by him.

A man – beyond question. Leithen saw that in him which had won him an enchanting wife and a host of friends. There was warmth, humour, loyalty. Something more, that something which had made Clifford Savory insistent that he must be brought back for the country's sake. There was a compelling charm about him which would always win him followers, and there was intellect in his brow and eyes. Leithen, accustomed all his life to judge men, had no doubt about Galliard.

But he was broken. As broken by fear as Lew had been at Sick Heart River, and, being of a more complex make-up than Lew, the mending would be harder. A man of a stiff fibre had been confronted by fear and had been worsted by it. There could be no settlement for Galliard until he had overcome it.

Leithen brooded over that mysterious thing, the North. A part of the globe which had no care for human life, which was not built to man's scale, a remnant of that Ice Age which long ago had withered the earth. As a young man he had felt its spell when he looked from the Clairefontaine height of land towards the Arctic watershed. The Galliard family for generations had felt it. Like brave men they had gone out to wrestle with it, and had not returned. Johnny, even the stolid Johnny, had confessed that he had had his bad moments. Lew – Heaven knows what aboriginal wildness was mingled with his Highland blood – had gone hunting for a mystic river and had then got the horrors of the unknown and fled from it. But he was bred to the life of the North and could fall back upon its ritual and defy it by domesticating it. Yet at any moment the fire might kindle again in him. As for Galliard, he was bound to the North by race and creed and family tradition; it was not hard for the gods of the Elder Ice to stretch a long arm and pluck him from among the flesh-pots.

What puzzled him was why he himself had escaped. He had had an hour of revulsion at Sick Heart River, but it had passed like a brief nightmare. His mind had been preoccupied with prosaic things like cold and weariness, and his imagination had been asleep. The reason was plain. He had been facing death, waiting stoically on its coming. There was no space for lesser fears when the most ancient terror was close to him, no room for other mysteries when he was nearing the ultimate one.

What had happened to him? Had he come out of the Valley of the Shadow, or had the Shadow only shifted for a moment to settle later on, darker and deeper? He deliberately refused to decide. A sense of reverence, almost of awe, deterred him. He had committed himself to God's hands and would accept with a like docility mercy and harshness. But one thing he knew – he had found touch with life. He was reacting to the external world. His mind had feelers out again to its environment. Therefore Galliard had assumed a new meaning. He was not a task to be plodded through with, but a fellow-mortal to be helped, a companion, a friend.

4

Johnny and the Hares reached camp when a sudden flurry of snow ended the brief daylight. Lew and the other Indian ran to receive them, and presently Galliard joined the group.

'Queer folk in the North,' Leithen thought. 'They don't make much fuss over a reunion, though it's three weeks since they parted.' Out of the corner of his eye he saw the team of dogs, great beasts, half wolf, half malamute, weighing a hundred pounds each, now sending up clouds of grey steam into the white snowfall. He had a glimpse, too, of Johnny, who looked tired and anxious.

The better part of an hour passed, while Leithen sat alone in the hut mending a pair of moccasins. Then Johnny appeared with a grave face, and handed him a letter.

'Things ain't goin' too well with them Hares,' he said. 'They've got a blight on 'em like Indians get. They're starvin', and they're goin' mad.'

The letter, written on a dirty half-sheet of mission paper, and secured between two pieces of birch-bark, was from the priest, Father Duplessis, who had taken Father Wentzel's place for the winter. It was written with indelible pencil in a foreign pointed script.

They tell me you are recovering health, my friend, and for your sake I rejoice. Also for my own, for I am enabled to make you an appeal. My poor people here are in great sorrow. They have little food, and they will not try to get more, for a disease has come upon them, a dreadful *accidie* which makes them impotent and without hope. Food must be found for them, and above all they must be roused out of their stupor and made to wish to live. I wrestle with them, and I have the might of the Church behind me, but I am alone and I am but a weak vessel. If you can come to my aid, with God's help we may prevail, but if not I fear this little people will be blotted out of the book of life.

# 5

That night after supper four men sat in council. Johnny made his report, much interrupted by Lew's questions, and once or twice the two Hares were summoned to give information. Johnny was a very weary man, for his bandy legs had broken the trail for the dogs through the snow-encumbered forest, and he had forced the pace for man and beast. His pale blue eyes, which had none of Lew's brilliance, had become small and troubled. One proof of his discomfort was that when he broke off to speak to his brother it was in the Cree tongue. Never before had Leithen heard him use his mother's speech.

Leithen found himself presiding over the council, for the others seemed to defer to him, after Lew had cross-examined his brother about what supplies he had brought.

'Father Duplessis says there's trouble in the Hares' camp,' he said. 'Let's hear more about it. Father Wentzel in the fall was afraid of something of the sort.'

Johnny scratched the tip of one of his bat's ears.

'Sure there's trouble. Them god-darned Hares has gone loony and it ain't the first time neither. They think they're Christians, but it's a funny kind of religion, for they're always hankerin' after old bits of magic. Comin' up in the fall I heard they'd been consultin' the caribou bone.'

He explained a little shamefacedly.

'It's a caribou's shoulder-blade, and it's got to be an old buck with a special head of horns. They'd got one and there's a long crack down the middle, and their medicine men say that means famine.'

Lew snorted. 'They needn't have gone to an old bone for that. This year the hares and rabbits has gone sick and that means that every other beast is scarce. The Hares ain't much in the way of hunters – never have been – but they know all about rabbits. That's how they've gotten their name. Maybe you thought they was so-called because they hadn't no more guts than a hare. That ain't right. They're a brave enough tribe, though in old days the Crees and the Chipewyans had the upper hand of them. But the truth is that they haven't much sense and every now and then they go plumb crazy.'

'You say they're starving,' Leithen addressed Johnny. 'Is that because they cannot get food or because they won't try to get it?'

'Both,' was the answer. 'I figured it out this way. As a general thing they fish all summer and dry their catch for the winter. That gives 'em both man's meat and dog's meat. But this year the white fish and pike was short in the lakes and the rivers. I heard that in the fall when we were comin' in. Well then, it was up to them to make an extra good show with the fall huntin'. But, as Lew says, the fall huntin' was a washout anyhow. Moose and caribou and deer were scarce, because the darned rabbits had gone sick. It happens that way every seven years or so. So them pitiful Hares started the winter with mighty poor prospects.'

Johnny spat contemptuously.

'For you and me that would've meant a pretty hard winter's

work. There's food to be got up in them mountains even after the freeze-up, if you know where to look for it. You can set bird traps, for there's more partridges here than in Quebec. You can have dead-falls for deer, and you can search out the moose's stamping-grounds. I was tellin' you that the moose were shifting further north. The Hares ain't very spry hunters, as Lew says, for they've got rotten guns, but they're dandies at trappin'. Well, as I was sayin', if it'd been you and me we'd have got busy, and, though we'd have had to draw in our belts, somehow or other we'd have won through. But what does them crazy Hares do?'

Johnny spat again, and Lew joined him in the same gesture of scorn.

'They done nothin'! Jest nothin'. The caribou shoulder-blade had 'em scared into fits. It's a blight that comes on 'em every now and then, like the rabbit sickness. If a chief dies they mourn for him, sittin' on their rumps, till they're pretty well dead themselves. In the old fightin' days what they lost in a battle was nothin' to what they lost afterwards lamentin' it. So they're takin' their bad luck lyin' down and it jest ain't sense. It looks as if that tribe was fixed to be cleaned out before spring.'

Johnny's contemptuous eyes became suddenly gentle.

'It's a pitiful business as ever I seen. Their old chief – Zacharias they call him – he must be well on in the eighties, but he's the only one that ain't smit with paralysis. Him and Father Duplessis. But Zacharias is mighty bad with lumbago and can't get about enough, and the Father ain't up to the ways of them savages. He prays for 'em and he argues with 'em, but he might as well argue and pray with a skunk. A dog whip would be the thing if you'd the right man to handle it.'

Johnny's melancholy eyes belied his words. They were not the eyes of a disciplinarian.

'And yet,' he went on, 'I don't know, but I somehow can't keep on bein' angry with the creatures. They sit in their shacks and but for the women they'd freeze, for they don't seem to have the strength to keep themselves warm. The children are bags of bones and crawl about like a lot of little starved owls. It's only the women that keep the place goin', and they won't be able to stick it for much longer, for everythin's runnin' short – food for the fire as well as food for the belly. The shacks are fallin' into bits and the tents are gettin' ragged, and the Hares sit like broody hens reflectin' on their sins and calculatin' how soon they'll die. You couldn't stir 'em if you put a charge of dynamite alongside of 'em – you'd blow 'em to bits, but they'd die broody.'

'Father Duplessis has the same story,' Leithen said.

'Yep, and he wants your help. I guess he's asked for it. He says it's a soldier's job and you and him are two old soldiers, but that he's a private and you're the sergeant-major.'

Galliard, who had been listening with bowed head, suddenly looked up.

'You fought in the War?' he asked.

Leithen nodded. His eyes were on Lew's face, for he saw something there for which he was not prepared. Lew had hitherto said little, and he had been as scornful as Johnny about the Hares. The brothers had never shown any pride in their Indian ancestry; their pride was reserved for the Scots side. They had treated the Hares with friendliness, but had been as aloof from them and their like as Leithen and Galliard. It was not any sense of kinship that had woke the compassion in Lew's face and the emotion in his voice.

'You can't be angry with the poor devils,' he said. 'It's an act of God, and as much a disease as T.B. I've seen it happen before, happen to tougher stocks than the Hares. Dad used to talk about the Nahannis that once ranged from the Peace to the Liard. Where are the Nahannis today? Blotted out by sickness of mind. Blotted out like the Snakeheads and the White Pouches and the Big Bellies. And the Hares are going the same way, and then it'll be the turn of the Chipewyans and the Yellow Knives and the Slaves. We white folk can treat the poor devils' bodies, but we don't seem able to do anything for their minds.'

No, it was not race loyalty. Leithen saw in Lew and Johnny at that moment something finer than the duty of kinship. It was the brotherhood of all men, white and red and brown, who have to fight the savagery of the North.

His eyes turned to Galliard, who was looking puzzled. He wondered what thoughts this new situation had stirred in that subtle and distracted brain.

'We'd better sleep over this,' he announced, for Johnny seemed dropping with fatigue . . .

Yet Johnny was the last to go to bed. Leithen was in the habit of waking for a minute or two several times in the night. When his eyes opened shortly after midnight he saw Johnny before the fire, not mending it, but using its light to examine something. It was the shoulder-blade of a caribou, which he had dug out of the rubbish-heap behind the camp. The Hares were not the only dabblers in the old magic.

# 6

Leithen slept ill that night. He seemed to have been driven out of a sanctuary into the turmoil of the common earth. Problems were being thrust on him, and he was no longer left to that narrow world in which he was beginning to feel almost at ease.

Of course he could do nothing about the wretched Hares. Father Duplessis' appeal left him cold. He had more urgent things to think about than the future of a few hundred degenerate Indians who mattered not at all in his scheme of things. His business was with Galliard, who mattered a great deal. But he could not fix his mind on Galliard, and presently he realized something which made him wakeful indeed and a little ashamed. At the back of his head was the thought of his own health. The curtain which had shut down on his life was lifting a corner and revealing a prospect. He was conscious, miserably conscious, that the chief hope in his mind was that he might possibly recover. And that meant a blind panicky fear lest he should do anything to retard recovery.

He woke feeling a tightness in his chest and a difficulty in breathing, from which for some weeks he had been free. He woke, too, to an intense cold. The aurora had been brilliant the night before; and now in the pale sky there were sun-dogs, those mock suns which attend the extreme winter rigours of the North. Happily there was no wind, but the temperature outside the hut struck him like a blow, and he felt that his power of resistance had weakened. This was how he had felt on the road to the Sick Heart River.

He was compelled by his weakness to lie still much of the day and could watch the Frizels and Galliard. Something had happened to change the three – subtly, almost imperceptibly in Galliard's case, markedly in the other two. Johnny had a clouded face; he had seen the Hares' suffering and could not forget it. In Lew's face there were no clouds, but it had sharpened into a mask of intense vitality, in which his wonderful eyes blazed like planets. The sight made Leithen uneasy. Lew had shed the sobriety for which he had been conspicuous in recent weeks. He looked less responsible, less intelligent, almost a little mad. Leithen, intercepting his furtive looks, was unpleasantly reminded of the man who had met him at Sick Heart River. As for Galliard, he was neither dejected nor exalted, but he seemed to have much to think about. He was doing his jobs with a preoccupied face, and he, too, was constantly stealing a glance at Leithen. He seemed to be waiting for a lead.

It was this that Leithen feared. For some strange reason he, a sick man – till the other day, and perhaps still, a dying man – was being forced by a silent assent into the leadership of the little band. It was to him that Father Duplessis had appealed, but that was natural, for they had served together under arms. But why this mute reference to his decision of the personal problems of all the others? These men were following the urge of a very ancient loyalty. Perhaps even Galliard. Who was he to decide on a thing wholly outside his world?

His own case was first in mind. All his life he had been mixed up in great affairs. He had had his share in 'moulding a state's decrees' and 'shaping the whisper of a throne'. He had left England when Europe was a powder magazine and every patriot was bound to put himself at the disposal of his distracted land. Well, he had cast all that behind him – rightly, for he had to fight his own grim battle. In that battle he seemed to have won a truce, perhaps even a victory, and now he was being asked to stake all his winnings on a trivial cause – the *malaise* of human kites and crows roosting at the end of the earth.

It may have been partly due to the return of his malady, but suddenly a great nausea filled his mind. He had been facing death with a certain courage because an effort was demanded of him, something which could stir the imagination and steel the heart. But now he was back among trivialities. It was not a surrender to the celestial will that was required of him, but a decision on small mundane questions – how to return a batch of lunatics to sanity, what risks a convalescent might safely run? He felt a loathing for the world, a loathing for himself, so when Lew sat himself down beside him he found sick eyes and an ungracious face.

'We've got to leave,' Lew said. 'We're too high up here for the winter hunting, and it'll be worse when the big snows come in February. We should be getting down to the bird country and the moose country. I reckon we must take the Hares' camp on our road to see about our stuff. There's a lot of tea and coffee left cached in the priest's cellar.'

Leithen turned a cold eye on him.

'You want to help the Hares?' he said.

'Why, yes. Johnny and me thought we might give the poor devils a hand. We could do a bit of hunting for them. We know the way to more than one moose *ravage*, and a few meals of fresh deer meat may put a little life into them.'

'That sounds a big job. Am I fit to travel?'

'Sure you're fit to travel! We've got the huskies and we'll go canny. It's cold, but you'll be as snug in a hole in the snow as in this camp. When you're in good timber and know the way of it you can be mighty comfortable though it's fifty under. Man! it's what's wanted to set you up. By the time the thaw-out comes you'll be the toughest of the bunch.'

'But what can I do? Hunt? I haven't the strength for it, and I would only be an encumbrance.'

'You'll hunt right enough.'

Lew's frosty eyes had a smile in their corners. He had clearly expected argument, perhaps contradiction, but Leithen had no impulse to argue. He was too weary in body and sick in soul.

It was different when Galliard came to him. Here was a man who had nothing to suggest, one who was himself puzzled. Confined for months to a small company, Leithen had become quick to detect changes of temper in his companions. Johnny never varied, but he could read Lew's mutations like a book. Now he saw something novel in Galliard, or rather an intensifying of what he had already observed. This man was afraid, more than afraid; there was something like panic in his face when he allowed it to relax from restraint. This tale of the Hares' madness had moved him strongly – not apparently to pity, but to fear, personal fear. It was another proof of the North's malignity and power.

He was clinging to Leithen through fear, clinging like a drowning man to a log. Leithen could bring the forces of a different world to fight the dominance of that old world which had mastered him. He wanted to be reassured about Leithen, to know that this refuge could be trusted. So he asked him a plain question.

'Who are you? I know your name. You know my friends. But I know nothing more about you ... except that you came out here to die – and may live.'

The appeal in Galliard's voice was so sincere that his question had no tinge of brusqueness. It switched Leithen's mind back to a forgotten world which had no longer any meaning. To reply was like recalling a dream.

'Yes, you are entitled to ask me that,' he said. 'Perhaps I should have been more candid with you ... My name is Edward Leithen – Sir Edward Leithen – they knighted me long ago. I was a lawyer – with a great practice. I was also for many years a Member of Parliament. I was for a time the British Attorney-General. I was in the British Cabinet, too – the one before the present.'

Galliard repeated the name with mystified eyes which seemed straining after a recollection.

'Sir Edward Leithen! Of course I have heard of you. Many people have spoken of you. You were for my wife's uncle in the Continental Nickel case. You had a big reputation in the States ... You are a bachelor?'

'I have no wife or any near relations.'

'Anything else?'

'I don't know. But I was once what I suppose you would call a sportsman. I used to have a kind of reputation as a moun-taineer. I was never sick or sorry until this present disease got hold of me – except for a little damage in the War.'

Galliard nodded. 'You told me you were in the War. As what?'

'I was chief staff officer of a rather famous British division.'

Galliard looked at him steadily and in his face there was some-thing like hope.

'You have done a lot. You are a big man. To think of you roosting with us in this desert! – two half-breeds, two Indians, and a broken man like me. By God! Sir Edward, you've got to help me. You've got to get well, for I'm sunk without you.'

He seized the other's right hand and held it in both his own. Leithen felt that if he had been a woman he would have kissed it.

# 7

Galliard's emotion gave the finishing touch to Leithen's depression. He ate no supper and fell early asleep, only to waken in the small hours when the fire was at its lowest and the cold was like the clutch of a dead hand. He managed to get a little warmth by burying his head in the flap of his sleeping-bag. Drowsiness had fled from him, and his brain was racing like a flywheel.

He had lost all his philosophy. The return of pain and discomfort after an apparent convalescence had played havoc with his stoicism. Miserably, penitently, he recalled the moods he had gone through since he had entered the North. At first there had been sullen, hopeless fortitude, a grim waiting upon death. There had been a sense of his littleness and the omnipotence of God, and a resignation like Job's to the divine purpose. And then there had come a nobler mood, when he had been conscious not only of the greatness but of the mercy of God, and had realized the vein of tenderness in the hard rock of fate. He had responded again to life, and after that response his body seemed to have laboured to reach the sanity of his mind. His health had miraculously improved ... And now he had lost all the ground he had made, and was down in the dust again.

His obsession was the fear that he would not recover and – at the heart of everything – lay the fear of that fear. He knew that it meant that his whole journey to the North had failed of its true purpose, and that he might as well be dying among the pillows and comforts of home. The thought stung him so sharply that he shut his mind to it and fixed his attention resolutely on the immediate prospect.

Lew and Johnny wanted to go to the Hares' assistance. Lew

said that in any case they must be getting down country. Once there they must hunt both for the Hares' sake and for their own. Lew had said that he, Leithen, would be able to hunt – arrant folly, for a few days of it in his present state would kill him.

Had he been a mere subaltern in the party he would have accepted this programme as inevitable. But he knew that whatever Lew might plan it would be for him to approve, and ultimately to carry out. The Frizels were old professionals at the business, and yet it would be he, the novice, who would have to direct it. His weakness made him strongly averse to any exertion of mind and body, especially of mind. He might endure physical torment like a Spartan, but he shrank with horror from any necessity to think and scheme. Let the Frizels carry him with them wherever they liked, inert and passive, until the time came when they could shovel his body into the earth.

But then there was Galliard. He was the real problem. It was to find him and save him that he had started out. He had found him, but he had yet to save him ... Now there seemed to be a way of salvation. The man was suffering from an ancient fear and there could be no escape except by facing that fear and beating it. This miserable business of the Hares had provided an opportunity. Here was a chance to meet one of the North's most deadly weapons, the madness with which it could affect the human mind, and by checking that madness defeat the North. He had seen this motive confusedly in Galliard's eyes.

He could not desert a man who belonged to his own world, and who mattered much to that world, a man, too, who had flung himself on his mercy. But to succeed in Galliard's business would involve more than hunting docilely in Lew's company with Lew to nurse him.

As he fell asleep to the sound of one of the Hares making up the morning fire he had the queer fancy that the Sick Heart River was dogging them. It had come out of its chasm and was flowing in their tracks, always mastering their course and their thoughts. Waters of Death! – or Waters of Healing?

## 8

They broke camp on a morning which, as Johnny declared in disgust, might have been April. In the night the wind had backed to the south-west and the air was moist and heavy, though piercingly cold. It was the usual thaw which, in early February, precedes the coming of the big snows.

The sledges were loaded with the baggage and the dogs harnessed. Johnny and one of the Hares were in charge of them, while Lew went ahead to break the trail. All of the men except Leithen had back-packs. He carried only a slung rifle, for Lew had vetoed his wish to take a share of the burden. The hut was tidied up, all rubbish was burnt, and, according to the good custom of the North, a frozen haunch of caribou and a pile of cut firewood were left behind for any belated wanderer.

Leithen looked back at the place which for weeks had been his home with a sentimental regret of which he was half-ashamed. There he had had a promise of returning health and some hours of what was almost ease. Now that promise seemed to have faded away. The mental perturbation of the last days had played the devil with his precarious strength. His breath was troubling him again, and his legs had a horrid propensity to buckle under him.

The first part of the road was uphill, out of the woods into the scattered spruces, and then to the knuckle of barrens which was the immediate height of land, and from which he had first had a view of the great mountain country where the Sick Heart flowed. That ascent of perhaps three miles was a heavy task for him. Lew mercifully set a slow pace, but every now and then the dogs would quicken and the rest of the party had to follow suit. Leithen found that after the first half-mile his feet were no longer part of his body, his moccasins clogged with the damp snow, and at each step he seemed to be dragging part of the hillside after him. His thighs, too, numbed, and he had a sickening ache in his back. He managed to struggle beyond the tree line into the barrens and then collapsed in a drift.

Galliard picked him up and set him on the end of one of the sledges. He promptly got off and again fell on his face. A whistle from Galliard brought Lew back and a glance showed the latter where the trouble lay.

'You got to ride,' he told Leithen. 'The dogs ain't too heavy loaded, and the ground's easy. If you don't you'll be a mighty sick man, and there's no camp for a sick man until we get over the divide into the big timber.'

Leithen obeyed, and finished the rest of the ascent in a miserable half-doze, his arms slung through the baggage couplings to keep him from falling off. But at the divide, where a halt was called and tea made, he woke to find his body more comfortable. He was able to swallow some food, and when they started again he insisted on walking with Galliard. They were now descending, and Galliard's arm linked with his steadied his shambling footsteps.

'You're getting well,' Galliard told him.

'I'm feeling like death!'

'All the same you're getting well. A month ago you couldn't have made that first mile. You are feeling worse than you did last week, but you've forgotten how much worse you were a month ago. You remember young Ravelston, the doctor man? I once heard him say that Nature's line of recovery was always wavy and up and down, and that if a man got steadily better without any relapse there was trouble waiting for him.'

Leithen felt himself preposterously cheered by Galliard's words. They were now descending into the nest of shallow parallel glens which ultimately led to Lone Tree Lake. They followed the trail which Johnny had lately taken, and though it required to be broken afresh owing to recent snow, it was sufficiently well marked to make easy travelling. Before the light faded in the afternoon it was possible for Leithen and Galliard to lag well behind the sledges without any risk of losing themselves. The descent was never steep, and the worst Leithen had to face were occasional slopes of mushy snow where the footholds were bad. He had a stick to help him, and Galliard's right arm. There was no view, for the clouds hung low on the wooded ridges, and streamers of mist choked the aisles of the trees. Exertion had for Leithen taken the sting out of the cold, and his senses were alive again. There were no smells, only the bleak odour of sodden snow, but the woods had come out of their winter silence. The hillside was noisy with running water and the drip of thawing spruces.

Galliard had the in-toed walk which centuries ago his race

learned from the Indians. He moved lightly and surely in difficult places where the other slipped and stumbled, and he could talk with no need to save his breath.

'You left England a month or two after I left New York. What was the situation in Europe in the summer? It was bad enough in the spring.'

'I wasn't thinking about Europe then,' Leithen answered. 'You see, I did not see how it could greatly concern me. I didn't give much attention to the press. But my impression is that things were pretty bad.'

'And in the United States?'

'There I think they took an even graver view. They did not talk about it, for they thought I would not live to see it. But again my impression is that they were looking for the worst. I heard Bronson Jane say something to Lethaby about zero hour being expected in September.'

'Then Europe may have been at war for months. Perhaps the whole world. At this moment Canadian troops may be on the seas. American, too, maybe. And up here, on the same continent, we don't know one thing about it. You and I have dropped pretty completely out of the world, Sir Edward.

'Supposing there is war,' he went on. 'Some time or other Lew and Johnny will get the news. They won't say much, but just make a bee-line for the nearest end of steel, same as they did in '14. They won't worry what the war is about. There's a scrap, and Britain is in it, and, being what they are, they're bound to be in it too. It must be a wonderful thing to have an undivided mind.'

He glanced curiously at his companion.

'You have that mind,' he said. 'You've got a hard patch to hoe, but you've no doubts about it.'

'If I live I shall have doubts in plenty,' was the answer. 'But *you* – you seem to fit into this life pretty well. You go hunting with Lew as if you were bred to it. You're as healthy as a hound. You have a body that can defy the elements. What on earth is there for you to fear? Look at me. I'd be an extra-special crock in a hospital for the sick and aged. You stride like a free man and I totter along like a sick camel. The cold invigorates you and it paralyses me. You face up to the brutishness of Nature, and I

171

shrink and cower and creep under cover. You can defy the North, but my only defiance is that the infernal thing can't prevent my escape by death.'

'You are wrong,' said Galliard solemnly. 'You have already beaten the North – you have never been in danger – because you know in your heart that you do not give a cent for it. I am beaten because it has closed in on me above and below, and I cannot draw breath without its permission. You say I stride like a free man. I tell you that whatever my legs do my heart crawls along on sufferance. I look at those hills and I am terrified at what may lie behind them. I look at the sky and think what horrid cruelty it is planning – freezing out the little weak sprouts of life. You would say that the air here is as pure as mid-ocean, but I tell you that it sickens me as if it came from a charnel house ... That's the right word. It's a waft of death. I feel death all around me. Not swift, clean annihilation, but death with torture and horror in it. I am in a world full of spectres, and they are worse than the Wendigo ghoul that the Montagnais Indians used to believe in at home. They said that you knew it was coming by the smell of corruption in the air. And I tell you I feel that corruption – here – now.'

Galliard's square, weather-beaten face was puckered like an old woman's. He had given Leithen his arm to support him, and now he pressed the other's elbow to his side as if the contact was his one security.

9

That night when Leithen stumbled into camp he found that even in the comfortless thaw Lew had achieved comfort. The camp was made in an open place away from the dripping trees. The big hollow which the men had dug with their snow-shoes was floored with several layers of spruce branches, and on a bare patch in the centre a great fire was blazing. The small tent had been set up for Leithen, but since there was no fall the others were sufficiently dry and warm on the fir boughs.

Movement and change had revived him and though his legs

and back ached he was not too much exhausted by the day's journey. Also he found to his surprise that his appetite had come back. Lew had managed to knock down a couple of grouse, and Leithen with relish picked the bones of one of them. All soon went to sleep except Johnny, who was busy mending one of his snow-shoes by the light of the fire.

Leithen watched him through the opening of his tent, a humped, gnome-like figure that cast queer shadows. He marvelled at his energy. All day Johnny had been wrestling with refractory dogs, he had been the chief worker in pitching camp, and now he was doing odd jobs while the others slept. Not only was his industry admirable; more notable still were his skill and resourcefulness. There was no job to which he could not turn his hand. That morning Leithen had admired the knots and hitches with which he bound the baggage to the sledges – each exactly appropriate to its purpose, and of a wonderful simplicity. A few days earlier one of the camp kettles was found to be leaking. Johnny had shaved a bullet, melted the lead, and neatly soldered a patch to cover the hole ... He remembered, too, what Galliard had said about the summons to war. Lew and Johnny were supremely suited to the life which fate had cast for them. They had conquered the North by making an honourable deal with it.

And yet ... As Leithen brooded in the flicker of the firelight before he fell asleep he came to have a different picture. He saw the Indians as tenuous growths, fungi which had no hold on the soil. They existed in sufferance; the North had only to tighten its grip and they would disappear. Lew and Johnny, too. They were not mushrooms, for they had roots and they had the power to yield under strain and spring back again, but were they any better than grassy filaments which swayed in the wind but might any day be pinched out of existence? Johnny was steadfast enough, but only because he had a formal and sluggish mind; the quicker, abler Lew could be unsettled by his dreams. They, too, lived on sufferance ... And Galliard? He had deeper roots, but they were not healthy enough to permit transplanting. Compared to his com-panions Leithen suddenly saw himself founded solidly like an oak. He was drawing life from deep sources. Death, if it came, was no blind trick of fate, but a thing accepted and therefore mastered. He fell asleep in a new mood of confidence.

# 10

In the night the wind changed, and the cold became so severe that it stirred the men out of sleep and set them building up the fire. Leithen awoke to an air which bit like a fever, and a world which seemed to be made of metal and glass.

The cold was more intense than anything he had ever imagined. Under its stress trees cracked with a sound like machine-guns. The big morning fire made only a narrow circle of heat. If for a second he turned his face from it the air stung his eyelids as if with an infinity of harsh particles. To draw breath rasped the throat. The sky was milk-pale, the sun a mere ghostly disc, and it seemed to Leithen as if everything – sun, trees, mountains – were red-rimmed. There was no shadow anywhere, no depth or softness. The world was hard, glassy, metallic; all of it except the fantasmal, cotton-wool skies.

The cold had cowed the dogs, and it was an easy task to load the sledges. Leithen asked Johnny what he thought the temperature might be.

'Sixty below,' was the answer. 'If there was any sort of wind I reckon we couldn't have broke camp. The dogs wouldn't have faced it. We'd have had to bury ourselves all day in a hole. Being as it is, we ought to make good time. Might make Lone Tree by noon tomorrow.'

Leithen asked if the cold spell would last long.

'A couple of days. Maybe three. Not more. A big freeze often comes between the thaw and the snows. The Indians call it the Bear's Dream. The cold pinches the old bear in his den and gives him bad dreams.'

He sniffed the air.

'We're gettin' out of the caribou country, but it's like they'll be round today. They're not so skeery in a freeze. You keep a rifle handy, and you'll maybe get a shot.'

Leithen annexed Johnny's Mannlicher and filled the magazine. To his surprise the violent weather, instead of numbing him, had put life into his veins. He walked stiffly, but he felt as if he could go on for hours, and his breath came with a novel freedom. Galliard, who also carried a rifle, remarked on his looks as they followed the sledges.

'Something has come over you,' he said. 'Your face is pasty with the cold, but you've gotten a clear eye, and you're using your legs different from yesterday. Feeling fine?'

'Fine,' said Leithen. 'I'm thankful for small mercies.'

He was afraid to confess even to himself that his body was less of a burden than it had been for many months. And suddenly there woke in him an instinct to which he had long been strange, the instinct of the chase. Once he had been a keen stalker in Scottish deer forests, but of late he had almost wholly relinquished gun and rifle. He had lost the desire to kill any warm-blooded animal. But that was in the old settled lands, where shooting was a sport and not a necessity of life. Here in the wilds, where men lived by their marksmanship, it was a duty and not a game. He had heard Lew say that they must get all the caribou they could, since it was necessary to take a load of fresh meat into the Hares' camp. Johnny and the Indians were busy at the sledges, and Lew had the engrossing job of breaking the trail, so such hunting as was possible must fall to him and Galliard.

He felt a boyish keenness which amazed and amused him. He was almost nervous. He slung his Zeiss glass loose round his neck and kept his rifle at the carry. His eyes scanned every open space in the woods which might hold a caribou.

Galliard observed him and laughed.

'You take the right side and I'll take the left. It'll be snap shooting. Keep your sights at 200 yards.'

Galliard had the first chance. He swung round and fired standing at what looked to Leithen to be a grey rock far up on the hillside. The rock sprang forward and disappeared in the thicket.

'Over!' said a disgusted voice. The caravan had halted and even the dogs seemed to hold their breath.

Leithen's chance came half an hour later. The sledges were toiling up a hill where the snow lay thin over a maze of tree roots, and the pace was consequently slow. His eyes looked down a long slope to a little lake; there had been a bush fire recently, so the ground was open except for one or two skeleton trunks and a mat of second-growth spruce. Something caught his eye in the tangle, something grey against the trees, something which ended in what he took to be withered boughs. He saw that they were antlers.

He tore off his right-hand mitt and dropped on one knee. He heard Galliard mutter '300', and pushed up his sights. The caribou had its head down and was rooting for moss in the snow. A whistle from Galliard halted the sledges. The animal raised its head and turned slightly round, giving the chance of a rather difficult neck shot.

A single bullet did the job. The caribou sank on the snow with a broken spine, and the Indians left the sledges and raced downhill to the gralloch.

'Good man!' said Galliard, who had taken Leithen's glass and was examining the kill.

'A bull – poorish head, but that doesn't matter – heavy carcase. Every inch of 350 yards, and a very prettily placed shot.'

'At home,' said Leithen, 'I would have guessed 120. What miraculous air!'

He was ashamed of the childish delight which he felt. He had proved that life was not dead in him by bringing off a shot of which he would have been proud in his twenties.

The caribou was cut up and loaded on one of the sledges, maddening the dogs with the smell of fresh meat. For the rest of the afternoon daylight Leithen moved happily in step with Galliard. The road was easy, the extreme cold was abating, he felt a glow of satisfaction which he had not known for many a day. He was primitive man again who had killed his dinner. Also there was a new vigour in his limbs – not merely the absence of discomfort and fatigue, but something positive, a *plus* quantity of well-being.

When they made camp he was given the job of attending to the dogs, whose feet were suffering. The malamutes, since their toes were close together, were all right, but with the huskies the snow had balled and frozen hard, and in biting their paws to release the congested toes they had broken the skin and left raw flesh. Johnny provided an antiseptic ointment which tasted evilly and so would not be licked off. The beasts were wonderfully tractable, as if they knew that the treatment was for their good. Leithen had always been handy with dogs, and he found a great pleasure in looking into their furry, wrinkled faces and sniffing their familiar smell. Here was something which belonged most intimately to the North and yet had been adapted to the homely needs of man.

That night he dined with relish off caribou steaks and turned early to bed. But he did not fall asleep at once. There was a pleasant ferment in his brain, for he was for the first time envisaging what life would be if he were restored to it. He allowed his thoughts to run forward and plan.

It was of his friends that he thought chiefly, of his friends and of one or two places linked with them. Their long absence from his memory had clarified his view of them, and against the large background of acquaintances a few stood out who, he realized, were his innermost and abiding comrades. None of his colleagues at the Bar were among them, and none of his fellow-politicians. With them he had worked happily, but they had remained on the outer rim of his life. The real intimates were few, and the bond had always been something linked with sport and country life. Charles Lamancha and John Palliser-Yeates had been at school and college with him, and they had been together on many hillsides and by many waters. Archie Roylance, much younger, had irrupted into the group by virtue of an identity of tastes and his own compelling charm. Sandy Clanroyden had been the central star, radiating heat and light, a wandering star who for long seasons disappeared from the firmament. And there was Dick Hannay, half Nestor, half Odysseus, deep in Oxfordshire mud, but with a surprising talent for extricating himself and adventuring in the ends of the earth.

As he thought of them he felt a glow of affection warm his being. He pictured the places to which they specially belonged: Lamancha on the long slopes of Cheviot; Archie Roylance on the wind-blown thymy moors of the west; Sandy in his Border fortress; and Dick Hannay by the clear streams and gentle pastures of Cotswold. He pictured his meeting with them – restored from the grave. They had never been told about his illness, but they must have guessed. Sandy at least, after that last dinner in London. They must have been talking about him, lamenting his absence, making futile inquiries . . . He would suddenly appear among them, a little thinner and older perhaps, but the same man, and would be welcomed back to that great companionship.

How would he spend his days? He had finished with his professions, both law and politics. The State must now get on without him. He would be much at Borrowby – thank Heaven he had not sold it! He would go back to his Down Street rooms, for though he had surrendered the lease he would find a way of renewing it. He had done with travel; his last years would be spent at home among his friends. Somebody had once told him that a man who recovered from tuberculosis was pretty well exempt from other maladies. He might live to an old age, a careful, moderate old age filled with mild pleasures and innocent interests ... On the pillow of such thoughts he fell asleep.

# 11

The snow began just as they reached Lone Tree Lake. At first it came gently, making the air a dazzle of flakes, but not obscuring the near view. At the lake they retrieved the rest of their cached supplies, and tramped down its frozen surface until they reached its outlet, a feeder of the Big Hare, now under ten feet of ice and snow. Here the snow's softness made the going difficult, for the northern snow-shoes offered too narrow a surface. The air had become almost mild, and that night, when a rock shelf gave them a comparatively dry bivouac, Leithen deliberately laid his blankets well away from the fire.

Next day they halted to hunt, looking for fresh meat to take to the Hares' camp. Johnny and Lew found a small stamping-ground of moose, and since in the snow the big animals were at a disadvantage, they had no difficulty in getting two young bulls. Leithen helped to drag in the meat and found that the change in the weather had not weakened his new vigour. His mind was in a happy maze, planning aimlessly and making pictures which he did not try to complete.

Lew watched him with satisfaction.

'I've got to learn you things,' he said. 'You haven't got the tricks, and you're wasting your strength, but' – and he repeated his old phrase – 'you're going to be the huskiest of the lot of us. And I seen you shoot!'

They reached the Hares' camp late on an afternoon, when the snow had so thickened that it had the look of a coarse-textured cloth ceaselessly dropped from the skies. Huts, tents, the little church were for the moment buried under the pall. Lew chose a camping site about a quarter of a mile distant, for it was important to avoid too close a contact at first with the stricken settlement.

Johnny and the Indians went off to prospect. Half an hour later Johnny returned with startled eyes.

'I got news,' he stammered. 'The Father told me – seems there was a dog-team got down to the Fort, and come back. There's fightin' in Europe – been goin' on for months. Seems it's them darned Germans again. And Britain's in it. Likewise Canada.'

# 12

The taller Indian spoke from behind Johnny.

'My father is dead,' he said, and slipped back into the dusk.

'Yes,' said Johnny, 'there's been a lot of deaths among them Hares. Their camp's like a field hospital. Talkin' of field hospitals, what about this war?'

'We'll sleep on that,' Leithen answered.

Lew did not open his mouth, nor Galliard. Supper was prepared and eaten in silence, and each man by tacit consent went immediately to his blankets. Leithen, before turning in, looked at the skies. The snowfall was thinning, and the air was sharpening again. There was an open patch in the west and a faint irradiation of moonshine. Tomorrow would be very cold.

His bodily well-being continued. The journey down from the mountains had left its mark, for his face was scarred by patches of frost-bite, his lips were inflamed, the snow-shoes had made the calves of his legs ache like a bad tooth, and under his moccasins his feet were blistered. Nevertheless he felt that vigour had come back to him. It reminded him of his mountaineering days, when he would return to London with blistered cheeks and aching shoulder muscles and bleared eyes, and yet know that he was far fitter than the smoothly sunburnt creature that emerged from a holiday at home.

But though his body craved for it his mind would not permit

of sleep. He had been living with life, and now suddenly death seemed to have closed down on the world. The tall Indian's cry rang in his ears like a knell.

What had become of the bright pictures he had been painting?

The world was at war again and somewhere in Europe men were grappling with death. The horrors of campaigning had never been much in his mind, for as a soldier he had been too busy to brood over the *macabre*. But now a flood of dimly remembered terrors seemed to flow in upon him – men shot in the stomach and writhing in no-man's-land; scarecrows that once were human crucified on the barbed wire and bleached by wind and sun; the shambles of a casualty clearing station after a battle.

His thoughts had been dwelling on his reunion with friends. Those friends would all be scattered. Sandy Clanroyden would be off on some wild venture. Archie Roylance would be flying, game leg and all. Hannay, Palliser-Yeates, Lamancha, they would all be serving somehow and somewhere. He would be out of it, of course. A guarded flame, a semi-invalid, with nothing to do but to 'make' his soul ... As he fell asleep he was ashamed of his childishness. He had promised himself a treat which was not going to come off, and he was whining about it.

He woke with a faint far-off tinkle in his ears. He had been dreaming of war and would not have been surprised if he had heard a bugle call. He puzzled over the sound until he hit on the explanation. Father Duplessis in his little church was ringing the morning Angelus.

That tinny bell had an explosive effect on Leithen's mind. This was a place of death, the whole world was full of death – and yet here was one man who stood stubbornly for life. He rang the bell which should have started his flock on their day's work. Sunk in weakness and despair they would remain torpid, but he had sounded the challenge. Here was one man at any rate who was the champion of life against death.

## 13

It was a silent little band that broke camp and set out in the late winter dawn. Johnny's face was sullen with some dismal pre-occupation, and Lew's eyes had the wildness of the Sick Heart River, while Galliard's seemed to have once again the fear which had clouded them when he was recovering from his exhaustion.

To his surprise Leithen found that this did not depress him. The bell still tinkled in his ears. The world was at war again. It might be the twilight of the gods, the end of all things. The globe might swim in blood. Death might resume his ancient reign. But, by Heaven, he would strike his blow for life, even a pitiful flicker of it.

The valley opened before them. Frost had stiffened the snow to marble, and they were compelled to take off their snow-shoes, which gave them no foothold. The sky was a profound blue, and the amphitheatre of peaks stood out against it in a dazzling purity, matched below by the unbroken white sheet of the lake. The snow was deep, for the near woods were so muffled as to have lost all clean contours, and when they came to the flat where the camp lay the wretched huts had no outlines. They might have been mounds to mark where the dead lay in some hyperborean grave-yard. Only the little church on the higher ground looked like the work of men's hands. From the adjoining presbytery rose a thin wisp of smoke, but elsewhere there was no sign of humanity.

Lew spoke at last.

'God! The Hares have gone to earth like chipmunks! Or maybe they're all dead.'

'Not all,' said one of the Indians, 'but they are dying.'

They soon had evidence. They passed a small grove of spruce and poplar, and in nearly every tree there was a thing like a big nest, something lashed to snowy boughs. Lew nodded towards them. 'That's their burying-ground. It's new since we was here before.' Leithen thought freakishly of Villon and 'King Louis's orchard close'. There were funny little humps, too, on the flat, with coverings of birch and spruce branches peeping from under the snow.

'Them's graves,' said Johnny. 'The big ones go up in the trees, the smaller ones are under them humps, and them of no account, like babies and old folk, just get chucked out in the drifts. There's been a power o' dyin' here.'

Lew turned to Leithen for orders.

'Which comes first?' he asked, 'Zacharias or the priest?'

'We will go to the presbytery,' was the answer.

# 14

There was at first no sign of life in the irregular street of huts that made the ascent to the presbytery. The roofs of some of them were sagging with the weight of snow, and one or two had collapsed. But there were people in them, for, now that they were seen at closer quarters, wraiths of smoke came from the vents, which proved that there were fires within, though very meagre ones. Once a door opened and a woman looked out; she at once drew back with a scared look like an animal's; a whimper of a child seemed to come from indoors.

Then suddenly there rose a wild clamour from starving dogs picketed in the snow. Their own dogs answered it and the valley resounded with the din. After the deathly quiet the noise seemed a horrid impiety. There was nothing in it of friendly barking; it was like the howling of a starving wolf pack lost and forgotten at the world's end.

The sound brought Father Duplessis to the presbytery door. He was about Leithen's own age, but now he looked ten years older than at Fort Bannerman. Always lean, he was now emaciated, and his pallor had become almost cadaverous. He peered and blinked at the newcomers, and then his face lit up as he came forward with outstretched hands.

'God be praised!' he cried. 'It is my English comrade-in-arms.'

'Get hold of the chief,' Leithen told Johnny. 'Take the Indians with you and make a plan for distributing the meat. Then bring Zacharias up here.'

He and Galliard and Lew followed the priest into the presbytery. In Father Wentzel's time the place had smelt stuffy, like a furniture store. Now it reeked of ether and carbolic, and in a corner stood a trestle table covered with a coarse linen cloth. He remembered that Father Duplessis was something of a doctor.

He was also most clearly a soldier, a soldier tired out by a long and weary campaign. There was nothing about him to tell of the priest except the chain which showed at his neck and which held a cross tucked under his shirt. He wore kamiks and a dicky of caribou skin and a parka edged with wolverine fur, and he needed all his clothing, for the presbytery was perishing cold. He might have been a trapper or a prospector but for his carriage, his square shoulders and erect head, which showed the discipline of St Cyr. His silky brown beard was carefully combed and trimmed. A fur skull-cap covered the head where the hair had been cut to the bone. He had the long, high-bridged nose of Picardy gentlefolk, and a fine forehead, round the edges of which the hair was greying. His blue eyes looked washed out and fatigued, but the straight lines of the brows gave an impression of power and reserve. The osseous structure of his face was as sharply defined as the features on a newly minted coin.

'Thank Heaven you have come,' he said. 'This campaign is too hard for one man. And perhaps I am not the man. In this task I am only a subaltern and I need a commanding officer.'

He looked first at Galliard and then at Leithen, and his eyes remained on the latter.

'We are fighting a pestilence,' he went on, 'but a pestilence of the soul.'

'One moment,' Leithen broke in. 'What about this war in Europe?'

'There is war,' said the priest gravely. 'The news came from the Fort when I sent a dog-team for supplies. But I know no more than that the nations are once again at each other's throats. Germany with certain allies against your country and mine. I do not think of it – Europe is very far away from my thoughts.'

'Supplies? What did you get?'

'Not much. Some meal and flour, of which a balance remains. But that is not the diet for the poor folk here. Also a little coffee for myself. See, I will make you a cup.'

He bustled for a minute or two at the stove, and the pleasant odour of coffee cut sharply into the frowst of the room.

'A pestilence of the mind?' Leithen asked. 'You mean – ?'

'In myself – and in you – it would be called *accidie*, a deadly sin. But not, I think, with this people. They are removed but a little way from the beasts that perish, and with them it is an animal sickness.'

'They die of it?'

'But assuredly. Some have T.B. and their sickness of the mind speeds up that disease. Some are ageing and it makes them senile, so that they perish from old age. With some it unhinges the wits so that the brain softens. Up to now it is principally the men who suffer, for the women will still fight on, having urgent duties. But soon it will mean the children also, and the women will follow. Before the geese return in spring, I fear, I greatly fear, that my poor people will be no more in the land.'

'What are you doing about it?'

Father Duplessis shrugged his shoulders and spread out his hands.

'There is little I can do. I perform the offices of the Church, and I strive to make them worship with me. I preach to them the way of salvation. But I cannot lift them out of the mire. What is needed is men – a man – who will force their life again into a discipline, so that they will not slip away into death. Someone who will give them hope.'

'Have you no helpers?'

'There is the chief Zacharias, who has a stout heart. But he is old and crippled. One or two young men, perhaps, but I fear they are going the way of the rest.'

# 15

Leithen had asked questions automatically and had scarcely listened to the replies, for in that dim, stuffy, frigid presbytery, where the only light came through the cracks in the door and a dirty window in the roof, he was conscious of something in the nature of a revelation. His mind had a bitter clarity, and his eyes seemed to regard, as from a high place, the kingdoms of the world and men's souls.

His will was rising to the same heights. At last, at long last, his own course was becoming crystal clear.

Memories of the war in which he had fought raced before him like a cinema show, all in order and all pointing the same truth. It had been waste, futile waste, and death, illimitable, futile death. Now the same devilment was unloosed again. He saw Europe as a carnage pit – shattered towns, desecrated homes, devastated cornlands, roads blocked with the instruments of war – the meadows of France and of Germany, and of his own kind England. Once again the free peoples were grappling with the slave peoples. The former would win, but how many free men would die before victory, and how many of the unhappy slaves!

The effluence of death seemed to be wafted to his nostrils over the many thousand miles of land and sea. He smelt the stench of incinerators and muddy trenches and bloody clothing. The odour of the little presbytery was like that of a hospital ward.

But it did not sicken him. Rather it braced him, as when a shore-dweller who has been long inland gets a whiff of the sea. It was the spark which fired within him an explosive train of resolution.

There was a plain task before him, to fight with Death. God for His own purpose had unloosed it in the world, ravening over places which had once been rich in innocent life. Here in the North life had always been on sufferance, its pale slender shoots fighting a hard battle against the Elder Ice. But it had maintained its brave defiance. And now one such pathetic slip was on the verge of extinction. This handful of Hares had for generations been a little enclave of life besieged by mortality. Now it was perishing, hurrying to share in the dissolution which was overtaking the world.

By God's help that should not happen – the God who was the God of the living. Through strange circuits he had come to that simple forthright duty for which he had always longed. In that duty he must make his soul.

There was a ring of happiness in his voice. 'You have me as a helper,' he said. 'And Mr Galliard. And Lew and Johnny. Between us we will save your Hares from themselves.'

Lew's face set, as if he had heard something which he had long feared.

'You mean we've got to feed 'em?'

Leithen nodded. 'Feed them – body and mind.'

Lew's eyebrows fell.

'You coming out in the woods with us? I guess that's the right thing for you.'

'No, that's your job, and Johnny's. I stay here.'

Lew exploded. Even in the dimness his eyes were like points of blue fire.

'Hell!' he cried. 'You can't do it. You jest can't do it. I was afeared you'd have that dam' foolish notion. Say, what d'you think life here would be like for you? You're on the road to be cured, but you ain't cured yet. Come out with me and Johnny and you'll be living healthy. We won't let you do too much. It's a mighty interesting job hunting moose in their *ravages* and you'll get some fine shooting. We'll feed you the kind of food that's good for you, and at night we'll make you as snug as a wintering bear. I'll engage by the spring you'll be a mighty strong man. That's good sense, ain't it?'

'Excellent good sense. Only it's not for me. My job is here.'

'Man, I tell you it's suicide. Fair suicide. I've seen plenty cases like yours, and I've seen 'em get well and I've seen 'em die. There's one sure way to die and that's to live in a shack or among shacks, and breathe stinking air and be rubbing shoulders with sick folks, and wearing your soul out trying to put some pep into a herring-gutted bunch of Indians. You'll be sicker than ever before a week is out, and a corp in a month, and that'll be darned little use to anybody.'

Lew's soft rich voice had become hoarse with passion. He got up from his seat and stood before Leithen like a suppliant, with his hands nervously intertwining.

'You may be right,' Leithen said. 'But all the same I must stay. It doesn't matter what happens to me.'

'It matters like hell,' said Lew, and there was that in his voice which made the presbytery a solemn place, for it was the cry of a deep affection.

'This is a war and I obey orders. I've got my orders. In a world where Death is king we're going to defy him and save life. The North has closed down on us and we're going to beat the North. That is to your address, Galliard.'

Galliard was staring at him with bright comprehending eyes.

'In this fight we have each got his special job. I'm in command, and I hand them out. I've taken the one for myself that I believe I can do best. We're going to win, remember. What does my death matter if we defeat Death?'

Lew sat down again with his head in his hands. He raised it like a frightened animal at Leithen's next words.

'This is my Sick Heart River. Galliard's too, I think. Maybe yours, Lew. Each of us has got to find his river for himself, and it may flow where he least expects it.'

Father Duplessis, back in the deep shadows, quoted from the Vulgate psalm, '*Fluminis impetus laetificat civitatem Dei.*'

Leithen smiled. 'Do you know the English of that, Lew? *There is a river, the streams whereof shall make glad the city of God.* That's what you've always been looking for.'

# 16

The place was suddenly bright, for the door had opened. A wave of icy air swept out the frowst, and Leithen found himself looking into a radiant world, rimmed with peaks of bright snow and canopied by a sky so infinitely far away that it had no colour except that of essential light.

It was the old chief, conducted by Johnny. Zacharias was a very mountain of a man, and age had made him shapeless while lumbago had bent him nearly double. He walked with two sticks, and Johnny had to lower him delicately to a seat. The Hares were not treaty Indians, but nevertheless he wore one of the soup-plate Victorian silver medals, which had come to him through a Cree grandmother. His heavy face had a kind of placid good sense, and age and corpulence had not dimmed the vigour of his eye.

He greeted Leithen ceremonially, realizing he was the leader of the newcomers. He had a few words of English, but Johnny did most of the interpreting. He sat with his hands on his knees, like a schoolboy interviewed by a headmaster, but though his attitude suggested nervousness his voice was calm.

'We are a ver' sick people,' he repeated several times. It was his chief English phrase.

What he had to tell was much the same story that Johnny had brought to the mountain camp. But since then things had slipped further downhill. There had been more deaths of children and old people, and even of younger men. They did not die of actual starvation, but of low diet and low spirits. Less than half a dozen went hunting, and not many more brought in fuel, so there was little fresh meat and too little firewood. People sat huddled in icy shacks in all the clothes they could find, and dreamed themselves into decay. The heart had gone out of them. The women, too, had ceased to scold and upbraid, and would soon go the way of their menfolk.

'Then our people will be no more,' said Zacharias grimly.

Leithen asked what help he could count on.

'There is myself,' said the chief, 'and this good Father. I have three sons who will do my bidding, and seven grandsons – no, five, for two are sick. There may be a few others. Say at the most a score.'

'What would you advise?'

The old man shook his head.

'In our fathers' day the cure would have been a raid by Chipewyans or Dog-Ribs! Then we would have been forced to be up and doing or perish. A flight of arrows is the best cure for brooding. Now – I do not know. Something harsh to get the sullenness out of their bones. You are a soldier?'

'The Father and I served in the same war.'

'Good! Soldiers' ways are needed. But applied with judgement, for my people are weak and they are also children.'

Leithen spoke to the company.

'There are a score of us for this job then. Mr Galliard and I stay here. Lew and Johnny go hunting, and will take with them whom they choose. We shall need all the dog-teams we can get to bring back meat and cordwood. But first there are several jobs to be done. You've got to build a shack for Mr Galliard and myself. You've got to get a mighty big store of logs, for a fire must be kept burning day and night.'

He was addressing Lew, whose eyes questioned him.

'Why? Because these people must be kept in touch with life,

188

and life is warmth and colour. A fire will remind them that there is warmth and colour in the world ... Tomorrow morning we will have a round-up and discover exactly what is the size of our job ... You've made camp, Johnny? Mr Galliard and I will be there by supper-time. Now you and Lew go along and get busy. We've got a lot to do in the next few days.'

The door opened again and disclosed the same landscape of primitive forms and colours, its dazzle a little dimmed by the approach of evening.

This second glimpse had a strange effect on Leithen, for it seemed to be a revelation of a world which he had forgotten. His mind swooped back on it and for a little was immersed in memories. Zacharias was hoisted to his feet and escorted down the hill. Father Duplessis prepared a simple meal. There was a little talk about ways and means after Lew left, Galliard questioning Leithen and getting answers. Yet all the time the visualizing part of Leithen's mind was many thousands of miles away in space and years back in time.

The stove had become too hot, so the door was allowed to remain half open, for the year had turned, and the afternoon sun was gaining strength. So his eyes were seeing a segment of a bright coloured world. The intense pure light brought a flood of pictures all linked with moments of exultant physical vigour. Also with friendships. He did not probe the cause, but these pictures seemed to imply companionship. In each Archie Roylance, or Clanroyden, or Lamancha was just round the corner waiting ... There was a July morning, very early, on the Nantillons glacier, on his way to make a traverse of the Charmoz which had once been famous. There was a moonlit night on an Aegean isle when he had been very near old mysteries. There were Highland dawns and twilights – one especially, when he sat on a half-submerged skerry watching for the wild geese – an evening when Tir-nan-og was manifestly re-created. There were spring days and summer days in English meadows, Border bent with the April curlews piping, London afternoons in May with the dear remembered smells fresh in his nostrils ... In each picture he felt the blood strong in his veins and a young power in his muscles. This was the man he once had been.

Once! He came out of his absorption to realize that these

pictures had not come wholly through the Ivory Gate. He was no longer a dying man. He had been reprieved on the eve of execution, and by walking delicately the reprieve might be extended. His bodily strength was like a fragile glass vessel which one had to carry while walking on a rough road; with care it might survive, but a jolt would shatter it ... No, that was a false comparison. His health was like a small sum of money, all that was left of a big fortune. It might be kept intact by a stern economy, or it might be spent gallantly on a last venture.

Galliard and Father Duplessis were sitting side by side and talking earnestly. He caught a word of the priest's: '*Dieu fait bien ce qu'il fait*' and remembered the quotation. Was it La Fontaine? He laughed, for it fitted in with his own mood.

He had found the right word both for Galliard and himself. They were facing the challenge of the North, which a man must accept and repel or submit to servitude. Lew and Johnny and their kind did not face that challenge; they avoided it by walking humbly; they conciliated it by ingenious subterfuges; its blows were avoided and not squarely met, and they paid the price; for every now and then they fell under its terrors.

He was facing, too, the challenge of Death. Elsewhere in the world the ancient enemy was victorious. If here, against all odds, he could save the tiny germ of life from its maw he would have met that challenge, and done God's work.

Leithen's new-found mission for life gave him a happy retrospect over his own career. At first, when he left England, he had looked back with pain at the bright things now forbidden. In his first days in the North his old world had slipped from him wholly, leaving only a grey void which he must face with clenched teeth and with grim submission. He smiled as he remembered those days, with their dreary stoicism. He had thought of himself like Job, as one whose strength lay only in humbleness. He had been crushed and awed by God.

A barren creed! He saw that now, for its foundation had been pride of defiance, keeping a stiff neck under the blows of fate. He had been abject but without true humility. When had the change begun? At Sick Heart River, when he had a vision of the beauty which might be concealed in the desert? Then, that evening in the snow-pit had come the realization of the tenderness behind the iron front of Nature, and after that had come thankfulness for plain human affection. The North had not frozen him, but had melted the ice in his heart. God was not only all-mighty but all-loving. His old happinesses seemed to link in with his new mood of thankfulness. The stream of life which had flowed so pleasantly had eternity in its waters. He felt himself safe in the hands of a power that was both God and friend.

Father Duplessis was speaking, and Galliard was listening earnestly. He seemed to be quoting the New Testament – 'Heureux sont les morts qui meurent dans le Seigneur.'

He had been inhuman, Leithen told himself, with the dreary fortitude of a sick animal. Now whatever befell him he was once again in love with his fellows. The cold infernal North magnified instead of dwarfing humanity. What a marvel was this clot of vivified dust! ... The universe seemed to spread itself before him in immense distances lit and dominated by a divine spark which was man. An inconsiderable planet, a speck in the infinite stellar spaces; most of it salt water; the bulk of the land rock and desert and austral and boreal ice; interspersed mud, the detritus of aeons, with a thin coverlet of grass and trees – that vegetable world on which every living thing was in the last resort a parasite! Man, precariously perched on this rotating scrap-heap, yet so much master of it that he could mould it to his transient uses and, while struggling to live, could entertain thoughts and dreams beyond the bounds of time and space! Man so weak and yet so great, the chief handiwork of the Power that had hung the stars in the firmament!

He was moved to a strange exaltation. Behind his new access of strength he felt the brittleness of his body. His stock of vigour was slender indeed, but he could spend it bravely in making his soul. Most men had their lives taken from them. It was his privilege to *give* his, to offer it freely and joyfully in one last effort of manhood. The North had been his friend, for it had enabled him, like Jacob, to wrestle with the dark angel and extort a blessing.

The presbytery had warmed up, and Galliard had fallen asleep. He slept with his mouth shut, breathing through his nose, and the sleeping face had dignity and power in it. It would be no small thing to release this man from ancestral fears and gird him for his task in the world. In making his own soul he would also give back Galliard his. He would win the world too, for now the great, shining, mystic universe above him was no longer a foe but a friend, part with himself of an eternal plan.

Father Duplessis' voice broke in on his meditation and seemed to give the benediction words. He was reading his breviary, and broke off now and then to translate a sentence aloud in his own tongue – '*Car celui qui voudra sauver sa vie la perdra; et celui qui perdra sa vie pour l'amour de moi, la retrouvera.*'

# 17

*From a report by Corporal S—, RCMP, Fort Bannerman, to Inspector N—, RCMP, Fort Macleod.*

'Pursuant to instructions received, I left Fort Bannerman on the 21st day of April, accompanied by Constable F—, and after some trouble with my dog-team arrived at the Hares' winter camp on Big Hare Lake at 6.30 p.m. on the 22nd. The last part of the journey was in the dark, but we were guided by a great blaze coming apparently from the camp which was visible from the outlet of the lake. At first I thought the place was on fire, but on arrival found that this evening bonfire had become a regular custom.

'Rumours of distress among the Hares had reached Fort Bannerman during the winter. Father Wentzel, on his return to the Fort, had predicted a bad time, and Father Duplessis, who replaced him, had sent an urgent message asking not only for supplies of food but for someone to go up and advise. I duly reported this to you, and received your instructions to take an early opportunity of visiting the camp. This opportunity I was unable to find for several months, since the Force was short-handed, owing to the departure of men to the provost company in France, and, as you are aware, I was compelled to make two trips to Great Bear Lake in connection with the dispute at the Goose Bay Mine. So, as stated above, I could not leave Fort Bannerman until the 21st inst.

'Constable F— and I were put up by Father Duplessis, and I received from him a satisfactory account of the condition of the

Hare tribe. They are now in good health, and, what is more important, in good heart, for it seems that every now and then they get pessimism, like the measles, and die of it, since it prevents their looking for food. It appeared that they had had a very bad bout in the winter, of the risk of which Father Wentzel had warned us. Up to the beginning of February they were sitting in their huts doing nothing but expecting death, and very soon getting what they expected. A schedule attached to this report gives the number of deaths, and such details as could be ascertained.

'The Hares were saved by an incident which I think is the most remarkable I have ever heard of in my long experience of the Territory. In the early fall a party went into the Mackenzie mountains, travelling up the Big Hare River to a piece of country which has been very imperfectly explored. Or rather, two parties who ultimately joined hands. The party consisted of an American gentleman named Galliard, a New York business man, and an Englishman named Leithen. It had with it two Hare Indians, and as guides the brothers Frizel. The Frizels, Lew and Johnny, are men of high character and great experience. They both served with distinction in the — Battalion of the Canadian Expeditionary Force in the last war, and have long been favourably known to the Police. The younger, until recently, was a game warden at the National Park at Waskesieu.

'I received further information about the Englishman, Leithen. It appears that he was Sir Edward Leithen, a famous London lawyer and a British Member of Parliament. He was suffering from tuberculosis, and had undertaken the expedition with a view to a cure. The winter in the high mountains, where the weather has been mild for a Mackenzie River winter, had done him good, and he was believed to be on the way to recovery.

'The party, coming out early in February, reached the Hares' camp to find it in a deplorable condition. Sir E. Leithen at once took charge of the situation. He had been a distinguished soldier in the last war – in the Guards, I believe – and he knew how to handle men. With Mr Galliard to help him, who had had large administrative experience in America, and with the assistance of Father Duplessis and the old chief Zacharias, they set to work at once.

'Their first job was to put some sense into the Hares. With the help of the Frizels, who knew the tribe well, a number of conferences were held, and there was a lot of straight talk. Father Duplessis said that it was wonderful how Sir E. Leithen managed to strike the note which most impressed the Indian mind.

'This, of course, was only the beginning. The next step was to organize the survivors into gangs, and assign to each a special duty. Food was the most urgent problem, for the Hares had been for a long time on very short commons, and were badly under-nourished. As you are aware, the moose have been moving north in recent years. The two Frizels, with a selected band of Hares, made up a hunting party, and, knowing how to find the moose stamping-grounds, were able to send in a steady supply of fresh meat. They also organized a regular business of trapping hares and partridges, at which the Hares are very skilful, but which they had been too dispirited to attempt.

'The tribe had also got short of fuel, so wood-cutting parties were organized. Sir E. Leithen insisted on a big fire being kept going by night and day in the centre of the camp, in order to hearten the people.

'Transport was a serious problem. The dogs of the tribe had been allowed to become very weak from starvation, and many had died, for the fishing in the summer had been poor and the store of dried fish, which they use for dog feed, was nearly exhausted. Sir E. Leithen made them start again their winter fishing through the ice in the lake. Here they had a bit of luck, for it turned out very productive, and it was possible to get the dogs back into condition. This was important, since the dog-teams were in constant demand, to haul in firewood from the wood-cutters and fresh meat from the hunters.

'The Frizels did the field work, and Sir E. Leithen and Mr Galliard managed the camp. I am informed by Father Duplessis that Leithen obtained almost at once an extraordinary influence over the Hares' minds. "Far greater than mine," the Father said, "though I have been living for years among them." This was partly due to his great ability and the confidence he inspired, but partly to the fact that he had been a very sick man, and was still regarded by the Hares as a sick man. The Indians have a superstitious respect for anyone whom they believe to be facing death.

'Sick man or not, in a month Sir E. Leithen had worked little short of a miracle. He had restored a degenerating tribe to something like health. He made them want to live instead of being resigned to die.

'And now, sir, I come to the event which kills all satisfaction in this achievement. It seems that the elder Frizel had repeatedly warned Sir E. Leithen that the work which he was undertaking would undo all the good of his sojourn in the high mountains, and would lead to certain death; but that Sir E. Leithen had declared that that work was his duty, and that he must take the risk. Frizel's prophecy proved only too true.

'I understand that his strength slowly declined. The trouble with his lungs revived, and, while he continued to be the directing mind, his power of locomotion gradually lessened. Lew Frizel, who came in frequently from the bush to inquire into his health, and implored him in vain to lessen his efforts, told me that by the end of March he had reached the conclusion that nothing could save him. The shack in which he lived was next door to the presbytery, and Father Duplessis, who has some knowledge of medicine, did his best to supply treatment. According to his account, the malady was such that only a careful life could have completed the cure begun in the mountains, and Sir E. Leithen's exertions by night and day were bound to bring it back in a violent form. The sick man, the Father told me, attended the Easter Mass, and after that was too weak to move. Myocarditis set in, and he died without pain during the night of April 19th.

'As I have already informed you, I arrived with Constable F—on the evening of the 22nd. The camp was in mourning, and for a little there seemed danger of the Hares slipping back to their former state of melancholy supineness. From this they were saved by the exhortations of Father Duplessis, and especially by Lew Frizel, who told them they could only show their love for Sir E. Leithen by continuing the course he had mapped out for them. Also, the tribe was now in a better mood, as spring was very near.

'Mr Galliard was anxious that Sir E. Leithen should be buried at a spot in Quebec Province for which he had a special liking. On April 24th we started by dog-team with the body, the party being myself, Constable F—, Mr Galliard, and the two Frizels. We had considerable difficulty with the ice in the Big Hare River, for the thaw-out promised to be early. We reached Fort Bannerman on the 25th, and were able, by radio, to engage a plane from Edmonton, Mr Galliard being willing to pay any price for it.

'I have since heard by radio that the destination at Quebec was safely reached. The two Frizels were dropped at Ottawa, it being their intention, at all costs, to join the Canadian Forces in Europe ...'

# 18

*An extract from the journal of Father Jean-Marie Duplessis, OMI, translated from the French.*

'In this journal, which I have now kept for more than twenty years, I shall attempt to set down what I remember of my friend. I call him my friend, for though our intercourse was measured in time by a few weeks, it had the intimacy of comradeship in a difficult undertaking. Let me say by way of prologue that during our friendship I saw what is not often vouchsafed to mortal eyes, the rebirth of a soul.

'In the fall I had talked with L. at Fort Bannerman. He was clearly a man in bad health, to whom the details of living were a struggle. I was impressed by his gentleness and his power of self-control, but it was a painful impression, for I realized that it meant a continuous effort. I felt that no circumstances could break the iron armour of his fortitude. But my feeling for him had warmth in it as well as respect. We had been soldiers in the same campaign, and he knew my home in France.

'When things became bad early in the New Year I was in doubt whom to turn to. Father Wentzel at Fort Bannerman was old and feeble; and I could not expect the Police to spare me a man. Besides, I wanted something more than physical assistance. I wanted a man of education who could understand and cope with the Hares' *malaise*. So when one of L.'s guides reached the camp in early February I thought at once of him, and ventured to send him a message.

'It was a shot at a venture, and I was not prepared for his ready response. When he arrived with Monsieur Galliard I was surprised by the look of both. I had learned from Father Wentzel that Galliard was a man sick in the spirit, and I knew that L. was sick in body. Now both seemed to have suffered a transformation. Galliard had a look of robust health, though there was that in his manner which still disquieted me – a lack of confidence, an air of unhappy anticipation, a sense of leaning heavily upon L. As for L., he was very lean and somewhat short of breath, but from my medical experience I judged him to be a convalescent.

'The first day the party spent with me I had light on the situation. L. was all but cured – he might live for years with proper care. But proper care meant life in the open, no heavy duties, and not too much exertion. On this one of the hunters, Louis Frizelle, insisted passionately. Otherwise, he said, and M. Galliard bore him out, that in a little time he would be dead. This L. did not deny, but he was firm in his resolution to take up quarters in the camp and to devote all his powers to saving what was left of the Hare tribe. On this decision plans were made, with the successful result explained in the Police corporal's report, which I here incorporate . . .

'At first I thought that L.'s conduct was that of a man of high humanitarian principles, who could not witness suffering without an attempt at relief. But presently I found that the motives were subtler, and if possible nobler, and that they involved his friend, M. Galliard. L., not being of the Church, made no confession, and he did not readily speak of himself, but in the course of our work together I was able to gather something of his history.

'We talked first, I remember, about the war in Europe. I was deeply apprehensive about the fate of my beloved France, which once again in my lifetime would be bled white by war. L. seemed curiously apathetic about Europe. He had no doubts about the ultimate issue, and he repeated more than once that the world was witnessing again a contest between Death and Life, and that Life would triumph. He saw our trouble with the Hares as part of the same inscrutable purpose of the Almighty, and insisted that we were on one battle-front with the allies beyond the Atlantic. This he said often to M. Frizelle, whom it seemed to comfort.

'I observed that as the days passed he showed an increasing

tenderness towards the Hares. At first I think he regarded their succour as a cold, abstract duty. But gradually he began to feel for them a protective and brotherly kindness. I suppose it was the gift of the trained lawyer, but he mastered every detail of their tribal customs and their confused habits of thought with a speed that seemed not less than miraculous. He might have lived most of his life among them. At first, when we sat at the conferences and went in and out of the huts, his lean, pallid face revealed no more than the intellectual interest which might belong to a scientific inquirer. But by degrees a kind of affection showed in his eyes. He smiled oftener, and his smile had an infinite kindliness. From the beginning he dominated them, and the domination became in the end, on their part, almost worship.

'What is the secret, I often ask myself, that gives one human being an almost mystical power over others? In the War I have known a corporal have it, when it was denied to a general of division. I have seen the gift manifest in a parish priest and lacking in an archbishop. It does not require a position of authority, for it makes its own authority. It demands a strong pre-eminence in brain and character, for it is based on understanding, but also, I think, on an effluence of sincere affection.

'I was puzzled at first by the attitude of Monsieur Galliard. He was a Catholic and had resumed – what he had for a time pretermitted – the observances of the Church. He came regularly to Mass and confession. He was ultimately of my own race, though *Les Canadiens* differ widely from *Les Français de France*. He should have been easy for me to comprehend, but I confess that at first I was at a loss. He was like a man under the spell of a constant fear – not panic or terror, but a vague uneasiness. To L. he was like a faithful dog. He seemed to draw strength from his presence, as the mistletoe draws strength from the oak.

'What was notable was his steady advance in confidence till presently his mind was as healthy as his body. His eye cleared, his mouth no longer twitched when he spoke, and he carried his head like a soldier. The change was due partly to his absorption in his work, for to L. he was a right hand. I have rarely seen a man toil so devotedly. But it was largely due to his growing affection for L. When the party arrived from the mountains he was obviously under L.'s influence, but only in the way in which a strong nature masters a less strong. But as the days passed, I could see that his feeling was becoming a warmer thing than admiration. The sight of L.'s increasing weakness made his face often a tragic mask. He fussed as much as the elder Frizelle over L.'s health. He would come to me and implore my interference. 'He is winning,' he would repeat, 'but it will be at the cost of his life, and the price is too high.'

'Bit by bit I began to learn about Galliard, partly from L. and partly from the man himself. He had been brought up in the stiff tradition of *Les Canadiens*, had revolted against it, and had locked the door on his early life. But it was the old story. His ancestry had its revenge, a revenge bound to be especially harsh, I fancy, in the case of one of his breeding. He had fled from the glittering world in which he had won success and from a devoted wife, to the home of his childhood. And here came a tangle of motives. He had in his blood the pioneer craving to move ever further into the wilds; his family, indeed, had given more than one figure to the story of Arctic exploration. He conceived that he owed a duty to the family tradition which he had forsaken, and that he had to go into the North as an atonement. He also seems to have conceived it as part of the penance which he owed for the neglect of his family religion. He is a man, I think, of sentiment and imagination rather than of a high spirituality.

'But his penance turned out severer than he dreamed. He fell into a *malaise* which, it is my belief, was at bottom the same as the Hares' affliction, and which seems to be endemic in the North. It may be defined as fear of the North, or perhaps more accurately as fear of life. In the North man, to live, has to fight every hour against hostile forces; if his spirit fails and his effort slackens he perishes. But this dread was something more than a rational fear of a potent enemy. There was superstition in it, a horror of a supernatural and desperate malevolence. This set the Hares mooning in their shacks awaiting death, and it held Galliard, a man of education and high ability, in the same blind, unreasoning bondage. His recovered religion gave him no defence, for he read this fear as part of the price to be paid for his treason.

'Then L. came on the scene. He saved Galliard's life. He appeared when Frizelle, in a crazy fit, deserted him, and he had come from England in the last stage of a dire sickness to restore Galliard to his old world. In L.'s grim fortitude Galliard found something that steadied his nerves. More, he learned from L. the only remedy for his *malaise*. He must fight the North and not submit to it; once fought and beaten, he could win from it not a curse but a blessing.

'Therefore he eagerly accepted the task of grappling with the Hares' problem. Here was a test case. They were defying the North; they were resisting a madness akin to his own. If they won, the North had no more terrors for him – or life either. He would have conquered his ancestral fear.

'Then something was added to his armour. He had revered L., and soon he came to love him. He thought more of L.'s bodily well-being than of his own nerves. And in forgetting his own troubles he found they had disappeared. After a fortnight in the camp he was like the man in the Scriptures out of whom the devil spirit was cast – wholly sane and at peace, but walking delicately.

# 19

'But L. was my chief concern. I have said that in him I witnessed the rebirth of a soul, but that is not quite the truth. The soul, a fine soul, was always there. More, though not of the Church, I do not hesitate to say that he was of the Faith. *Alias oves habeo quae non sunt ex hoc ovili*. But he had been frozen by hard stoicism which sprang partly from his upbringing and partly from temperament. He was a strong man with an austere command of himself, and when he had to face death he divested himself of all that could palliate the suffering, and stood up to it with a stark resolution which was more Roman than Christian. What I witnessed was the thawing of the ice.

'He had always bowed himself before the awful majesty of God. Now his experience was that of the Church in the thirteenth century, when they found in the Blessed Virgin a gentle mediatrix between mortal and divine. Or perhaps I should put it thus: that he discovered that tenderness and compassion which Our Lord came into the world to preach, and, in sympathy with others, he lost all care for himself. His noble, frosty egoism was merged in something nobler. He had meant to die in the cold cathedral of the North, ceasing to live in a world which had no care for life. Now he welcomed the humblest human environment, for he had come to love his kind, indeed, to love everything that God had made. He once said (he told me he was quoting an English poet) that he "carried about his heart an awful warmth like a load of immortality".

'When I first met him at Fort Bannerman he seemed to me the typical Englishman, courteous, aloof, the type I knew well in the War. But now there seemed to be a loosening of bonds. He talked very little, but he smiled often, and he seemed to radiate a gentle, compelling courtesy. But there was steel under the soft glove. He had always the air of command, and the Hares obeyed his lightest word as I am certain they never obeyed any orders before in their tribal history. As his strength declined he could speak only in a whisper, but his whispers had the authority of trumpets. For he succeeded in diffusing the impression of a man who had put all fear behind him and was already in communion with something beyond our mortality.

'He shared his confidences with no one. Monsieur Galliard, who had come to regard him with devotion, would never have dared to pierce his reserve. I tried and failed. With him I had not the authority of the Church, and, though I recognized that he was nearing death, I could not offer the consolations of religion unless he had asked for them. I should have felt it an impiety, for I recognized that in his own way he was making his soul. As the power of the sun waxed he liked to bask in it with his eyes shut, as if in prayer or a daydream. He borrowed my Latin Bible and read much in it, but the book would often lie on his knees while he watched with abstracted eyes the dazzle of light on the snow of the far mountains.

'It is a strange fact to chronicle, but I think his last days were his happiest. His strength was very low, but he had done his work and the Hares were out of the pit. Monsieur Galliard tended him like a mother or a sister, helped him to dress and undress, keeping the hut warm, cooking for him and feeding him. The hunters, the Frizelles and the Hares, came to visit him on every return journey. Old Zacharias would remain for hours near his door in case he might be summoned. But all respected his privacy, for they felt that he had gone into retreat before death. I saw him oftenest, and the miracle was that, as the spring crept back to the valley, there seemed to be a springtime in his spirit.

'He came often to Mass – the last occasion being the High Mass at Easter, which for the Hares was also a thanksgiving for recovery. The attendance was now exemplary. The little church with its gaudy colouring – the work of old Brother Onesime, and much admired by Father Wentzel – was crowded to the door. The Hares have an instinct for ritual, and my acolytes serve the altar well, but they have none for music, and I had found it impossible to train much of a choir. L. would sit in a corner following my Latin with his lips, and he seemed to draw comfort from it. I think the reason was that he was now sharing something with the Hares, and was not a director, but one of the directed. For he had come to love those poor childish folk. Hitherto a lonely man, he had found a clan and a family.

'After that Easter Sunday his body went fast downhill. I do not think he suffered much, except from weakness. His manner became gentler than ever, and his eyes used often to have the pleased look of a good child. He smiled, too, often, as if he saw the humours of life. The huskies – never a very good-tempered pack, though now they were well fed – became his friends, and one or two of the older beasts would accompany him out of doors with a ridiculous air of being a bodyguard. One cold night, I remember, one of them suddenly ensconced itself in an empty box outside the presbytery door. I can still hear L. talking to it. "I know what you're saying, old fellow. 'I'm a poor dog and my master's a poor man. I've never had a box like this to sleep in. Please don't turn me out.' " So there it remained – the first time I have seen a husky with ambitions to become a house dog.

'He watched eagerly for the signs of spring. The first was the return of the snow buntings, shimmering grey flocks which had wintered in the south. These he would follow with his eyes as they fluttered over the pine woods or spread themselves like a pied shadow on the snow. Then the mountain we call Baldface suddenly shed most of its winter covering, the noise of avalanches punctuated the night, and the upper ribs were disclosed, black as ink in the daytime, but at evening flaming into the most amazing hues of rose and purple. I knew that he had been an alpinist of note, and in these moments I fancy he was recapturing some of the activities of his youth. But there was no regret in his eyes. He was giving thanks for another vision of the Glory of God.

'The last time he was able to go abroad Monsieur Galliard and I assisted him down to the edge of the lake. There was still a broad selvedge of ice – what the Canadian French call *batture* – but in the middle the ice was cracking, and there were lanes of water to reflect the pale blue sky. Also the streams were being loosed from their winter stricture. One could hear them talking under their bonds, and in one or two places the force of water had cleared the boulders and made pools and cascades ... A wonderful thing happened. A bull moose, very shaggy and lean, came out of the forest and stood in an open shallow at a stream's mouth. It drank its fill and then raised its ugly head, shook it and stared into the sunset. Crystal drops fell from its mouth, and the setting sun transfigured the beast into something magical, a beneficent dragon out of a fairy tale. I shall never forget L.'s delight. It was as if he had his last sight of the beauty of the earth, and found in it a pledge of the beauty of Paradise; though I doubt if there will be anything like a bull-moose in the Heavenly City ... Three days later he died in his sleep. There was no burial, for Monsieur Galliard wished the interment to be at his old home in Quebec. The arrival of two of the R.C.M.P. made it possible to convey the body to Fort Bannerman, whence it would be easy to complete the journey by air.

'Such is my story of the end of a true man-at-arms whose memory will always abide with me. He was not of the Church, but beyond doubt he died in grace. In his last hours he found not peace only, but beatitude. *Dona aeternam quietem Domine et lux perpetua luceat ei.*'

# 20

The chief beauty of the Canadian spring is its air of fragility. The tints are all delicate; the sky is the palest blue, the green is faint and tender, with none of the riot of an English May. The airy distances seem infinite, for the mind compels the eye to build up other lands beyond the thin-pencilled horizons.

A man and a woman were sitting on the greening turf by the well of the Clairefontaine stream. The man wore a tweed suit of a city cut, but he had the colour and build of a countryman. The woman had taken off her hat, and a light wind was ruffling her hair. Beneath them was a flat pad of ground, and on it, commanding the sources of both the north- and south-flowing rivulets, was a wooden cross which seemed to mark a grave.

The eyes of both were turned northward where the wooded hills, rising sometimes to rocky scarps, shepherded the streams to the Arctic watershed.

Galliard slowly filled a pipe. His face had filled out, and his jaw was firmer. There were now no little lines of indecision about his mouth. Also his eyes were quiet and content.

For a little the two did not speak. Their eyes followed the slender north-flowing stream. It dropped almost at once into a narrow ravine, but it was possible to mark where that ravine joined a wider valley, and where that valley clove its way into the dark tangle of forested mountains.

'What happens away up there?' the woman asked. 'I should like to follow the water.'

'It becomes a river which breaks into the lowlands and wanders through muskegs and bush until it reaches the salt. Hudson's Bay, you know. Dull, shallow tides at first, and then the true Arctic, ice-bound for most of the year. Away beyond are the barrens, and rivers of no name, and then the Polar Sea, and the country where only the white bear and the musk-ox live. And at the end a great solitude. Some day we will go there together.'

'You don't fear it any more?'

'No. It has become part of me, as close to me as my skin. I love it. It is myself. You see, I have made my peace with the North, faced up to it, defied it, and so won its blessing. Consider, my dear. The most vital forces of the world are in the North, in the men of the North, but only when they have annexed it. It kills those who run away from it.'

'I see,' she said after a long pause. 'I know what you mean. I think I feel it ... But the Sick Heart River! Wasn't that a queer fancy?'

Galliard laughed.

'It was the old habit of human nature to turn to magic. Lew Frizel wanted a short cut out of his perplexities. So did I, and I came under the spell of his madness. First I came here. Then I went to the Ghost River. Then I heard Lew's story. I was looking for magic, you see. We both had sick hearts. But it was no good. The North will always call your bluff.'

'And Leithen? He went there, didn't he?'

'Yes, and brought Lew away. Leithen didn't have a sick heart. He was facing the North with clear eyes. He would always have won out.'

'But he died!'

'That was victory – absolute victory ... But Leithen had a *fleuve de rêve* also. I suppose we all have. It was this little stream. That's why we brought his body here. It is mine, too – and yours – the place we'll always come back to when we want comforting.'

'Which stream?' she asked. 'There are two.'

'Both. One is the gate of the North and the other's the gate of the world.'

She faced round and looked down the green cup of the Clairefontaine. It was a pleasant pastoral scene, with none of the wildness of the other – the white group of farm buildings in the middle distance and the patches of ploughland, and far beyond a blue shimmer which was the St Lawrence.

The woman laughed happily.

'That is the way home,' she said.

'Yes, it is the way home – to our home, Felicity, which please God will never again be broken. I've a lot of atoning to do. The rest of my life cannot be long enough to make up to you for what you have suffered.'

She stroked his hair. 'We'll forget all that. We're starting afresh, you know. This is a kind of honeymoon.'

She stopped and gazed for a little at the glen, which suddenly overflowed with a burst of sunlight.

'It is also the way to the wars,' she said gravely.

'Yes, I'm bound for the wars. I don't know where my battle-front will be. In Europe, perhaps, or maybe in New York or Washington. The North hasn't sent me back to malinger.'

'No, of course not. But, anyhow, we're together – we'll always be together.'

The two by a common impulse turned their eyes to the wooden cross on the lawn of turf. Galliard rose.

'We must hurry, my dear. The road back is none too good.'

She seemed unwilling to go.

'I feel rather sad, don't you? You're leaving your captain behind.'

Galliard turned to his wife, and she saw that in his eyes which made her smile.

'I can't feel sad,' he said. 'When I think of Leithen I feel triumphant. He fought a good fight, but he hasn't finished his course. I remember what Father Duplessis said – he knew that he would die; but he knew also that he would live.'

## MORE ABOUT PENGUINS, PELICANS
## AND PUFFINS